WHA

J. M. Q. DAVIES attended Greek schools during his childhood in Thessaloniki and read Modern Greek and German at Oxford before pursuing an academic career in English and Comparative Literature, teaching at the Universities of California, Alberta, Melbourne, Darwin and Waseda. He is the author of a monograph, *Blake's Milton designs: the dynamics of meaning* (1993), has edited a collection of essays, *Bridging the gap: literary theory in the classroom* (1994), and written articles on modern fiction, literary theory, fantasy and new literatures in English. He is well known as a translator of German literature and more recently for his translations from Modern Greek — namely the works of Konstantinos Theotokis — and was shortlisted for the New South Wales Premier's Translation Prize in 2015 and 2017.

J. M. Q. DAVIES : OTHER TRANSLATIONS OF THEOTOKIS
Slaves in their chains (Angel Classics, 2014).
The life and death of Hangman Thomas (Colenso Books, 2016)
Corfiot Tales (Colenso Books, 2017)

J. M. Q. DAVIES : TRANSLATIONS FROM GERMAN
German tales of fantasy, horror and the grotesque (Longman Cheshire, 1987)
Arthur Schnitzler, *Selected short fiction* (Angel Classics, 1999)
Arthur Schnitzler, *Dream story* (Penguin, 1999)
Thomas Schipperges, *Prokofiev* (Haus, 2003)
Arthur Schnitzler, *Round dance and other plays* (Oxford World's Classics, 2004)
Hugo von Hofmannsthal, *Selected tales* (Angel Classics, 2007)

COLENSO BOOKS : OTHER TRANSLATIONS FROM MODERN GREEK
TRANSLATED BY MARJORIE CHAMBERS
Iakovos Kambanellis, *Three plays: The courtyard of wonders — The four legs of the table — Ibsenland* (2015)
Yannis Ritsos among his contemporaries: twentieth century Greek poetry (2018)
Chistophoros Milionis, *Kalamas and Acheron: rivers of Hades* (2020)
Panayotis Tranoulis, *Keratochori: my life in the furnace* (2020)
TRANSLATED BY THEODORE STEPHANIDES
Karaghiozis: three modern Greek shadow-play comedies (2020)

What price honour?

— ◆ —

The convict

— ◆ —

TWO NOVELLAS

BY

KONSTANTINOS THEOTOKIS

TRANSLATED FROM THE GREEK

BY

J. M. Q. DAVIES

WITH A FOREWORD BY DAVID RICKS

COLENSO BOOKS
2020

This translation first published September 2020
by
Colenso Books
68 Palatine Road
London N16 8ST
colensobooks@gmail.com

Reprinted with minor corrections December 2020

ISBN 978-1-912788-14-9

What price honour? was first published as *Η τιμή και το χρήμα*
in serial format in the periodical *Νουμάς* in 1912, and in book form
by Χρωμοτυπολιθογραφείο Αφών Ασπιώτη, Corfu, in 1914.

The convict was first published as *Ο κατάδικος*
by Βιβλιοπωλείον Γ. Ι. Βασιλείου, Athens, in 1919.

The portrait of a young woman on the front cover
is *Wishbone* (*Γιάντες*) by Nikolaos Gyzis (1878)
in the National Gallery, Athens.
The image, downloaded from Wikimedia Commons,
is in the public domain.

CONTENTS

An asterisk in the text indicates that comments on the preceding word or phrase will be found in the Notes.

FOREWORD

by

David Ricks

Modern Greece holds a distinguished place in the world's poetry, and no self-respecting reader does without Cavafy, Seferis, and Ritsos: indeed, all three have had a significant life in translation and a marked (sometimes too marked) influence on foreign poets. Yet the Greeks have had much to offer in the field of fiction — shorter fiction, especially. Just as we can trace a distinguished line in Greek poetry from Independence to today, with many connecting threads and no few creative antagonisms, so too Greek shorter fiction has its own multifarious tradition from the 1880s. Three older contemporaries of Konstantinos Theotokis now accessible to the English speaker provide reference points: Alexandros Papadiamantis (1851–1911), G. M. Vizyinos (1849–1896), and Andreas Karkavitsas (1866–1922); as indeed does the only modern Greek novelist who has a firmly established readership in translation, Nikos Kazantzakis (1883–1957).[1]

One way of thinking about Theotokis' distinctive contribution in this context is prosaically regional: his prose fiction is set in his native island of Corfu, and this adds new landscapes and new historical–social–psychological territory to that which those other authors made their own: Papadiamantis' Skiathos, Vizyinos' Thrace, Karkavitsas' (adopted) Thessaly, and Kazantzakis' Crete.

---

[1] Papadiamantis' short novel *The Murderess* has been newly translated by Liadain Sherrard (Limni, Evia: Denise Harvey, 2011), and forty-seven of his short stories, translated by various hands, are available from the same publisher as *The Boundless Garden* (2011 and 2019). Vizyinos' six canonical tales have now been freshly translated by Peter Mackridge in *Thracian Tales* and *Moskov Selim* (Athens: Aiora, 2014 and 2015). Karkavitsas' short novel, *The Beggar*, appeared in a translation by William F. Wyatt, Jr (New Rochelle, NY: Aristide Caratzas, 1982) and his rather programmatic *The Archaeologist* (along with a couple of other shorter pieces) will appear in Penguin, translated by Johanna Hanink, in 2021.

FOREWORD BY DAVID RICKS

The Ionian Islands, and Corfu in particular, have had their own history, with its own kind of social tensions; and it is worth recalling that at the time of the restoration of democracy in Greece in 1974 Corfu, easily presented as a Greco-Italian isle of carefree Phaeacians, had the highest illiteracy rate in Greece. But Theotokis does more than cover new territory in this basic sense: as discussed in the Introduction to this volume, he seeks to compress in these two novellas a good deal of anguished speculation.

The project, though not perfectly executed in every respect, was an ambitious one, and differently ambitious from the contemporaries I have mentioned. Papadiamantis' writing (though less blandly pious than many readers would have it) is permeated by Eastern Orthodox traditional life and values: this stands in contrast with Theotokis' free-thinking stance which led him to translate Lucretius into demotic Greek and to espouse the socialism which Papadiamantis deplored. Yet unsparing attention to the special pressures placed on ordinary lives by the clash of tradition and modernity, of the monetary economy and the true price of things, is something the two writers share. With Vizyinos, likewise, both a contrast and a fruitful tension are clear: where the son of Thracian peasants and lapsed seminarian weaves intellectually intricate patterns that come close to eluding final analysis — and never more so than where religion is involved — Theotokis' ardent note of social protest is clear. Karkavitsas, a closer contemporary, gives fuller rein to the petty enmities of peasant life, as Theotokis does, but generates out of this in *The Beggar* (1896) a sort of mock-epic grandeur; in *The Archaeologist* (1904) he succumbs to the lure of the *roman à thèse* which drew Kazantzakis so strongly and which perhaps ensnares Theotokis' longest novel, *Slaves in their Chains*, more than the two short novels in the present volume.

Another way of looking at Theotokis, however, is to look back at him through writers who are at the height of their powers today. This involves no more than a glance just across to the Greek mainland and to novellas and short stories set in the Epirus of today (or a past within living memory). Michalis Makropoulos (b. 1965) and Dimitra Louka (b. 1970) are heirs to Theotokis — conscious heirs, it should be noted — in their unflinching presentation of the rigours of peasant life, the inhumanity of authority, the shock of violence (including sexual violence and coercion), and the religion-haunted yet God-forsaken peasant heart. To read the two novellas in this volume is, not just to be taken to a historical and literary past worth knowing in its own right, but to be put in contact with a powerful vein of writing which continues to ramify more than a century on.

J. M. Q. Davies' commitment to making Theotokis better known in English is a distinctly ambitious one, now extending to a fourth volume (and a third for Colenso Books).[2] As recently as thirty years ago, just a single Theotokis story was available in English — the savage 'Face Down' from *Corfiot Tales*. Now, thanks to Davies' tenacity and dexterity, the full range of Konstantinos Theotokis' Corfu can be as closely encountered by the English speaker as Verga's Sicily or Pavese's Piedmont.

David Ricks
Professor Emeritus of Modern Greek
and Comparative Literature
King's College London
September 2020

---

[2] For details of the earlier volumes, see the page facing the title page or the Bibliography (page 197).

TRANSLATOR'S INTRODUCTION

Corfu, the fairest of the Ionian Isles with its temperate climate and picturesque forts and bays and olive groves, has been coveted and contested since Homeric times. After a thousand years under Byzantine rule, it was raided repeatedly by pirates and invaded by the Normans, the Angevins, the Genoese and more permanently by the Venetians, who from 1386 colonized it as a source of olive oil for landless Venice and an entrepôt on the silk road. They established a semi-feudal Italian-speaking aristocracy, some drawn from Greek families who had fled after the fall of Constantinople to the Turks in 1453; they built an arsenal and repair yards for their galleys and extended the town's fortifications, successfully resisting major Turkish sieges in 1537 and 1716; and though nominally Catholic they tolerated the Orthodox religion of the locals and accepted Jewish refugees from Spain. And for four centuries, while mainland Greece and most of the Aegean islands remained under Ottoman rule, the Ionian Islands, and Corfu in particular, served as a cultural conduit between East and West.

Napoleon was no less conscious of Corfu's strategic location at the entrance to the Adriatic than the Venetians and in 1797 the French invaded, raising a 'Tree of Liberty' in the town square and burning the *Libro d'Oro*, the Venetian honour roll of the local nobility, only to be ousted by a Russian–Turkish coalition, which established a short-lived Septinsular Republic of the Ionian Islands. The French returned in 1807 and administered the island for a further seven years. In 1815 at the Congress of Vienna the Ionian Islands became a British Protectorate, governed by a sequence of colourful High Commissioners, with the nominal assistance of a senate, drawn like its first president Emmanouil Theotokis from the local nobility, a popular assembly and a constitution. In 1821 the Greeks on the mainland rose up against the Turks, generating a wave of philhellenism, spearheaded and partly financed by Lord Byron, and attracting adventurers from across Europe cashiered after the Napoleonic Wars. Sir Thomas

Maitland, the first High Commissioner, mindful of Britain's treaty obligations to the Turks, dealt robustly with Ionian freedom fighters and agitators from the *Philiki Etairia*, the secret society started in Odessa. But when in 1827 the war reached a stalemate and the Powers intervened, it was the Corfiot Count Ioannis Kapodistrias who was chosen as the first President of the fledgling nation. And it was the (Zante-born) Corfiot poet Count Dionysios Solomos whose demotic 'Hymn to Liberty' would later furnish verses for the Greek national anthem.

Corfu Town still has a Venetian feel to it, with its crumbling mansions, narrow streets, arcades and campanile, and its parades of its patron Saint Spyridon in his reliquary four times a year. And during most of their fifty-year rule the British garrisoned there remained almost as isolated from the locals socially as in India during the Raj. But administratively they were progressive, ending the nocturnal confinement of the Jews within the ghetto, legislating to curb the nobles' exploitation of the peasants, and building roads, bridges, aqueducts, schools, hospitals and prisons, all of which helped to revive the economy following the Napoleonic Wars, increase law and order and reduce the isolation of the villages. And early in the Protectorate the eccentric philhellene, Lord Guilford — whose fondness for dressing up like Plato exemplified the widespread Western assumption that the Greeks and their language had remained unchanged since Antiquity — spent his personal fortune establishing the Ionian Academy, the first modern Greek institute of higher learning. But welcome though the British were initially, their efforts were steadily undermined by nationalist Ionian radicals, or *Rizospastai*, who continued to press for union with the mainland, which after the assassination of Kapodistrias in 1832 had become the Kingdom of Greece under the Bavarian King Otto. And in 1864, following a report by William Gladstone — who bemused the islanders by addressing them in ancient Greek — the British ceded the Ionian Islands to Greece, securing in return their own candidate, the Danish-born King George I, as Otto's successor on the Greek throne.

The Union was in line with the Greek nationalist movement which later adopted the *Megali Idea*, the irredentist 'Grand Idea' of liberating the Greeks of Ottoman-ruled Crete, Thessaly, Epirus, Macedonia and Asia Minor and reuniting them within a new Byzantium — a movement which would lead to the Balkan Wars of 1912–13, the 1919 Greek incursion into Asia Minor and the ensuing disastrous and chaotic 1922 evacuation of the Greeks of Smyrna. But Union put paid to Corfu's leadership aspirations, deprived its nobles of a source of patronage and made the islanders liable for mainland taxes and military service. Nevertheless, for affluent Westerners the Islands retained their romantic charm throughout the *Belle Epoque,* the Habsburg Empress Elizabeth building her sea-view Achilleon outside Corfu Town (purchased by the German Kaiser after her assassination), the Greek royals making the High Commissioners' residence Mon Repos their family retreat, and scholars and archaeologists like Heinrich Schliemann exploring Cephalonia, Ithaca and Lefkada for their Homeric associations. The exotic allure of the Islands also comes across in the rich travel literature of the period, which provides fascinating glimpses of place-seeking noblemen, unemployed professionals, feuding peasants, anathematizing priests, folk costumes, puppet shows and village dancing.[1]

Nowhere is the genius loci of Corfu — its enchanting ambience and its social and spiritual life as it emerged into the modern world — more vividly conveyed than in the fiction of Konstantinos Theotokis (1872–1923), multilingual aristocrat turned socialist, patriot, Sanskrit scholar, translator, folklorist and scion of the distinguished Theotokis family, entered initially into the *Libro d'Oro* during the seventeenth century. His father, Count Markos, Orthodox by faith and a librarian responsible for Corfu's Venetian archive, considered the French Revolution and democracy as the

---

[1] Especially illuminating as a companion to Theotokis' fiction is Sophie Atkinson's *Artist in Corfu* (first published 1911) — see the Bibliography (page 199) and Notes on pp. 191, 192 and 194 for pages 10, 23 and 115.

contrivances of Jews and Masons and was given to extolling the achievements of his ancestors. When already in his forties, he married the patrician seventeen-year-old Angeliki Polyla and sired ten children, thus ensuring continuation of the line and leaving his bachelor elder brother Alexandros to manage the estate. Konstantinos, affectionately known as Dinos, was the eldest son and the apple of the family's eye — gifted, precocious and (like so many of his characters) hot tempered, speaking Italian with his mother, staging amateur theatricals taken from Goldoni with his siblings, observing the night sky from the rooftop through his telescope, and at school showing a special aptitude for maths and science. As a student in fin-de-siècle Paris however he turned prodigal, flaunting his aristocratic status, neglecting his studies, squandering the allowance his doting uncle secretly mortgaged the estate to send to him, and in 1891 fleeing to Venice to escape the flu epidemic without taking a degree. There, still only nineteen, he fell in love with and rashly proposed to Ernestine von Malowitz, a German-speaking Bohemian baroness, Catholic, convent-educated and almost as old as his own mother. Summoned to the rescue, Count Markos warned Ernestine of his son's temperamental nature and modest expectations, but she held her youthful suitor honour-bound. After a year awaiting his majority at his father's insistence, writing a first novel in French about Greek bandits, *Vie de montagne* (1895), and being lionized by Corfiot society, he married Ernestine in Prague and settled in the family's rundown country house or *archontiko* of Karousades in the north of Corfu opposite Albania.

Here Theotokis spent the best part of the next twenty years as an independent man of letters, immersing himself in European literature and philosophy, particularly Schopenhauer and Nietzsche, translating from Lucretius, Shakespeare, Goethe, Heine, Flaubert and Turgenev as part of the ongoing contemporary drive to edify a backward post-Ottoman Greek nation, and writing powerful fiction mainly in the realist or *verismo* mode of Giovanni Verga. In 1896–97, inspired by his friend Lorentzos Mavilis, poet, Sanskrit scholar and ardent nationalist (later killed in the First Balkan War), Theotokis mustered a troop of his retainers in support of the uprisings against the Turks in Thessaly and Crete. Mavilis also influenced his decision to write in demotic Greek, and his rustic *Corfiot tales*, a Nietzschean prophecy entitled *Passion* (1899) and several short allegorical stories began to appear serially in the demotic periodicals *Techni* and *Noumas*.

After the death of their only daughter from meningitis in 1900, he and Ernestine became increasingly estranged, she taking refuge in her Catholic faith, he burying himself in work, while occasionally attending to the medical needs of the villagers and their livestock and transgressing with the peasant maidens — who regarded this as not only a duty but an honour.

In 1908 during two semesters at Munich University Theotokis became more seriously interested in Marxism as an alternative to the romantic nationalism of Mavilis, leading to a rift between them; and on his return he helped form a local socialist club. *What price honour?* (1912), his first short social novel, reflects the influence of these ideas and the extent of his disaffection with his own class. During the First World War, distrustful of German imperialism, Theotokis sided with the pro-Entente position of prime minister Eleftherios Venizelos in the National Schism, and against King Constantine I (married to the Kaiser's sister) who favoured Greek neutrality. After the War, when Ernestine's Bohemian inheritance was confiscated by the new Czechoslovak state, he was for the first time obliged to earn a living in Athens as a civil servant. During these his final years *The convict* (1919) and *The life and death of Hangman Thomas* (1920) were published, as was his masterly *Slaves in their chains* (1922). He died painfully of stomach cancer in 1923, declaring shortly before the end that he felt he still had ten years' work left in him and exhorting mankind to 'be good to one another'.

His posthumous literary fortunes were affected adversely by his outsider status among the Athenian literati and by a metropolitan readership no longer interested in tales of rural life. But in 1927 the poet Irini Dendrinou, who had been his co-editor on the short-lived journal, *Corfiot Anthology* (*Kerkyraïki Antholoyia*) and, in 1935, first reissued his stories from *Noumas* under the title *Corfiot tales*, paid tribute to him as a writer of European stature whose own fiction cried out to be translated. And since then his work has come to be acknowledged as a qualitative benchmark by a wide range of contemporary Greek writers.

All Theotokis' realistic fiction is both immensely readable, reflecting his genuinely democratic outlook, and meticulously crafted. Two of his seminal artistic mentors were Shakespeare, whose tragic heroes and mingling of the serious and the comic he so often emulated, and Flaubert, whose *Madame Bovary* (1859) he translated and admired as both a tragedy of provincial life and as a formal masterpiece. And like both these writers he sought to dramatize the inner world of man's drives and ruling passions. As early as *Vie de montagne*, quoting from Sophocles' *Antigone*, he had written, 'Passion, you are everywhere, in the miser's love of gold, in the hedonist's debaucheries, in high-minded sentiments and innocent longings, in forbidden loves, in hatred, crimes and bloodshed, everywhere!' And all of the *Corfiot tales* focus on the primal passions, collectively building up a picture of the closed, clannish and fiercely patriarchal peasant world that Theotokis had been familiar with since childhood. Several turn on honour killings, sometimes narrowly averted, highlighting the plight of peasant women and Corfu's cultural affinities with neighbouring Albania and Sicily. Some, like 'Illicit love' which broaches the taboo topic of incest, are more psychologically probing. Read sequentially, their formulaic element, influenced in part by the contemporary interest in folksong, emerges more clearly and several of the recurrent characters and dramatic situations — the sexually exploitative squire, the go-between, the outspoken underdog, the fratricide — are later interpolated in the longer works. All the stories unfold against a timeless backdrop of village weddings, folksongs, dancing, Orthodox church services and seasonal activities.

Also rustic in setting is *The life and death of Hangman Thomas*, a dark tragicomic novel of infatuation in old age, in which Thomas, a sly old peasant nicknamed 'the hangman' by the village children becomes besotted with his neighbour's attractive wife Maria, who, in league with her rapacious brother-in-law and the village priest, manages to outfox and fleece him. One of the things the poet Kostis Palamas (1859–1943) admired about Theotokis' fiction was the range of literary influences it seamlessly assimilates. This is especially evident in *Hangman Thomas*, with its balanced structure, its echoes of Heinrich Mann's *Professor Unrat* (1905),[2] and its Goldoni-like knockabout scenes, Naturalist deathbed sequence and grim Expressionist finale. At a symbolic level the tale is both a parable of capitalist greed and a re-enactment of the eternal dialectic between love and death. While as a study of folk customs and morality, technically known as *ethographia*, it is a mine of information, almost incidentally shedding light on dowries, funeral rites, inheritance customs, superstitions, rural hygiene, poverty and destitution.

Slaves in their chains, Theotokis' longest, most personal and savagely satirical work, which took over a decade to complete, is the tragicomic saga of a noble family's descent into moral and financial bankruptcy, unable to compete in the modern capitalist world. The ironically named Count Alexandros Ophiomachos Philaretos ('dragon slayer' and 'lover of virtue'), pressured by a Jewish loan-shark who also serves him as a go-between, blackmails his elder daughter emotionally into marrying an affluent parvenu doctor, despite her love for a patrician but consumptive poet and would-be revolutionary. In a climactic scene of rage and humiliation the Count smashes his ancestral portraits, and after his other children go off the rails, King-Lear-like he goes mad with grief. Though the novel is not strictly a

[2] Better known outside Germany in Josef von Sternberg's 1930 Expressionist film version, *Der blaue Engel* (*The blue angel*), starring Marlene Dietrich. Professor Rat in Mann's novel is nicknamed Professor Unrat by his pupils (the prefix turning 'Councilor' into 'Excrement'), and when he becomes infatuated with a cabaret dancer he loses his job and, like Thomas, ends up a spiteful and demonic outcast.

roman a clé, some of the caricatured minor figures were sufficiently identifiable to cause a stir in Corfiot society. All these works portray passion not as in, say, Blake or Nietzsche or D. H. Lawrence, as a redemptive force, but in the tradition of ancient Greek and Shakespearean tragedy or Thomas Hardy as a dangerous and destructive one.

What price honour? [3] (1912) and *The convict* (1919) are no less powerful but much more optimistic works. The first, written before the First World War during the time when Theotokis was most actively engaged with socialism, is a proto-feminist work dedicated to Irini Dendrinou (see page 3), who since his alienation from Ernestine had increasingly become his muse. The second seeks a rapprochement between socialist and traditional Christian ideals, and focuses on a peasant Innocent who constitutes a redemptive mirror image, as it were, of the demonic protagonist of *Hangman Thomas*. Both works avoid tendentiousness and both, but particularly *The convict*, see social change as emanating ultimately from individual moral action.

What price honour? is set in Corfu Town's working suburb of Mandouki, to which many impoverished villagers were migrating in the 1900s, and explores the shifting class divisions of the times, the clash between town and village mores and the corrupting effects of the capitalist cash nexus. The narrative is dominated by Siora (Signora) Epistimi, one of Theotokis' redoubtable female protagonists. Saddled with an alcoholic husband, she is the family breadwinner, working for low wages in a textile factory,[4] lending money at extortionate rates, selling smuggled goods on the black market and saving every penny towards her three daughters' dowries. Complications set in when Andreas, a debt-ridden patrician caique-owner turned smuggler, is smitten with her

---

[3] *Honour and cash* would be a more literal translation of the Greek title, and the one I have used hitherto in writing about Theotokis.
[4] Amazing though it seems today, Corfu was among the first regions of Greece to start industrializing.

blooming eldest daughter, Rini. He finds himself torn between marrying a humble working girl and, as his cunning uncle and willing go-between advises, securing a dissolute heiress to redeem the family's fortunes. When Siora Epistimi is pressured to provide a larger dowry at the expense of her other daughters, she resists, and stung by neighbourhood gossip, she in turn pressures Andreas to do the honourable thing, after which events quickly spiral out of her control.

Formally *What price honour?* makes exemplary use of what Verga termed *prosa dialogata*, lightening the narrative with intensely dramatic scenes using vivid colloquial dialogue, for which Theotokis had an unerring ear. Two episodes replete with dramatic irony are particularly memorable, one in the tavern, where Epistimi's bibulous husband Trinkoulos gives away more than he should; the other where Andreas' uncle pays Epistimi a visit and reveals his trump card. Throughout the novel contending points of view are finely balanced, and reversals and epiphanies of the kind Aristotle recommended in the *Poetics* enhance suspense. And Corfiot daily life — the men talking politics in the tavern, the gossips keeping an eye on their promenading daughters, the motorist speeding by, tooting as if he were the Kaiser, the nobles heading to the villages for sex or chatting in Italian at the market, the cries of fishmongers and butchers — is captured with a freshness and economy that bring the Greek caricatures of Osbert Lancaster to mind.

The convict is a more profound and searching work which dramatizes the existential quandaries of mankind in an unjust post-Darwinian world where God is dead and traditional values are being eroded. It is also considered Theotokis' most experimental and aesthetically satisfying novel, refining many of the narrative devices he had developed earlier. As so often in the *Corfiot tales*, adultery is again the catalyst. Arathymos' wife Margarita is enjoying secret trysts with the younger macho Petros Pepponas, and when she tells him she suspects her husband's ploughman Tourkoyannis may be watching her, he advises her to sell the ox-team (part of her dowry) to get rid of him. And in the horrendous events that follow, Petros and Tourkoyannis are counterpointed to reveal the extremes of nobility and depravity that man is capable of. As an *ingénu* or Holy Fool, Tourkoyannis has affinities with Dostoyevsky's Prince Myshkin in *The idiot*, Theotokis' most immediate literary source of inspiration.[5] But his peasant robustness, his capacity for firmness, even violence, and his devotion and loyalty to Margarita throughout his Job-like trials make him arguably more plausible and human. His cunning adversary and accuser Petros is his polar opposite — proud, wilful, charismatic, obsessed with Margarita and driven by jealousy and envy to extremes. Though there are echoes of *Othello* and of Nietzsche's Superman in his portrayal, in the Corfiot context Petros is an insightful study of the psychopathology of sexual passion and frustration in patriarchal honour cultures; and Margarita speaks for all women of her class and time when she tells him ruefully that she is the one with everything to lose, and indeed she reaps the whirlwind as events unfold.

In the socialist context, where Siora Epistimi in the earlier novel is representative of the proto-industrial proletariat, Tourkoyannis the unmarried itinerant labourer epitomizes the rural poor. And his assumption of a pastoral role in prison suggests that Theotokis, like Tolstoy whom he admired and emulated in the disposal of his property, hoped a corrupt degenerate society might ultimately be redeemed by honest peasant virtues.[6] Beyond this, Tourkoyannis' obscure origins (despised as the son of a Christian Albanian whore and an unknown Turk), his fondness for Margarita's children and the slaughtered oxen, his betrayal, mockery of a trial, suffering and

---

[5] The influence of *The Idiot* is also apparent in Margarita's sense of being followed and in the money-burning episode. *Crime and punishment,* which Theotokis sent to Dendrinou in Italian translation, is echoed *inter alia* in the murder, the psychology of guilt explored through inner monologues and the false confession.

[6] Theotokis has however been criticized for never really confronting the issue of land reform, and after his death the Greek Communist Party denounced him as never a true believer.

assumption of another's guilt all suggest that he is also a type of Christ. Yet in the context of the ongoing wars between Turks and Christians, his nickname implies that he is a syncretistic conciliatory paradigm, transcending specific faiths. He often quotes the biblical commandments, but the core message of his homespun preaching — that happiness comes only to those who do good, or having sinned repent — is simple and universal. Just how difficult repentance and forgiveness are psychologically is illustrated by the story of his prison protector Cain (interpolated from *Corfiot tales*), unable to forgive the brother who had cuckolded him — a paradigm which recalls Dostoyevsky's dictum that hell is the inability to love. Tourkoyannis also poses the radical existential question raised by Schopenhauer, when he asks himself 'whether divine Providence were making him pay for the misdeeds of others so that sinful souls might be redeemed, or whether perhaps he was suffering in vain because a blind irrational will governed this world'. Ultimately he finds salvation in service to others and as an illiterate soothsayer, or folk Zarathustra, he is also an artist figure. When in her 1927 tribute Dendrinou commented on his noble renunciation of Margarita, like herself a married woman, she was thus perhaps tacitly acknowledging the novel's autobiographical footprint.

Formally *The convict* is Theotokis' most experimental novel, with a wide expressive range stylistically. The forward momentum of the plot, though as inexorable as that of *What price honour?* is frequently delayed and the time sequence displaced, the central crime for instance being first summarily reported then nightmarishly recalled, increasing the suspense. There are sensuous scenes of copulation in the long grass, Dostoyevskean inner monologues and Naturalist exposés of prison horrors, all seamlessly integrated. The mood of individual scenes is often complex. The tavern scene around the card table, in which Petros puts Arathymos in a towering rage with sly insinuations about his wife's honour, is electric but quite funny. The almost Hogarthian trial sequence, which brilliantly satirizes the lax Corfiot legal system, has hilarious moments too, as when Tourkoyannis brings the house down by suggesting his chastity could be tested by physical examination. Characters are counterpointed and scenes of love and violent death reiterated to suggest their archetypal status and the Nietzschean 'eternal recurrence' of events. Particularly effective are the two mirror image ploughing scenes, the opening one with Tourkoyannis and Arathymos, the later one, identically phrased, without them — an experiment Theotokis was to repeat in the opening and closing chapters of *Slaves in their chains*.

Despite Theotokis' classic standing within Greece, internationally he has been overshadowed by the ensuing generation of Greek novelists, for instance Stratis Myrivilis and Ilias Venezis, who fictionalized the traumas of the First World War and the Asia Minor Catastrophe, and more famously the prolific Cretan Nikos Kazantzakis, all of them translated into English in the 1950s and and 1960s. Although *What price honour?* and *The convict* both appeared in French relatively soon after their publication, translated as *L'honeur et l'argent* (1929) and *Le condamné* (1933) by Léon Krajewski, who was the French consul in Corfu for many years, this is the first time either has appeared in English.

Both works reflect Theotokis' desire to demonstrate the versatility of the demotic, and the attempt in this translation is to present a simulacrum which balances the contending claims of accuracy and idiomatic English while also reflecting the different styles, voices, syntactic intricacies and musicality of the originals. Theotokis uses Greek concisely and nuances are easily lost in translation. Epistimi's frequent exclamation *Ba!* can express surprise, doubt or outright denial and requires amplification; *psofios* meaning 'dead' is normally reserved for animals and when she applies it to Andreas' late father it becomes a withering insult. In *The convict* an adulteress is referred to as the *androyinochoristra* — the 'woman who comes between man and wife' — an inimitable marvel of compression. Some idioms translate naturally, clutching at straws, as against clutching at mirrors, for instance; but occasionally the Greek idiom is so expressive in dramatic context that a literal rendition seems preferable, as with 'natter, natter from the lad, soon the old lady wants it bad,' the standard equivalent of the English, 'if at first you don't succeed, try, try, try again'.

Body language is both culturally and dramatically important in Theotokis. Very Greek gestures like the confidentially lowered voice, the sage batting of the eyes, the shrug or the arm raised in a curse can be hard to convey. The physical manifestations of emotional states are imagined by Theotokis with clinical precision and require careful phrasing to avoid sounding merely rhetorical. In *What price honour?* the themed snatches of folk song and sea-shanty, garnered from Theotokis' ethnographic studies, have been freely rendered.

In the translations all family names are given in the nominative case of the masculine form, including those of women, which in Greek usage are normally in the genitive case.

The stylistic virtuosity of *The convict* with its many literary echoes makes it more challenging to translate than the earlier work. Engaging and plausible virtuous protagonists are notoriously harder to create than convincing villains, as has been recognized since Blake and Shelley extolled the dramatic power of Milton's Satan. And finding the right speech register for Tourkoyannis, which does not make him sound too clownish or a simpleton or too preachy, is to some degree a hermeneutic leap of faith. Theotokis seems to select religious vocabulary such as a pious peasant might be expected to use, while foregrounding its psychological rather than its doctrinal implications. The inner monologues of Tourkoyannis, Petros and Margarita, with their Proustian retrospective time shifts, though sometimes lengthy are integral and have not been trimmed. The terse exchanges between characters in the court and tavern scenes, the lyrical evocations of the Corfiot landscape with oxen straining at the plough, and the matter-of-fact inventories of peasant domiciles, all involve slight shifts in linguistic register.

The translation of *What price honour?* is based on the Greek text originally published by Keimena in 1969, with illustrations by Markos Zavitsianos (Athens: Nefeli, 1993); that of *The convict* on the Greek text edited with an introduction by Stathis Protaios (Athens: Damianos, c. 1959). The principal sources for the biographical information and for some of the critical comments in this Introduction are *The early years of Konstantinos Theotokis* by the author's brother Spyridon M. Theotokis (1983), Philippos Philippou's *Konstantinos Theotokis: slave of passion* (2006), and the standard critical works by Emilios Chourmouzios and Yannis Dallas — all in Greek, full details in the Bibliography (pages 197–198).

I should like to thank George Georghallides for responding to numerous queries, David Ricks, Anthony Hirst and my wife Poh Pheng for their invaluable criticism and suggestions, and David Ricks especially for also providing the Foreword.

J. M. Q. Davies
Sydney and Windermere, 2020

What price

honour?

LETTER OF DEDICATION
TO
IRINI DENDRINOU

Gracious Madam,

I should like to dedicate to you a work that I have long been promising, a work worthy of your name, your artistic soul and my infinitely high regard for you. The delay was less for want of motivation than for lack of strength, and I would therefore ask you to accept my tribute of this modest story with your customary indulgence. It was written, Madam, before the Balkan Wars that were the prelude to Europe's current disastrous hostilities, and was first published in *Noumas* while that conflict was still raging. Evidently it was the fate of my peaceable tale to appear, amid all these historic upheavals and the rivers of blood staining mother earth, as a timid protest as it were against so illogical a system, the existence of which requires so much irrational killing and the misery of so many people. What a waste of life there has been during all these years! But let us at least hope that the current distressing blood-bath may be inscribed in the annals of human destiny as the final one. I know, gracious Madam, how much your tender heart is affected by all this misery, and so I cherish the hope that you will derive some pleasure from my humble story, if not as a work of art, then at least as something perhaps compatible with your philanthropic ideals, your deep learning and your brilliant mind, which all who know you cannot but admire.

With kind regards,

K. T.
Corfu
15 September 1914

I

Like the good housewife that she was, Siora Epistimi Trinkoulos*
rose from her bed at dawn, slipped into her underskirt, tidied her
hair a little and stepped out for a moment into the cobbled lane.
The neighbours were still fast asleep. She glanced up at the patch
of sky which was steadily getting lighter though two or three stars
were still twinkling, looked down the narrow lane to where the sea
stretched ash-gray and calm to the mountains of the mainland,
then re-entered her house to kindle a fire in her little kitchen. She
was a tall slim middle-aged woman of about forty-five, with a
wrinkled face and a mass of white hair, but her eyes were still
young and lively.

'It's going to be a hot day,' she thought opening the little
kitchen window. But as there was still not enough light, she put a
match to the blackened oil-lamp hanging from a nail on the russet
smoke-stained wall above the stove, looked round for the coffee
pot, then reached down for some charcoal and in a few moments
had dextrously kindled a fire inside the iron stove, blowing it first
with her mouth then using the bellows. Meanwhile she was
thinking, 'Six bolts of sackcloth at four francs a bolt . . . six
fours . . . that's twenty-four francs.* By the day after tomorrow,
Saturday, there should be another three bolts ready, so that'll make
thirty-six francs all told. I'll put them in the chest of drawers with
the rest, and when I've saved a hundred I'll give it all to him to
deposit in the bank. So long as he doesn't get wind of it
beforehand, the old drunk, because he'll burn it in the tavern in
no time! Little does he care about our children, our sunburned
young daughters, who are growing up apace. Look at my Rini,
there's no denying she's a woman already. If I'd left things to him,
what would become of her! What we own is thanks to my stout
arms, otherwise we wouldn't have a change of linen.' And she
sighed and shook her head.

Still working the bellows, she shouted towards the bedroom, 'Hey, Rini, what's wrong with you this morning! Get up, young lazybones! Early to rise makes a maid wealthy and wise! D'you hear me? Or are you pretending not to? Come on, wake up now!'

'It's not dawn yet, mother,' answered Rini from the bedroom with a yawn, wanting to lie in a little longer.

'It's nearly midday,' her mother shouted back relentlessly. 'Get up. You must get used to rising early. One day you'll have a husband and I don't want my in-laws cursing me.'

Suddenly there was the sound of hurried footsteps in the lane.

'What could that be,' the housewife wondered, listening intently.

And putting down the bellows, she went and stood near the door. Three men were running up the lane from the sea shore. One was weighed down by a heavy sack he was carrying, the other two taking some of the weight to enable him to move faster. The housewife understood at once what was afoot.

'They're smugglers,' she told herself. 'They must have run into trouble. They're panting with fear and exhaustion, poor fellows.'

By this time the men had reached her house and had dropped the sack right there on her doorstep.

'Save us,' one of them cried frantically, 'hide it.'

She recognized the voice at once. 'I can't, my dear Andreas, even for you. The authorities already suspect us.'

But just then her daughter, also half-dressed and tousled after sleep, came up behind her and stretching her rosy-cheeked fair head over her mother's shoulder said in a compassionate voice, 'Surely you're not going to refuse Andreas?'

Andreas meanwhile went on breathlessly, 'There's no time to lose. They're after us. Do what you like — turn us in if you can live with it.' And without more ado he and his companions took off up the lane as fast as they could go.

'How's this for trouble first thing in the morning, I wish I'd not got up!' exclaimed Siora Epistimi, folding her arms and looking glumly at the sack. 'Take a horse to water and willy-nilly make him drink! And there was I telling you to get up early!'

'Come on, mother,' replied Rini with a smile. 'Grab the other end and we'll drag it inside.'

And without another word the two women gripped the sack firmly and eased it carefully into the house. Rini closed the door, loosened two or three floorboards, and moments later the sack had vanished into the cellar and the flooring was back in place as if nothing had happened.

But by now the father was shouting from the bedroom, 'Why are you making all that racket? You'll land yourselves in jail, and me as well, then you'll be to blame for what happens to the children.'

'How dare you talk to me like that!' Siora Epistimi retorted, pretending to be angry. 'After you've ruined us, squandered all you ever had on gambling, drink and God knows what. And now you start simpering about the children, you old drunk! Where's our blessed daily bread supposed to come from?'

'We're not that badly off, woman,' he replied, sitting up in bed and facing the bedroom door, where his wife was now standing looking fierce, ready for a quarrel.

'You bring it home each day of course,' she replied, her fists on her hips. 'Where were you yesterday and the day before, and where are you off to again this evening? The tavern, right? And you have the face to lecture me!'

'Well, whatever may or may not happen,' he replied submissively, wanting to have done, 'you'll be the one to blame. But enough of all this talk. Why don't you make my coffee so we can all go about our business.'

'All you think of is your stomach,' she answered in a gentler voice. 'What's wrong with you, poor fellow?' And she returned to the kitchen, where by now the charcoal fire was dying and the water still only lukewarm.

But hearing a fresh clatter of footsteps, she went back to the door.

'It's the police,' she told herself undaunted, 'we'd better have a word with them.'

'Hey, Missus,' shouted one of them, 'did they come this way?'

'Who?' she replied smiling.

'Didn't you hear anything? They laid into us — God damn their fathers — and then gave our chief and us the slip. You didn't see anyone pass by?'

'Me?' she replied crossing herself. 'I've just got up — you can see I'm still only half dressed . . . But I might have heard footsteps running up the next lane. Have a look. They were heading into town, I think. If you're quick you might still catch them.'

The policemen glanced at one another, silently conferring. 'A waste of time,' said one of them. 'They've got away. Good luck to them for now.'

'Let's call it a day, we need a break after being roughed up like that.'

They said goodbye to the housewife and sauntered off casually towards the shore, twirling their worry beads.

II

Several days had passed. The whole business seemed to have blown over. Every morning at dawn, Siora Epistimi would set out to weave sackcloth in the factory, and every evening she would return home with a few bundles of hemp for her daughter to spin, though Rini was also responsible for the household chores and getting her younger siblings off to school. More or less every night Siora Epistimi's husband would get drunk.

It was evening and she had just got back. Looking round the cramped room that served as hall, dining room and parlour, she satisfied herself that everything was in its proper place, and after taking off her headscarf and tossing it on a chair, she went on into the kitchen. There Rini was busy preparing supper.

'Where are the children?' she asked.

'Must be playing in the road.'

'How much did the whitebait cost?'

'Twenty cents. Our Paul fetched it after school.'

Siora Epistimi proceeded to soap her hands, intending to assist her daughter, but just then someone hailed her from outside.

'I'm coming, I'm coming,' she replied, drying her hands and going to open the door. But when she saw who it was she said courteously, 'Ah, it's you, is it, Andreas? Good evening. Come in.'

Andreas did as he was bidden. He was a tall broad-shouldered man of thirty, with a suntanned face and a long curling moustache. He was wearing a large soft hat, a broad red sash around his waist and a linen jacket thrown casually over his shoulders. His clean shirt and waistcoat were unbuttoned, exposing his chest, and his shirtsleeves were rolled up.

'Good evening, Siora Epistimi,' he replied as he stepped inside.

'Have a seat,' she said, indicating a chair beside the table and closing the door.

The room by now had become quite dark, but Epistimi lit a

lamp at once.

'What happened to the sugar,'* he asked in a low voice.

'It's safely hidden,' she replied, sitting down opposite him.

'Things have quietened down. We'll come and pick it up tonight — unless you yourself are interested?'

'No, my lad, I don't think so! Just let me have a pound or two for saving your skin. The authorities aren't playing games. No, no, I really don't think so! . . . On the other hand, if it were worth my while . . . Otherwise, I'll leave it outside the door and you can pick it up. How much are you asking?'

'Half a franc.'

'No, no! Take it away! It's selling openly in all the country stores for half a franc, and more wagonloads are arriving all the time. Thirty cents and you've a deal.'

'That wouldn't cover my freight costs with the caique. As a special favour, let's say forty-five.'

'Am I not entitled to make a few cents' profit too? I'll have to lug it into town and sell it piecemeal to various noble homes I know are interested. It's hard risky work and I might get caught. Bah! I'm better off at home minding my own business. No, I won't take it.'

'Let's call it forty. I'll forget about the freight.'

'How much is there?'

'Fifty-five okas, that's a hundred and fifty-five pounds, sixty-two francs all told.'*

'That's what I worked it out at too.' And with this she rose and going over to her chest in the corner of the room, opened a drawer and brought him the money.

'You've a bargain,' he told her as he took the notes. Then after a moment's thought he added, 'I'll make you another proposition.'

'Mother,' said Rini coming from the kitchen, 'you need to fetch some oil.'

'Wait until our visitor has left. It's not closing time yet.'

Rini made no reply but lingered near the door to hear what they were saying. Andreas then put his elbows on the table in a businesslike way and went on in a low voice, 'My affairs, Siora

Episitimi, are in a mess. My late father, poor soul, left me unpaid debts. With the expense of marrying off my sister we have added to them. Our house is mortgaged and my brothers abroad don't even write to me. Evidently they don't want to know. So I'm forced to work for myself to bring in a bit of money. I thought of purchasing a few head of cattle on the mainland and smuggling them over, but I'm short of ready cash. I know you have plenty, praise the Lord. Will you let me have five hundred francs for a few days — with interest of course?'

'Ah, if only, my lad. A poor woman like me! Where would I find that much, or even half. With what I've just given you I'll be scrimping, and if I don't sell the sugar I can't clothe my children. You know my husband, he's a wastrel.'

'Come now, my dear Siora Epistimi, these are excuses.'

'On the other hand . . . But you've seen the way the customs inspector has been hounding you. Light the other lamp, Rini dear, it's hellish dark in here. If he catches you red-handed with the cattle, there goes my money. You could hardly land them without being seen, and as you know he won't take bribes. I don't have that kind of cash, my lad, I really don't.'

'Let me tell you something, my dear Siora Epistimi,' he replied even more softly, as if to avoid being overheard, and rhythmically moving his head and left hand for emphasis. 'I like my affairs to be secure! After what happened to us the other day, I went round to see Siora Athagias and said to her, "You should get rid of this inspector, he's not good for the party." She offered to write to her husband in Athens. Letters to and fro, I told her, would take time and mean delays. "Send a telegram," I urged her. And so together we went to the telegraph office, she sent her husband, the minister, a telegram and the customs inspector was transferred immediately. He has already left Mandouki* so there won't be a soul around for days. It's a good deal. I'll sign whatever guarantees you wish.'

Rini brought the lamp in, placed it on the table and stayed to listen. But Siora Epistimi remained sceptical.

'Don't be afraid,' he urged her.

'You arranged that very neatly,' she said at last, 'but . . .'

'Let him have the cash, mother, you won't lose it,' coaxed Rini sweetly, 'you do business with all sorts of people and you don't trust Andreas?'

'You stick to your frying, my lass, I don't want you mixed up in everything, like parsley.'

Andreas, raising his head just then, stared in wonderment at Rini. For the first time he saw her as a fully-fledged woman. He had always considered her a little girl and up till now had never really paid attention to her. She smiled at him. An instinctive voice within him said, 'That would be nice,' and he too smiled. After looking down a moment, he gazed at her again and saw that she was still smiling at him coolly, her eyes clear and honest, like a lily-bud waiting for a sunbeam to open it, purest white and fragrant. Meanwhile in response to his own involuntary thought he asked himself, 'What? What would be nice?'

By now Siora Epistimi was saying, 'Only with a notarized contract, mind you. Otherwise, nothing doing.'

'Of course, of course,' he replied. 'What else — on trust alone?' And although he had the impression that Rini was encouraging him, he went on brooding: 'Hasn't the family come down in the world enough already?' he asked himself. 'Father employed others to sail the caique while he slept at ease in bed and the money kept rolling in, whereas now we ourselves have to work and are continually hounded, barely making a crust and a poisoned one at that. What do you want with her? Why get involved? Do you want to be degraded and humiliated further by marrying into such a low-class family?' And yet there very close to him was Rini, manifestly radiating youth, since even without looking at her he was conscious of her presence, and instinctively he imagined the girl inhaling, her virgin breasts expanding and her heart beating beneath her soft white chest; and when involuntarily he raised his eyes again she seemed even more beautiful, and he realized that he was utterly captivated by her pure beguiling gaze.

'So for every ten francs you'd pay back twelve,' continued Siora Epistimi.

'Agreed,' he answered with a happy smile.

Now Rini too was smiling complacently, as if eager to fly into his broad embrace and share the joy she had helped mediate for him. Her curiosity about him had been aroused and her eyes sparkled as if she were enchanted by his presence.

And automatically he again said to himself, 'Who knows?'

'But how?' he added. 'By what means?' Ah, at least if she had a little cash, which he could then use to sort out his affairs and again hold his head high in society. But how much would the good Siora Epistimi let him have? As little as possible no doubt, so she'd have something left for her old age. She had other children too and would have to find a dowry for each daughter. No, she wouldn't give him much. And for Andreas marriage was his last hope. But then again, in his heart he knew that nowhere else would he find a sweeter bud just waiting for a ray of love, to open up, purest white and fragrant.

Meanwhile Siora Epistimi went on haggling: 'Why don't we say for every eighty and you'll return a hundred?'

'Yes,' he replied, 'agreed,' and he got up to go.

But from that day forward Andreas looked at Siora Epistimi's daughter with different eyes, and whenever he came across her he would greet her joyfully.

III

Every evening numerous tradesmen knocking off work in town would make their way back to the suburb: masons in their sun-baked caps, their clothes and footwear splashed with whitewash; carpenters in their everyday gear; lean workers from the various factories, looking dazed and thoughtful from the noise of the machinery; porters in bare feet; boatmen, peasants, craftsmen of all kinds. And the road was made even more lively at that hour by the constant stream of carriages and carts going to and fro between town and country, some returning home, others heading to the taverns to relax and dine.

The most celebrated place in the suburb for good wine was Tragoudis' tavern, a wine store on the main street with stone windowsills and lintels painted blue, which by that time of day was already lit up and crowded. Inside, to left and right along the plastered walls were long wooden tables flanked by narrow benches packed with people. To the right a party of youngish men were drinking wine and singing boisterously; at another table several villagers were quietly enjoying their frugal supper and talking in shy subdued voices, as if afraid of those who had arrived from town. The air was heavy with the pungent smell of wine, raw garlic, cooking, tobacco smoke and human sweat, and a haze obscured the light shed by the few lamps hanging from the walls.

'Bring us some wine, a couple of pints,'* shouted a thick voice from the carousing company, which had just come to the end of a song, drawing out the final note melodiously.

'This year, you know,' cried someone else, 'even wine's so dear, no one in the whole island gets drunk.'

Just then Andreas entered the tavern with two companions and bade everyone good evening. All three of them were dressed alike, with soft black hats and red sashes, their jackets thrown over their shoulders. One was younger than Andreas, the other much older, a sunburned and robust man who, though shorter, resembled him in features and complexion. All three sat down on a bench that still happened to be free and called out to the proprietor for wine.

That evening Andreas was in a jovial mood. He shoved his broad hat back, rolled up his sleeves as if preparing for work, and noticing that everyone was looking at him, announced in his strong voice, 'You know, lads, with the elections upon us, you should all vote for the minister!* He's the one who'll provide jobs for the poor. Roads, factories, theatres, you name it, he'll build them on Corfu. And as for you villagers, he'll make over the nobles' property to you, he says, for ever. Hasn't he already started? So be sure you vote for him, my friends. You should not only let him have your vote but your womenfolk as well!'

The whole tavern erupted into laughter. Evidently they were enjoying Andreas' remarks. One of the villagers, a frail unshaven old fellow, among the few still wearing baggy trousers, replied, 'I've known many a government, way back to the British, in my time. Forget those days. The nobles then did anything they pleased! It's true Kostandas* — God rest his soul — made a little progress. Who'd deny it? But good luck to the incumbent! He'll support the poor.'

Then one of Andreas's companions, the younger one, nudged him, observing in an undertone, 'Your father-in-law!'

'Who?' asked Andreas laughing as he glanced towards the door, where a small elderly man was just entering, thin, shabbily dressed with a sparse beard and pale spent eyes.

'Trinkoulos, of course,' the other replied, 'Siora Epistimi's husband.'

'Enough of your jokes, Andonis, if you don't mind,' he replied with a serious expression. Then he shouted to the newcomer, 'Come over here, Uncle Thanasis, come and have a drink on us.'

His older companion appeared vexed by this suggestion, but Andreas looked at him and smiled.

'Good evening, lads,' said the old man, coming over. 'Ah, if I'm late home I'll never hear the end of it from Siora Epistimi.

She stays up to spite me. And now the children are older, they side with her as well.'

By this time Andonis had poured him a glass and with a gesture invited him to drink.

'Even Rini?' asked Andreas.

His older companion glanced at him and shook his head sadly.

'To your health, lads,' said Trinkoulos, raising his glass, and after downing it replied, 'Oh, my Rini never says a word. But Siora Epistimi is always going on about Rini this and Rini that, because, she says, she's now a strapping wench. She's ripe for marriage and needs money spent on her, a dowry and all that. And I, she says, don't bring home a penny. That's a bit unfair, as what little I earn she stashes away with her own money in the chest. There's only one key and she keeps that to herself. And yet, lads, she's always whinging and complaining that she's poor and hasn't a bean, whereas I happen to know she's sitting on . . . a considerable sum.' And he laughed.

'Really, a fair amount, eh?' asked Andreas, curious.

'I've not seen it though, my boy, I don't know the colour of the notes. You'd know that better than I. When she lent you the five hundred francs the other day, I signed the contract, because, she says, that's what the law requires. But I neither handled them nor saw them. You've repaid the money since, I know, but . . . How did your little business go anyway, Andreas?'

'Under this government, need you ask? As God intended. We too made a tidy profit. Much better than expected. Have another drink, Uncle.'

'Just one more, for friendship's sake, and then I must be off!' Then after a pause, as if recollecting something he had failed to mention, he added, lowering his voice, 'Yet she's such a worthy housewife. A blessing to the family. We're not short of anything — the Lord be praised. With the interest you paid her, she's completed Rini's dowry and now has everything prepared, down to the bridal veil. What more could one ask of a wife? She's even put aside the cash that Rini will be getting.'

'How much might that be?' asked Andreas again curiously.

16

'You're a pain in the neck, Andreas,' his older companion told him, 'is that how one inquires about other people's womenfolk, for God's sake? What's it got to do with you, I'd like to know.'

'Let him ask, Spyros,' said the old man. 'Girls are for marrying, and if they have money I think it's as well for word to get around, because not all of them do. Very few, in fact. But in any case, Siora Epistimi won't tell me how much she's giving Rini. Well, good night everyone... Whoever marries our daughter, she says, should choose her for her character and not for her money. Well, good night all... But I'd estimate she'll be giving her three hundred... Good night.'

As he spoke these last words, the old man had finally got to his feet and, as if frightened by all his indiscretions, was now anxious to be off. And his tired old face expressed all his displeasure at being obliged to withdraw so early from the tavern he loved more than his own home.

'Not much,' remarked Andreas as the old man departed.

Everybody in the tavern wished him good night.

'What d'you expect her to give? Her eyes?' observed Spyros peevishly.

Thereupon Andreas began to sing:

Here and there just now and then, you chance upon a prize,
And that's a girl with golden hair, who also has dark eyes.

His two companions sang along with him, one in a rich tenor, the other in a deep bass; and when they reached the final phrase the whole tavern joined them in a medley of voices, drawing out the last note as long as possible.

But once the song had ended Andonis remarked with a wry smile, 'Didn't I say you fancied Rini! And you playing honest Injun with me, eh? Why were you asking about her dowry? But pay no attention to the old drunk. Madame Trinkoulos has money coming out of her ears. All Mandouki knows it. And with a bit of skill you could extract a great deal more from her. She's sharp as a needle, mind you. As much again perhaps. And what a girl! I doubt there's another like her in the suburb.'

17

'Even that's not much,' replied Andreas in a disgruntled tone.

'Listen, lads,' said Spyros with a serious expression. 'Don't discuss other people's womenfolk here in the tavern. Sing, crack jokes, talk politics, do whatever else you want. But leave such matters out of it! Trinkoulos' daughter may be a very fine girl indeed, but is she for the likes of us? Just think about it! What stock is she descended from compared to ours? Were she given a thousand, that still would not make it right. If you're going to marry, Andreas, you must choose someone of breeding and restore our family's fortunes in every respect. I've already had a word to him about somebody, Andonis, and if he heeds my advice he's saved. He shouldn't pay attention to the rumours, I want what's best for him.'

'You mean that Savvas woman's daughter, don't you, Uncle?' replied Andreas testily. 'Not even if . . .'

'No names, only the village,' Spyros repeated gravely. 'We agreed, such discussions are unseemly in a tavern. Sing, discuss, do whatever else you like, we said. Not only does she have the thousand francs we need, she also comes from a well-known family. So what if people slander her? Let them, who's to stop them? When you marry her, that'll shut them up. It's envy that sets people's tongues a-wagging. How does the old saying go? If envy were a nit . . .'

'The whole town would soon get bit,' Andonis completed the saying with a laugh and began to sing:

A thousand wicked rumours buzz around a woman with a stain.
The thousand rumours fly away, the woman and her stain remain.

The whole tavern laughed uproariously.

'But seriously, Uncle,' Andreas resumed, 'I reckon nothing's going to come of any of that, and when my time is up I'll cark it penniless and single.'

'You're still young, my boy. You don't know what you may achieve,' replied Spyros.

'But I do know what I need to do,' declared Andreas. 'Now I've discovered temperance and application, by Saint Spyridon I'll work hard. And if we continue to do as well as this, in a year or two I'll have cleared the debt and put my affairs in order. I don't intend to hang around for dowries! So long as the government doesn't fall and things go sour on us!' And he shouted, 'You're all voting for the minister, right lads?'

'Even if we do vote for him here,' remarked a builder as he stood sipping his wine, 'it won't make any difference. What will the other districts do, just tell me that! Here he could win all eight, and the villages support him. But what about elsewhere? I'll guarantee you in writing, this government will fall.'

'We all know,' replied Andreas, 'you're not a party member because you couldn't get your snout into the trough over that theatre contract, but the results won't go your way.'

The other man looked round the room and, realizing that no one agreed with him, did not reply.

'I have to say,' Andreas continued, addressing his companions in a lower voice, 'if what this cock is crowing happens, then of course marriage may be the only option. The debts can't be paid off in two months. The woman you mentioned, Uncle, d'you think she'd have a thousand?'

'And more,' he replied, delighted. 'God willing, I'll arrange everything for you. One day my lad you'll thank me for it.'

'But the other girl has such glorious eyes!' Andreas sighed, shaking his head.

'Trinkoulos' Rini, you mean?' said Andonis, smacking his lips as he sipped his wine. 'Yes, her glances pierce one's heart. She's quiet, unaffected and hard-working. Oh, if only I were free!'

'By Saint Spyridon I'd marry her,' declared Andreas tilting back his hat, 'but what can I do! It's the money, you see. I wouldn't be all that concerned about her family. Even the nobles marry their own servants and worse. Didn't one of them marry a whore picked up on the street, and now calls on all the mansions with her decked out in silk? I'd not be ashamed of Rini, Uncle, I assure you.'

'Take her, Andreas,' urged Andonis, 'she's just the woman for your family.'

'What are you telling him, for God's sake,' said Spyros. 'She's not suitable for us, she hasn't any money. I've already told him what he needs to do.'

'If only Epistimi would let her have the thousand, you'd soon see,' said Andonis.

'If my family weren't so hard up,' declared Andreas, 'then even if she had nothing but the clothes on her back, I'd marry her for her fair hair and stunning eyes! . . . And she looks at one so innocently, so sweetly! I've only recently realized how beautiful she is. She's become a really gorgeous woman. She's blossomed all of a sudden. There's not another like her, even in town. What does money matter, confound it wherever it's displayed!'

'You say that because you haven't any,' remarked his uncle slyly, wrinkling his brow. 'Marry the woman I'm proposing and see if you don't bless me for it. A life of bliss, I tell you. What does money matter? Money is the god that makes this world go round! Try eating love!' And he pretended to play the violin across his stomach. 'Keep your guard up, Andreas, make sure you don't become embroiled and get stuck with her. Don't keep wandering down her lane. I'm told you've even been chatting her up publicly.'

'I've known her since she was a child, why shouldn't I talk to her?'

'Because she's now a woman,' replied his uncle sternly.

By now the villagers had left for home. And at one of the other tables many voices launched into yet another song:

> *When I pass on, please bury me beneath the tavern floor,*
> *So that the guests will tread on me, and the waitress I adore.*

When the song came to an end the whole tavern rocked with laughter. The place had become more crowded. The little barefoot serving lad could hardly keep up with washing the glasses, and some of the more inebriated were becoming rowdy. The conversation was general. They talked about boats, about the steamers which arrived laden with coal and took on board the island's olive oil; about the oil markets which that year had done a roaring trade; about the money coming into the economy. Then they discussed the taxes imposed by the government, by every government, preparing for war, to dispatch the country's wealth, earned by the sweat of working men, to line the pockets of the foreigners, the rich of Germany, France, Italy and England. And every now and then the discussion would be interrupted by another song like this one:

> *When I wooed a maiden with my money things went wrong,*
> *But I had rather more success with tambourine and song.*

IV

One Sunday afternoon Siora Epistimi Trinkoulos, as usual on feast days, was sitting with the other housewives in the suburb's little square. Each had brought her own stool from home, and they were all seated in a row on the street in front of the houses. Before them the sea, dark blue and serene, stretched away to the mountains of the mainland, which at that hour were still obscured by the heat-haze. On a steeper stretch of the beach two fishing boats, one only partly built the other nearly finished, awaited the craftsmen to resume work on them the following morning. Black fishing nets draped over a taut rope were drying in the sun. A warm breeze was blowing in from the sea and the heat was still intense. The girls of the suburb were promenading up and down the broad street in clusters, all without headscarves, their hair well combed, their white pinafores immaculate, some with a rose or carnation pinned to their bosom, all laughing and chatting volubly and occasionally stealing sidelong glances at the young men lolling against the house walls, likewise clad in their Sunday best and eyeing them as they went by. The housewives watched their daughters proudly and went on gossiping amongst themselves.

'Our priest's daughter,' Siora Epistimi was saying, 'has been extremely lucky. She hasn't a penny, poor thing. But he's prosperous enough.'

'Depends how you look at things,' replied a fat middle-aged woman dressed in white. 'He's a fine young man, Siora Epistimi, bless you, but he's a seaman. Bread earned at sea is often bitter .'

'Even so,' remarked an ugly old crone dressed in black, leaning on her stick, 'at least the priest managed to marry her off. Would that ours were so lucky. One can only live in hope.'

Just then a large motorcar came speeding past, blowing its horn and trailing a cloud of noxious fumes.

'Devil take you and your honking,' cried another housewife in

22

her fifties, her dark hair immaculately combed, her fat arms folded across her chest. 'Now they've brought out these machines to frighten poor honest folk. Ah, these rich people! They have everything.' And she shook her fist after the motorcar, which by now was out of sight.

'That's the way God has made the world,' observed Siora Epistimi smiling, 'and we poor folk make a living from the rich.'

'She's right,' two or three matrons agreed appreciatively.

'What a stench,' the woman who hated the rich continued, 'anything the Kaiser does, that fellow thinks he must do too! Now he's going about tooting his horn so people will take him for the Kaiser.* Confound the wretch! When the government keeps shovelling napoleons* into his filthy maw, even I know how he got rich. Ten years ago he was a nobody, I tell you.' And she affirmed this with a nod.

'Don't talk nonsense, Siora Christina,' said Epistimi seriously, 'he's a benefactor to the poor. He provides a living for a hundred women and as many men.'

'Ha, ha, ha!' the other laughed maliciously. 'It's they who make him rich, you mean! Only the other day out at Alefki he ran over a ewe and found himself in trouble, but again he got away with it scot free.'

'Oh, enough of such unchristian talk!' said some other woman.

'A fine young lass, your daughter, Siora Christina,' Epistimi remarked, pointing to a girl just passing with her friends.

'A weak vessel, though, poor thing! Hasn't a penny. And your Rini, Siora Epistimi, still at home? How come she hasn't joined the others yet?'

'She should be here any minute. She was getting ready when I left.'

Two coaches heavily laden with passengers, baskets, sacks and vegetables and drawn by lean ill-kempt exhausted nags, were passing by just then and raising a cloud of dust.

'They're choking us,' declared the woman who hated the rich, and spat.

'Those are the Ayiris estate's coaches heading out to the

23

villages. Now every village has its coach service.'

'Who was the nobleman inside?' asked someone.

'I know him alright,' remarked Christina spitefully. 'He's the one from Lefkoraki. Everything there belongs to him: farms, men, women, girls! Nowadays the villages have become regular bawdy houses, worse even than town! What are the poor villagers supposed to do? If they don't submit, they starve to death.'

'Same old tune from Siora Christina,' said Epistimi, 'enough of all that. Let people go about their business.'

'Has your Rini shown up yet?'

'I don't see her.'

'Good news, we hear, Siora Epistimi, bless you. Is it true?'

'What?'

'Oh, something about Andreas Xis.'

'Ah, we're humble folk,' replied Siora Epistimi, closing her eyes sagely, 'and he's from a good family. We couldn't aspire so high. On the other hand, if that's what fate ordains for her . . .'

'Quite right! Quite right!' concurred several women.

'But he's so young!'

'It's a pity,' remarked the woman who hated the rich, 'that the Xis family is now a great deal poorer. But they're the sort who will survive. They're well connected! But watch out, Siora Epistimi, that . . . he doesn't cheat you. His late father was the same. He ruined one or two girls here in our suburb too, confound him.'

'He did when they made a pass at him! But surely you know the sort of girl my Rini is?'

'Where does the apple fall?' said someone.

'Underneath the apple tree,' another rounded out the saying.

'She wouldn't do it, my dear, not for all the riches in Corfu,' added a third.

'That's why I trust her,' said Epistimi proudly. 'She's our daughter, brought up here in this suburb. They chat now and then and I permit it. Chatting doesn't mean there's any hanky panky going on, you know. But only out in the street! I don't want her to ruin her chances, in case he asks for her hand in writing.'

'Deep in conversation, ladies,' remarked an attractive middle-aged woman as she came up carrying her chair and squeezed in among them. 'Talking about Rini, are you? So does Siora Epistimi know?'

'Do I know what, Konstandina?' she asked with a serious expression.

'It's her proud secret,'* said the housewife who hated the rich. 'If you ask me, everything's been settled, that's why she's not worried.'

'Well. I wish you every joy,' said the new arrival. 'I've just come from our neighbourhood. The young people were chatting in the street for quite a while, unconcerned that we were watching. But I have to say, it's a bit unseemly that . . . she's now taken him inside.'

Siora Epistimi, startled, was on her feet at once. 'What's this, Konstandina,' she exclaimed trying to appear calm, 'no, no, my Rini would never do such a thing! My old man must have asked him in. When I left he was still in bed. He told me he wouldn't be going out until this evening.'

But even she didn't believe what she was saying and already she was pursuing another line of thought: 'I must find out where that old drunk has got to. He's hardly going to stay at home on Sunday. But how could Rini ask him in! Surely she knows the world has eyes?'

Aloud she added, 'I'll go and see what's up. I'll bring Rini here and she can tell you all herself what happened. My girl has neither blemishes nor secrets.'

The women smiled. Another motorcar drove by at top speed and Christina again launched into her tirade. By then Epistimi was hurrying home.

When she arrived she saw that it was all too true. The neighbour's account had been correct. Admittedly the front door was not shut, but there in the room that served as dining room and parlour, with its fine chest of drawers, stood Andreas and her daughter, both in their Sunday best, happily chatting away and smiling at each other. Epistimi, having approached the house with trepidation, stood a moment in the lane observing them. And though her honourable heart was frantic with anxiety and her palms and brow drenched in cold sweat for very shame, at that moment her daughter, in the flower of youth, seemed to her more beautiful than ever, and Andreas no less handsome, as if made to be her daughter's consort. And despite herself she thought, 'If only he would marry her!' — followed at once by the reason, coming from deep within her heart: 'That would silence all the gossip! How could the old drunk leave the house! What excuse can I now find to save our reputation?' And rushing into the house, she barricaded the door with the chest. For a few seconds all three of them just stood there, stunned and motionless, no one quite knowing what to do next. Rini had gone pale with fear and shame and was on the point of fainting, like some pale flower wilting before it has blossomed. Andreas pretended to be unconcerned but his heart was pounding; the mother didn't know whether to wail and beat her breast, or curse and swear, or talk politely and try if possible to save the disastrous situation. What had they been up to all this time alone? How long had she had him in the house? Finally she decided to speak out. Rini heaved a sigh.

'Andreas,' said Epistimi in a low but steady voice, 'are you trying to bring shame on my humble home?'

'Oh mother,' cried Rini bursting into tears, 'Oh, Mother!'

'No,' replied Andreas, a shade ruddier than usual.

'Did you not consider' she went on, 'that we are poor vulnerable folk, that we have nothing but our reputation and our faith in God, that our family has no other means of support besides me, a wretched woman and as good as widowed since my husband's worse than useless?' And she began to weep.

'Oh Mother!' Rini sighed again, 'he will explain. He has a heart of gold. He wouldn't stoop to anything dishonourable.'

'Why did you invite him in? And why, Andreas, did you enter? The neighbour is proclaiming it all round the square, and she's every right to do so. Who will have my daughter, now you've ruined her reputation?'

'Listen,' replied Andreas, nettled, 'the whole suburb knows I'm a man of honour. You know it yourself. What more can I say? Love doesn't follow the wishes of the parents, it occurs spontaneously. And I intend to marry your Rini.'

'There's no alternative,' sighed the mother propitiated, 'it's the only way our honour will be saved.'

'If you wish,' Andreas went on airily, 'summon the priest and best man right now and we'll have done. But Siora Epistimi, you know my family is hard up. My hapless father left me debts I'm constantly having to repay. Which responsibility should I embrace first? Rend my heart and you'll find your Rini there. I've loved her ever since that evening when her eyes first seared my heart. But how am I to support her, how am I to raise a family?'

'Is that what's worrying you? Won't God assist? Aren't both of you hard-working? Then who else need you rely on?'

'No, Siora Epistimi, I'm on the brink of ruin. They'll sell my house. I'll be shamed in the eyes of the world.'

'But as we're both hard-working, who else need we rely on?' Rini too now pleaded amid her tears. 'If we love each other, would we exchange our life together, albeit in a hut, for all the riches in the world?'

'I want to make you a proper wife, I refuse to drag you into misery. What'll you give, Siora Epistimi?'

'My daughter,' she replied proudly, wiping her eyes, 'and my blessing! Why don't you behave like the honourable man you are? Do you not love her? Then marry her. God will provide. We are poor folk. You know that!'

'Without a penny?' he asked uneasily.

'You've damaged her reputation! She's vulnerable now, poor thing. I'll let her have three hundred francs, no more.'

'That's almost nothing,' he said folding his arms. 'What could I begin to do with that?'

'You've damaged her reputation,' the mother repeated sharply. 'If your intentions are honourable, prove it. Otherwise you'll have her on your conscience!'

'Give me six hundred, then at least I can clear my house of debt. Confound these money matters!'

'Let him have it Mother!' cried Rini weeping and stretching her clasped hands towards her mother. 'You'll be purchasing my happiness. No other man in all the world, not even a prince, could love me as much as Andreas does, nor any woman love him as much as I do.'

'What's this?' she replied giving her a stern look. 'You did wrong, and I'm now supposed to be unjust to all your siblings? Two young fillies are growing up after you apace and the lad is on the streets. What more can I do for all of you? Haven't I done everything I could? That's all I have!'

'Then it's out of the question,' declared Andreas, tears in his eyes.

At this Siora Epistimi flew into a rage. She raised her hand aloft and, pale in the face and her eyes blazing, cried, 'That's the way your family has always been. Always! And they deserved their ruination! And now you're following their example. Accursed fellow, what have I ever done that you should violate my tranquil home and the best girl in the suburb? May any gold you lay your hands on turn to dust!'

'Don't curse him,' cried her daughter, clutching her breast in alarm. 'He never intended this to happen, Mother. He loves me. Let him have the cash!'

'And as for you,' she continued, rounding on her furiously, 'since you've turned out like this, you brainless girl, and lost your youthful innocence, go and have your head shaved in some nunnery, you wretch. Ah, I've lost all patience with you!' And collapsing into a chair, she buried her honest face in her hands and began weeping bitter silent tears.

All three of them by now were weeping.

'But surely!' said Rini timidly, her hands clasped and gazing at Andreas through her tearful eyes, 'as we're both hard workers, who else need we rely on!'

'I just can't do it,' said the young man in anguish. 'Tomorrow we'd be on the street. I won't drag you into poverty and scorn.'

They again lapsed into silence for some time. The room was getting dark now, as the sun had set. There was not a sound except for the mother's quiet breathing as she sat there motionless. It did not occur to anyone to light a lamp that evening.

Now it was Rini who became angry and in her despair she rebelled. 'You, Mother,' she said hoarsely, 'you are responsible, not Andreas — and over such a trivial sum. You have the money but you won't give it. You've a thousand or twelve hundred francs, I know for certain, and every day you do business deals which increase your stash. And now . . . and now you want to shut me in a nunnery, after I've worked for you, put together my own dowry through hard work, so the rest of your children can have more. Oh, Mother! Oh, Mother!'

'Three hundred francs are yours,' she replied in a thick voice, without raising her head.

'I will marry you,' Andreas murmured in her ear. 'Just be patient!' And hurriedly he stepped out of the door.

After a while Epistimi calmed down. Her daughter continued to stand there, as if rooted to the spot, and didn't say a word.

'Light the lamp, will you,' her mother said peremptorily at last, raising her head as if nothing had happened. And when the light was brought in she continued in a matter-of-fact tone, 'well, let's now take stock. What has happened? You made a mistake. You will pay for it of course. But it's not the end of the world. Right? You've only been talked about. But you have your three hundred francs. It was not your fate to marry Andreas. Now you'll marry somebody of humbler standing. That's what it comes down to. All you need do till then is behave yourself.'

'No, Mother, Andreas is the man I'm going to marry. No one else,' and with that she went into the kitchen.

Just then the old man, thin stooping and inebriated, entered the house. He had caught the last of this exchange and, with drooping eyes and an inane smile on his pale lips, he asked, 'What's up?'

'You can be mighty proud of your daughter today!' his wife replied. 'And it's all your fault. If you'd been at home instead of in the tavern, nothing would have happened.'

'What, my Rini?' he asked on the point of tears at once.

'Yes, your Rini,' she replied. 'He came in here . . .'

'Andreas wants to marry me,' their daughter interrupted, wailing from the kitchen, 'but he wants six hundred francs and she won't give it him. She won't secure my fate.'

'Let him have it,' sighed the old drunk compassionately. 'Let him have it, woman.'

'What about our other girls? And us? And the lad?'

'Let him have it, woman, God will provide for us too!' and he shuffled towards the bedroom to sleep it off.

'No! No way!' shouted Epistimi after him.

V

Summer had passed; the days had grown shorter and the scorching summer temperatures had eased. Siora Epistimi continued to work all week in the factory, while also doing other jobs to bring in money, and every Sunday she would come to the little square beside the sea, where the two fishing boats were now completed, and chat with the other housewives until evening. Her daughter continued to look after the household and spin hemp as usual, as if nothing had happened. Every evening in Tragoudis' tavern people ate, drank, got tipsy and sang songs. Andreas seemed to have forgotten his beloved, and was constantly sailing his caique to the mainland and loading it with contraband, trying to sort out his affairs while the current government was still in power — which everyone predicted would not be for much longer.

It was late. A fresh breeze was blowing, making the deep blue sea quite choppy, and the caique plied the waves, its huge sails billowing. Andreas seated in the stern was at the tiller and his two shipmates, his uncle and Andonis, were singing sea shanties in the bow, and between songs they would nibble salt rusks and sip a little watered wine from a flagon by their side.

The caique cut swiftly through the waves and the town, its lighted streetlamps reflected in the sea, gradually receded as the vessel steadily gathered speed.

'Lower the jib, Uncle,' Andreas commanded. 'There's a storm brewing.'

The uncle, used to following orders, complied at once. Then having finished the task and secured the sail he replied, 'By the time the storm takes hold, we'll be in Sayada.* We're well ahead of it, don't worry. So long as the weather doesn't trap us there.'

'Let's get there first,' said Andonis, 'and God will provide.'

They again lapsed into silence, then all three launched into a sea shanty:

> *Rolling sea, cruel sea, your billows roaring endlessly,*
> *Others gaze admiringly, but all I see's your treachery.*

The vessel was now riding the waves, pitching to port and starboard, and every so often salt foam would spray over them and wet the sails and rigging, which exuded an odour of tar.

'If there were women on board this evening,' chuckled Andonis after a while, 'they'd all be seasick by now and we'd have no end of fuss.'

'We're all three of us unmarried sea dogs,' replied the uncle laughing, 'and you have to start talking about women!' And after a moment he continued, 'Why not have done with the whole subject and make yourself rich, nephew, instead of working like a stevedore? The Savvas woman asked me again the other night. What should I tell her?'

'Hold that sail steady! — What should you tell her? I hardly know myself. If it weren't for the other girl, by Saint Spyridon I'd say yes, as the debts are a huge worry.'

'You're right,' said Andonis much put out, 'it would be nice if one could do as one pleased, but it can't be helped, so say your prayers, Andreas, and listen to your uncle.'

The foam-crested waves were now getting higher. The wind was blowing in their faces and occasionally snatching at their clothes, so that they had to shout to hear each other. The vessel was lurching erratically.

'Talking of the other girl, Trinkoulos' daughter,' the uncle resumed, 'I heard from some women in the market that she's getting married — to a poor but decent peasant.'

'Who, Rini!' Andreas yelled, jumping to his feet and letting go the tiller. 'Rini is going to marry someone else!'

The vessel, left without a helmsman for a moment, was immediately in peril. It turned in the wind; the mainsail flapped about as it sagged and billowed.

'God help us,' cried the uncle hastening to gather in the sail. 'You'll drown us all tonight, you and your Rini! Keep your wits about you, we're not sailing on a lake.' And a moment later, seeing Andreas back at the helm, he continued, 'What did you expect her parents to do? Let her moulder on the shelf? She has three hundred francs, so her suitor has ignored the rumours about you and her.'

'Rumours fiddlesticks. Even without a penny she's worth all the rest!'

'Well said,' agreed Andonis.

'Forget about her. She wasn't worth it,' said his uncle.

They again fell silent. On they sped, cresting and descending the waves, which were now larger and more frequent and often drenched them as Andreas didn't bother to steer clear of them. His mind was preoccupied with other matters. In the bows the two deckhands ate their brine-drenched rusks, drank their wine and now and then launched into seafaring songs:

> *In the middle of the ocean, there is this little well;*
> *Sailors drink its water and refuse love's binding spell.*

Meanwhile Andreas was mulling things over. What, another man, his inferior, was going to snatch away the girl he adored and knew would make him happy? Oh, how the idea turned his stomach, how it wrung his pounding heart!

The wind now whistled in the rigging and the mast, and the sea grew wilder, as if the elements too were troubled by his grief. Rini would be in another's arms, another would caress her virgin body, she would become another's wife, all because he didn't have the cash to clear his family debt and Siora Epistimi refused to let him have the larger sum he needed.

The wind kept getting stronger and whistling louder, the foaming sea became more turbulent and frequently a wave would break over the caique, overflowing like the tumult in his heart.

Ah, he couldn't bear to see this marriage go ahead! He would not be able to go on living on the island. He would be racked by jealousy. His whole life would be disrupted by tempestuous passion, hatred and a thirst for bloodshed, his heart would never know the sweetness of tranquillity!

'Confound the money!' he shouted out. Just then a huge wave drenched him and the caique threatened to keel over.

'Lower the mainsail,' he commanded.

'But money's necessary,' his uncle replied as he carried out the order.

'Money's necessary,' he repeated to himself deeply perturbed, as if he were confronting death, 'and the other woman has it, even though she might be neither beautiful, nor sweet-natured, nor honourable like Rini. She has money and to spare. With it the debts could be paid off, the mortgage on the houses cleared, all the business matters set in order, and the good life would begin. Whereas Rini, alas, would mean humiliation! But also love, excitement, joy. Life at home with Rini would be one long holiday — singing, kisses, happiness, delight! Ah, where are such things to be found in life without love?' And he heaved a sigh. Instead she would be marrying another! Another would be taking her away from him, depriving him of his whole life's happiness. Oh, how could he put up with that, how could he stand by and watch it happen, hear about it from afar, or bear even to imagine it? And instead he would have a woman on his arm whom he was marrying simply and solely for her purse!

'Confound the money!' he cried out again.

A strong gust and a large wave caused the caique to shudder alarmingly. The sea, lashed by the wind, was seething; the stars in the sky above had disappeared; there was a rumbling of distant thunder and large raindrops started falling from the clouds. The caique rode the storm, ascending and descending the mountainous waves, travelling at a fair speed.

'Money, bless it, is absolutely necessary,' replied his uncle from the bows, 'and the Savvas woman's daughter has plenty of it. Love alone won't fill your stomach. Don't forget that!'

He knew it all too well; that was why he had avoided Rini up till now and tried to repress and overcome the love he felt for her within his heart. And now jealousy was making it resurface more powerful than ever — fierce, fiery, destructive like the raging sea, swaying his reason, driving him relentlessly towards poverty.

No, he would not let another man take her from him. 'Ah, Siora Epistimi, Siora Epistimi!'

The vessel continued to ride the storm and in the bows the two sailors, unperturbed, sang shanties as they gazed at the dark sea. But by now the lights on the mainland had appeared.

'I *shall* have your daughter!' he again said to himself with firm determination. 'I'm the one who's going to marry her, not the other fellow. And you must let me have the six hundred francs I asked for. Because I need it and without it I am doomed and will go under. You have to let me have it. I'd snatch her from the church, from the bridegroom's arms, to prevent the marriage!'

Now that they were approaching land, the wind and the seas abated and the boat sliced through subsiding waves.

'Why didn't I do anything earlier?' he went on ruminating. 'Because I didn't want to force you to give me the cash. But this has put a spanner in the works! You're marrying her to someone else and ruining my life. Ah, Siora Epistimi, wasn't I worth a modest sacrifice?'

The wind by this time had subsided and the sea was calmer. The two sailors were still singing shanties in the bows and the boat was sailing peacefully. Andreas' heart was also more at ease, as he had now made up his mind.

'Drop the anchor,' he commanded. And to himself he added, 'Come hell or high water, she'll be mine!'

VI

As every evening, Rini had lit the lamp in the little room that served their home as both dining room and parlour, and was in the kitchen kindling the charcoal to get supper ready. Her mother had not yet returned from the factory. Now that the days were shorter Rini would work making sackcloth in the evenings too. Her siblings were not at home. The young woman was visibly upset, her face pale, her eyes downcast, her fair hair hanging down her back in two thick braids, and every so often she would heave a sigh.

'What am I to do?' she kept asking herself. 'Men are all the same. Everyone tells me Andreas is sure to have forgotten me. Ever since that evening I've neither seen nor heard from him again. He wanted a fat dowry, and as I didn't have it he deserted me. He was more interested in that than me.' And with a bitter smile she shook her head. 'Should I pledge my word now?' she continued, 'should I wait a bit? But wait for what? The poor but decent man who wants to marry me has not asked for a dowry. He'll take me as I am. And I'm industrious and used to work, I can make a living anywhere, so who else would we need to rely on? Ah, Andreas was afraid of descending further into poverty! But didn't my mother, a poor woman, manage to raise our family, despite father's being a wastrel? And wouldn't I have been capable of doing the same? Oh, if he'd married me he'd soon have seen. He'd have had no cause for regret. But he was afraid. He wanted me seated in an armchair, acting the lady of the manor, for fear his name might be dishonoured, as none of the women in his family had ever had to work. What rotten fusty ideas! No wonder he has descended into poverty. Ah, my humble suitor is not concerned about such things. What am I to do? What am I to do? Am I supposed to remain single all my life? But don't I too deserve to have my own home, husband and family . . . to raise my own children, a valiant little band growing up around me like carnations?'

And a voice within her heart exhorted her to accept the poor man, and not jealously hanker after the other man's affections, or aspire to a higher station than befitted her. 'Higher, higher!' she reflected with a smile of derision. 'They are up to their ears in debt, those Xises, and still they don't give in. They clutch at straws to avoid further disasters. Just as well they have government connections, otherwise by now they'd have gone under. All they worry about is not losing status, not going out to work like the rest of the world. They are ashamed of any sort of work and become their own worst enemies. As a result he's got me too into this pickle. Oh, I feel sorry for my honest suitor! . . . I'll accept him.'

She had made up her mind. But just then she heard a knock at the door; and when she opened, there was Andreas standing before her. She blushed, her heart began to pound and in her agitation she could neither step forward, nor retreat, nor find anything to say. And he meanwhile was gazing at her passionately, as if eagerly devouring all her youthful beauty with his eyes to satisfy his love. His broad chest heaved, his nostrils quivered, his neck-veins bulged and his face was even ruddier than usual, and yet he was trembling from head to foot.

They gazed at one another and their eyes betrayed their love. And now all the young girl's calculations, all her sober reflections suddenly collapsed in the presence of the man who had made her suffer, and she sensed her resolution melting as she gazed at the man whom her heart had first and truly loved. She would do anything to please him. She'd readily sacrifice her whole being for his happiness.

Meanwhile in a gentle voice, apprehensive lest she forego any of the infinite sweetness of those irrevocable moments, she said to him, 'Ah, if the dam were not about to overflow, you wouldn't have turned up.'

'Are you going to marry him?' he asked her going pale.

'What else can I do? After you've abandoned me so long?' And with her hanky she dried a tear. Then she added with mingled joy and sadness, 'But who knows if even this poor man will want me now. Ah, Andreas, they'll have seen you come!'

Then suddenly reason returned to her and she was able to assess all the consequences clearly. In a flash a host of thoughts ran through her mind: the neighbours, her mother, the bridegroom, her honour, Andreas' reluctance to marry a poor woman, her mother's obstinacy over the money, her whole life wrecked. And while Andreas continued to gaze at her, not quite knowing how to make his intentions known, she added, 'They'll have seen you, mother will be back, what have you done to me!'

He nodded. 'They did notice me,' he told her quietly with a serious expression. 'Any minute now your mother will return.'

'Ah, you've ruined me!' Rini replied, clasping her hands in despair. 'Now he will forsake me too. But I won't hold it against you. Love must have compelled you!' And she smiled amid her tears.

'Love and jealousy,' he answered.

Just then she glanced through the door, which had remained open, and noticed Konstandina the neighbour lurking in the street. She went white as a sheet with shame and thought of closing the door at once, but didn't dare.

'They're watching us,' she told him in alarm.

'Let's go then,' he said resolutely.

She was shaken. She now had to make a decision, a clear and irrevocable decision that would weigh heavily on the rest of her life. And even as she was asking doubtfully, 'Go where?' and he responding calmly, 'Home with me. I'll marry you. Don't you want me?', she reflected that they had been seen — no doubt about it — and any minute now her mother would be back, become irate and start raising merry hell. And what about the groom? Oh, she didn't give a fig about the groom. The poor and honourable man who had asked for her hand was not the man she loved. Yes, she could marry him as a stay in life, but her heart's desire was standing there before her! But what of the shame awaiting her? Why receive Andreas, why not run into the street and raise the alarm, as her mother had instructed her, saying this was the only way to gain an honest reputation and respect?

'Let's go, we've not much time,' he urged again. 'There will be shouting, arguments and endless fuss once she gets back.'

Rini closed her eyes. And as in a nightmare she imagined her mother, tall, lean, wrinkled, her still youthful eyes ablaze, come storming in, screaming her head off and laying about them with her fists, while a crowd gathered outside to watch the pantomime. But again reason reassured her: even if her mother should arrive and start shouting and chastising her, wouldn't she be appeased the moment Andreas opened his mouth?

'Coming?' he urged her again, pulling her gently towards the door.

'Let go of me,' she replied. 'Let's wait for her. Let's tell the neighbour who's watching why you've come and she'll support us too.'

But Andreas now became impatient. 'Alright then stay,' he told her. 'Stew at home and suffer. Either do as I say or forget it. I'm off.'

'Ah woe is me!' she said weeping.

'Pack your clothes.'

'You're going to demand more money. That's why you want me to leave. Oh my God, what am I to do!'

'Let's go!'

She stood there a moment considering, tears streaming down her cheeks, then bowed her head, as if to indicate that she was submitting to a higher power. If she said no, her reputation would be ruined forever and her life become a perpetual torment. Hastily she began to pack her clothes. Andreas stepped outside a moment to summon his companions to carry them, and as he walked up the lane he told the neighbour who was looking at him mockingly, 'I shall marry her tonight!'

VII

No more than a few minutes had elapsed since the young people's departure when, as every evening, Siora Epistimi came hurrying home. But on this occasion she was stopped by the neighbour waiting under the streetlamp at the top of the lane.

'I was just on my way to the factory to find you,' Konstandina burst out without so much as a good evening. 'He ran off with her, not two minutes ago!'

'What? Who?' she asked, going pale.

'Andreas, with your Rini, my poor Epistimi!'

She was completely stunned. There was a buzzing in her ears as of a thousand circling bees; the houses, street and stars seemed to spin round and a dark fog descended on her mind. For several moments she stood rooted to the spot, her heart pounding, feeling as though all beneath her feet were plunging into the abyss and she about to die.

'Courage,' said her neighbour sympathetically, noticing her turmoil.

'My Rini?' she said in a faltering voice, her lips very pale.

Suddenly Siora Epistimi became incensed: 'It's all that drunkard's fault again! I had my suspicions and told him to be watchful. But all in vain! Now the damage has been done!' Then she added in alarm, 'Oh, he's going to fleece us!'

But at once a ray of hope flashed through her mind: 'Did you say they only just left?' she asked.

'Not two minutes ago. Were you to run, they'd still be in the main street.'

She took a deep breath. All her instincts were urging her to run, catch up with them and snatch her from him before she became his mistress, not to refuse him altogether but to protect her family and the money she had scraped together franc by franc, toiling with her honest hands every day of her life. She knew that all was now at stake since clearly Andreas would not marry her daughter unless she gave him the sum he had requested, or even more perhaps. That was why he had abducted her.

All these considerations had flashed through her mind at lightning speed, as such ideas always come to us in torrents at important moments in our life. And without further ado she decided to run after them.

By now she was hastening down the main street of the suburb, elbowing through the crowd, pushing children out of her way, indifferent to the fact that the shopkeepers and people on the street were watching her with curiosity. She must catch up with them. On and on she ran. And as the moments sped by she increased her pace. Ah, by now Andreas would be conducting her upstairs into his house; she wouldn't be in time. Her palms and brow were drenched in a cold sweat, she was panting hard, her heart felt about to burst. Every minute seemed an age. Alas, she would be too late! On and on she ran. Two coaches that had collided briefly blocked her way and she was obliged to wait. She was beside herself with impatience and her heart was in her mouth. 'A life's in peril, hurry!' she shouted at the coachmen, who ignored her, and not knowing what else to do she went on running on the spot, as if she might progress by marking time. Ah, she was losing all these precious moments! The girl was in serious danger. Perhaps he was already taking her to bed. 'Move, for heaven's sake, move!' she yelled at them again.

At last the road was clear and, determined to make up for lost time, she set off again at the double. But in her heart she felt despairingly that she would be too late 'Hurry, hurry!' she kept saying to herself.

Eventually she reached Andreas' residence, a modest well maintained two-storey villa down one of the suburb's narrow side streets leading to the sea. All was quiet in the lane and Andreas' house appeared to be locked up. 'Oh, perhaps they're not here after all,' she thought, as she stood there panting, discouraged and uncertain what to do. She looked about. At the house next door she caught sight of Andreas' uncle, who was sitting nonchalantly smoking on his doorstep, so she shouted out to him, 'Spyros, where's your nephew?'

Scarcely able to control her impatience and anxiety, she beat her fists against her head. 'Where is he?' she again demanded.

Taking his time, the uncle approached and calmly said 'Good evening.'

'Come on, where is he?' she repeated angrily.

'What's the matter, Siora Epistimi,' he answered with a smile, 'you seem out of sorts this evening!'

'Where is he, tell me at once!'

'Let me think a moment.'

'Heartless man, it's vital!'

The uncle rubbed his hands together. 'He's probably with his aunt out at Aliades,' he said casually. 'But if you take my advice, Siora Epistimi, you will run along home now.' And he gave her a sly wink.

The woman realized he was making fun of her and immediately she was overwhelmed with rage. The whole dishonourable clan was laughing at her, while her daughter was in peril, might — alas! — already have been ruined! Her first impulse was to fling herself upon him, scratch his eyes out, bite him, strangle him like a raging lioness when her cubs are snatched from her. But why waste precious time over the old liar. And suddenly it flashed through her mind that Andreas might indeed have brought her daughter home with him, and that all this had been prearranged expressly to deceive her. Now she directed all her pent up rage and fury at the door. She flung herself against it with all her might, kicking at it with her foot and knee, pounding it with her fists and butting it with her head, doing all she could to break it down. And at the top of her voice she shouted, 'Open up, you mongrels, you're both upstairs, I know it!'

But the door would not give way. Siora Epistimi could imagine everything as clear as daylight, as if the walls were all transparent and she tall enough to look inside and see what was going on upstairs. Yet still it would not open.

By now all the neighbours were watching gloomily from every

door and window, as she desperately and futilely went on battering herself against the stout front door, and frequently they remarked amongst themselves, 'The poor mother!' At last one of the windows above her head swung open. At once her rage subsided. They had finally responded.

'Come home, you little bitch,' she cried in a hoarse voice, exhausted after her exertions. 'I won't lay a finger on you.'

Rini, weeping bitterly at the window, did not answer. Instead Andreas, pale and shaken, replied in a trembling voice, scared as if he were on the point of committing murder, 'She's mine! I intend to marry her!'

'Ah!' the mother cried and collapsed on the doorstep.

The neighbours looked on in silent sympathy for the suffering woman, as if a single heart beat in one and all. Everyone waited expectantly to see the outcome.

Siora Epistimi, overwhelmed with shame, was by now getting to her feet. She covered her face with her headscarf and, tottering a little, started to make her way home. Then she paused a moment and without raising her head heaved a heavy sigh and said, 'I won't curse the pair of you, Andreas, but get this clear: she has three hundred francs and not a penny more, do what you will.'

'I don't want anything,' replied the young man from the window, his love-sated heart just then feeling expansive and ready to empathize with the suffering of every creature. 'I don't want anything,' he declared again.

The mother continued on her way; and Rini, now comforted and smiling amid her tears, embraced him passionately and said, 'Oh, Andreas! We're both hard-working, so who else need we rely on?'

VIII

Winter had set in. A cold damp rainy miserable winter. Siora Epistimi went off to the factory at crack of dawn each morning, while at home Rini's household chores were now seen to by the second daughter, who had been withdrawn from school expressly. Each evening at Tragoudis' tavern people gathered to eat, drink, get tipsy and carouse; on the rare Sundays when the sun did come out, the same housewives still gathered round the suburb's little square, and only Siora Epistimi, who had become more taciturn and almost never laughed, no longer joined them, staying at home instead and waiting for her drunken husband to return. But the Corfiot minister's government had fallen. The island, as everyone anticipated, had endorsed all eight of his party's candidates, but the other provinces, tired of seeing the same names year after year, remembered an elderly former prime minister who cunningly promised them the moon, and the incumbent party suffered a rout.

In Mandouki they were now cracking down on smuggling.

It was late one Sunday afternoon around Carnival time.* The rain was pouring down and it was bitterly cold. Wrapped in two thick ancient jackets, Andreas' uncle Spyros had gone to see Siora Epistimi, and they were now conversing in the small room that served her as both dining room and parlour.

'When's the wedding?' the woman of the house had asked, after sending the children over to a neighbour to be free to speak her mind.

'Their eyes will grow dim before they see a wedding,' he replied slyly, seating himself at the table and stroking his thick moustache. 'Business has gone from bad to worse.'

'But didn't he promise? And didn't he even say he doesn't want a dowry?'

'He did, dear kinswoman. But consider — times are very hard.

44

We're constrained by the weather and by the authorities, who are now pursuing us like rabid dogs! Our government has fallen, as you know, and the new customs inspector they've appointed is the very devil. He wants to put us out of business. The new government, he says, is determined to stamp out smuggling, because, he says, it's bleeding the nation dry. All a pack of lies! Everywhere else the new ministers will be protecting their own cronies back on their home turf. What else would one expect? We smugglers, dear kinswoman, are the life force behind every party, both here and in town and in the villages. The people are like a flock of sheep — they go where we throw fodder. We control the tide in an election, you might say, or the direction of the current, because people are like a river in spate when they go to vote. Do you understand, dear kinswoman? Without us, you see, the party system wouldn't work. Let the lying newspapers and the chattering hypocrites say what they like — no sane government goes after smuggling. Individual smugglers not of their party — yes, but not smuggling itself. Isn't this true, dear kinswoman?'

'Yes,' she said indifferently, bored with his long-windedness, 'but how about telling me when he's going to marry her?'

'All in good time, dear kinswoman, we'll come to that. But didn't I just tell you it will be a good while yet? That nephew of mine, he's always been a little stupid. Well, as I was saying, dear kinswoman, no one goes after smuggling. That's a big mistake. It's a business venture too, as honourable as any other. And to tell the sober truth, which no one will admit to, it's not right that it should be hounded. It does everyone a favour, it saves them from all those unjust taxes. What does it matter if all those guzzlers in Athens eat a little less? Those same people who shout about millions in lost revenue, their mouths this wide' — and he made a gesture — 'd'you think they don't buy cheap goods when they get the chance? Of course they do. For example, the ladies you supply with sugar and other stuff in town, don't they bless you for it? But here the customs inspector is the very devil. You see, he wants promotion. He too has been promised his stripes, no doubt, and so day and night goes after us. And the weather? Really foul, dear kinswoman: put paid to our ventures all this winter. Housebound and hungry! Even so we braced ourselves and got the better of them — both the inspector and the weather. What choice was there? We had no cash to pay for a wedding for Andreas. We had to work to stay afloat. Weddings cost money, whatever one does, the world over, Mandouki the same. Isn't that so?'

Siora Epistimi tried to interrupt him, but he didn't give her a chance. 'I know what you're going to say,' he continued, 'but he just couldn't do it, bless you! Nor would I have allowed it. What, marry at night like some common bandit? No one in our family has ever done that, and are we to start now? We didn't have a bean. You yourself know that. His father's debts consumed all our efforts. We were operating with other people's cash, paying interest, paying wages, losses here, losses there, so nothing much was left to put bread on the table. See what I mean? And that stupid nephew of mine kept on saying he didn't want a dowry. He didn't want to look ridiculous, he said, after announcing it from the window.'

'And so now he wants one?' said the woman shaking her head gravely, sensing where all this garrulous preamble was heading.

'Have a little Christian patience, will you, let me finish. You don't know half our troubles yet.'

'I won't give anything.'

'Don't give then, fine. Do as your conscience dictates No one's going to grab you by the throat. As I was saying, he didn't like to ask. He was expecting to bring in enough to cover costs, poor fellow, but we've been continually housebound, constantly hounded. That's where his scruples have landed us. I told him myself, "Love alone won't fill your stomach. Go on, take your dowry," I said. "No!" "But you have all these pressing debts you need to pay." "If I don't, *tant pis*." That's all very well for now. But you see, dear kinswoman, here in the suburb as in town, if someone has debts, his creditors will come after him, obtain a ruling, have him sent to jail, seize his property, his house even, should he have one. It's not like in the villages, you know. The villagers have become our teachers. Cunningly, they've agreed amongst themselves that no one will pay up, and yet they neither have their property impounded, nor go to jail. And naturally every government protects them over this to secure their votes! Here, such times have not arrived yet.'

'He's really plaguing me this evening,' Siora Epistimi thought to herself. 'I can't believe such greed!' And losing patience, she asked, 'Tell me, Spyros, what does Rini have to say about all these troubles?'

'Rini? What can the poor girl say. God grants her patience. She weeps and carries on, but so what? She stays closeted at home. Where should she go, unmarried as she is, poor thing? She's ashamed to show her face. But what can she do? And she goes on and on about the wedding. But a wedding now?'

'What do you mean, *now*?' she asked anxiously.

'We'll come to that too, dear kinswoman, be patient. So far we've managed to muddle through in our affairs, much as one does with most things in life, you might say. We always managed to put something aside. Eventually we'd have had the wedding. We'd have worked day and night paying off the debts, in a year or two the old rogue now ruling would have been voted out, or carked it, our minister would have been back protecting us again and we'd have been making all the money we could wish for with no trouble. Now Rini has started saying, "We can't go on like this, just hoping for the best. That leads nowhere. We're hard-working, aren't we?" she says. "We don't need anybody else! Let's get married one fine night," she says, "and let's be rid of the houses consuming us and live like everybody else who's poor."'

'And isn't she right?'

'She is. But what about our reputation? Are we to be impoverished through our own incompetence and become the laughing-stock of all our enemies? Ah, no! I won't let my nephew do that to us. Better he should remain single all his life. Are we to adopt this womanish way of thinking too? What would that achieve? Nothing. The man, my dear kinswoman, is the one who directs the family. The woman stays at home and raises her children. Isn't that the way? But Rini has other ideas, not at all like ours. She says she's prepared to work. But who could bear the public scorn! Neither my sister nor my mother, nor my sister-in-law, nor my nieces ever went out to work, and are we to start now?'

Frustrated, Siora Epistimi gave a little cough. She knew all this and more. Why was the cunning old rogue so tiresome? She could see a mile off what his motive was and where his preamble was heading. Rini and Andreas were living in poverty. That's why they weren't getting married. If she had their welfare at heart, she should help them out. Yes, but they were deceiving themselves! Siora Epistimi had other children, two growing fillies and a boy. She had to consider her family, her old age and her weak drunken husband. She knew what she could afford to give them. But no, not a penny more. If Andreas didn't want the three hundred francs, so much the better. She would keep the money and so be it, let them stay unmarried. Not much harm in that. Aloud she said, 'He may have three hundred, not a penny more.'

'Don't be in such a hurry, have a little Christian patience! My nephew as I've said, dear kinswoman, even though a full-grown man, is a rather stupid fellow and, like the proverbial apple, fell for her. I kept telling him, "Don't get involved with Trinkoulos' daughter, she doesn't have the money you require. Don't play around with other people's womenfolk." He wouldn't listen. "Marry some other girl who has. I'll find you one. I already have someone on the slipway." No response. Plain stupid. What can you do! Since then everything has gone wrong for him — everything, as you'll no doubt have heard. That devilish customs inspector seized the caique full of contraband — God damn his father! Andreas was distraught. Since then his whole life has turned sour. He neither eats nor drinks nor sleeps. He's constantly brooding and complaining. Good thing they didn't catch him too! Nor us either! Andreas was in bed asleep that night. Andonis and I managed to escape, but the caique and the goods went to the devil. Now his debts have increased of course. No way can he raise money for new ventures. The interest remains unpaid. Worries by the sackful. And now Andonis and I sit glumly twiddling our thumbs. Andreas has become unrecognisable since the calamity — a different man — and justifiably so, poor fellow. The funds he kept in circulation and earned a living from have now dried up! He had been hoping to increase them. Now all he talks about is the Savvas woman's cash, and he kicks himself for not having taken my advice. But what can I do now? He should have listened to me in the first place. Then he would not have harmed your family either, and today he would be his own master. Well, let him kick himself.'

He fell silent, watching to see what impression his last words had made on the good woman. But Trinkoulos' wife remained impassive.

'The worst of it is,' he continued, 'Rini too has realized she's had a raw deal. So she's for ever weeping instead of trying to console him. You know bitterness can sometimes numb a person, even to dishonour, and turn his heart to stone? That's how it is with Andreas. Ever since all this happened he hasn't given your Rini a thought. He clutches at straws trying to save himself from going under, and battles on without regard for anybody else. That's bad. And, poor lad, I let him know it. "You made a mistake? Learn to live with it!" But he won't listen. I even said to him, "Look, nephew, what happened, happened. It can't be helped. You're much poorer now and you'll have to make a living to support your wife if you're not to send her out to work. Go on, accept Siora Epistimi's dowry, then you can start another venture." "No, he says, I told her I didn't want a dowry." And he stuck to his word as obstinately as a cursèd Jew sticks to his faith. "But Siora Epistimi has the money," I told him. "She can help you if she wants." But all to no avail. "What difference," he said, "would her measly three hundred make? Better for us all to starve to death." "Look, if you ask, she may give you more." "No, he says, my word's my word." "Yes, but you gave it at a time when you had your own caique and the rich entrusted you with cash, which you used to make a living." "No way," he says. "You'll have me on your conscience too, you know, because now I'm unemployed and when I'm hungry sunshine doesn't satisfy my stomach." "No, he says, absolutely not!" "Alright then, no. Let's see what happens. Go your own headstrong way again, don't listen to me. See what a pickle you're in? What are you hoping for? Some windfall? Ah, perhaps you think Rini might bring you good luck? But haven't you seen the kind of luck she brings? Since that girl's been on your hands, haven't you lost everything?" Of this he needed no convincing. "Shall I go and see Trinkoulos' wife then?" "No," he said. "Very well." '

'Have you still not finished?' Siora Epistimi asked him, thoroughly vexed. 'I have other matters to attend to.'

'You're showing us the door are you, dear kinswoman,' he replied with a sly chuckle. 'Never mind. I'm almost done. Poor hapless Rini, fat chance she'll see her wedding! It's a good month now that we've been surviving without work. Our meagre savings have all gone. Now they are sending legal documents round to the house. We're doomed. Andreas has become totally irrational. They are going to take possession of his home, and you should see him, he's like a rabid dog. He feels ashamed! And now he keeps going on about emigrating and abandoning us all, and the whole time your Rini weeps nonstop. He's become quite abusive too. Well, let him kick himself. Good luck to him!'

'And what's going to happen to Rini, my poor unhappy daughter?' asked Epistimi much distressed, suddenly realizing he was telling her the truth.

'Who knows! It seems to be her fate,' he replied with secret glee, pretending to be sorry, 'to remain husbandless through no fault of her own, poor thing. And if you knew how much she loves him! But what can she do? She'll have to return home.'

'Home!' exclaimed the mother horrified; she got up to light the lamp, as by now night had fallen. 'Home!' she said again. The cunning old uncle, she realized, was not lying to her. Andreas would indeed emigrate. Forced now to struggle for his survival and his social standing, he would fight a lone battle against all creation rather than admit defeat. And leave her daughter to face public scorn. Her family would thus be even further shamed. And her poor wretched daughter had not been to blame, since destiny, a higher power, had swept her into his arms, as the wind blows the leaves from the trees and whips up the foaming waves.

Meanwhile her visitor was saying, '"Look here," I told him, "before you leave, at least let me go to Trinkoulos' wife and explain things to her." He did not answer me. "For better or for worse, let me go round." "What's the point in your going, Uncle?" he replied. "D'you think Trinkoulos' wife doesn't know everything already? If she wanted to help, wouldn't she contact me herself?" "After you've deprived her of her child and of her honour, *she* contact *you*? Come now!" "She's determined to humiliate me. D'you know, Uncle, it would serve her right if I sent Rini back to her and married the Savvas woman's daughter. What d'you think, would she still let me have her?" "If she could, she would," I said, "but you're not going to do anything so dishonourable. Better to emigrate." "D'you think I'd be frightened of old Trinkoulos?"* he said.'

'Ah, so you've discovered our weakness,' said Epistimi, alarmed and furious. 'The two of you have planned all this together. What a rogue that Andreas is! What schemes his mind's been hatching. I'm amazed you have the face to come and talk to me like this. But that's the way you lot have always been. Your clan was devious from the beginning!'

'Don't abuse us, dear kinswoman, bless you, or I might lose my temper too,' he replied lighting a cigarette. 'He'd never do such a thing, nor would we permit it. You swear at me, whereas I came round with good intentions. I want you to act in time. And I came to tell you all this, believe me, without his knowing anything about it. His house is mortgaged to the tune of six hundred francs, as he mentioned to you at the start. If you'd let him have them, all would now be well. And for you, it wasn't all that much. Rini would now be married, the mistress of the ancient well-regulated house of Xis, and you yourself at peace. Wasn't Andreas worth a little more? What are six hundred miserable francs? A bagatelle! The Savvas woman's daughter has over a thousand.'

'And will he then marry Rini?' sighed the good woman, wavering.

'Don't be in such a hurry all of a sudden,' he replied putting a finger to his temple. 'If he had the six hundred he would be able to clear the mortgage on his house. But I must consult him. I told you he doesn't yet know I've come to see you. One tile is some protection from the rain, there's no denying, but it's not a roof! A man needs to eat as well. He says he'll emigrate. He won't work for others here. He has no caique, and a caique like the one we lost would cost four hundred.'

'So he wants a thousand!' exclaimed the woman angrily. 'Be off now, and do as you please, the pair of you. You came here to twist my arm. Weren't you ashamed!'

'Very well then,' he replied ominously and got up to go.

'Be off, before I tell you where to go! Three hundred is her share, if he wants it he can have it, if not you can drown her for all I care. Not a penny more!'

Just at that moment old Trinkoulos returned home, frail, stooping, inebriated, tottering. His spent eyes were blurry from the evening's tippling and his thin face was rubicund. He too had heard his wife's last words and now said to her, 'Let him have the six hundred francs, woman, I told you so from the beginning. Now look where we've ended up!'

'They want a thousand, you old drunk,' his wife cried furiously, 'and it's all your fault. What am I to give next, my eyes?'

'You've got the cash,' the drunk man said to her, nodding his head stupidly. 'You've got it. Let him have it.'

'A thousand is absolutely everything I've saved! D'you want him to take our shirts as well and beggar us?'

'We'll work,' he replied, 'give him the cash.'

And with this he staggered towards the bedroom to sleep it off, just as Andreas' uncle was stepping out into the street.

IX

The sad truth was that Andreas *had* changed. The struggle for existence and his efforts not to lose his social standing had worn him down. By this time it had also prevailed over his love. And now Siora Epistimi's answer made him stubborn.

When his uncle delivered it to him that night at a small café in their suburb, he went home with a heavy heart, muttering to himself, and he now blamed all his misfortunes on his mistress, on her ill luck, on her weak-mindedness in not knowing how to force her mother to assist them.

'Both mother and daughter,' he said to himself as he ascended the stairs, 'are dead set on reducing me to servitude, like themselves. Perhaps Siora Epistimi may even be rejoicing at my ruin.'

Upstairs he found Rini in the bedroom, seated by a small table with a lighted lamp, needle in hand, mending the household linen; he gravely bade her good evening.

Rini read his mood at once and with a sigh asked sadly, 'What's up now? She won't let us have it, eh?'

'No, she won't,' he replied dryly.

She tried to smile and a moment later said to him, 'Don't assume Mother won't give you what she promised, though perhaps when our need is greater.'

'Are you serious?' he retorted much put out. 'When could our need possibly be greater? This week they are selling off my house, and as you know, we have no other cash. Tomorrow I'll have to find work.'

'Had he really decided to?' she asked herself elated. 'Oh, if it were really so, all her misery would be at an end, from now on a new life would begin and every step they took would improve their lot.' She went over to him, a smile on her lips and a faint blush on her pale face. At that moment she wanted to throw

53

herself into his arms, thinking she would win him back. 'We are both young,' she said to him tenderly, 'and if the house is sold we'll build another better one. I too will work alongside you. I've learned my mother's skills, and we'll struggle on together. Don't despair. God will assist us. So long as we are happy, then confound the money.'

It was not the first time she had spoken to him in this vein. But Andreas didn't want to hear about happiness on such terms. He had cursed wealth too and never coveted it. Otherwise he would not of course have chosen her, but this didn't mean he wanted to face ruin. If Siora Epistimi had given him all he had requested the previous summer, everything would now be different. He'd have cleared his house of debt, he'd still be in possession of his caique and be doing more or less alright. He'd not have been obliged to take risks under adverse conditions, as his debts would have been less pressing, allowing him to bide his time and undertake less profitable but safer ventures. Whereas, as things were, her ill luck had turned everything topsy-turvy and the six hundred francs would be a mere drop in the ocean. How could he ever hope to ply the waves again after such a catastrophe? And so just then Rini's words exasperated him instead of soothing him.

Staring at the floor he replied in a thick voice, 'Confound the money. Wasn't I the first to say so? But where am I to find enough to clear the house of debt, to build another caique, to be the man I was before you came here? It's all your fault.'

'All my fault?' she said, looking at him bitterly. 'How can you say that? Did I send you all sailing to the mainland? Did I ever once reproach you? With everything you did you went your own headstrong way, and even now you won't submit to necessity. You don't want to work honestly, trusting in God. You just sit waiting for disaster to engulf you. What do we lack, for heaven's sake, the way we are? Strength, health, youth — don't we have all of these? And don't we also . . . have our love?'

'Love won't feed us,' he replied brutally.

'Allow me,' she sighed looking at him tearfully, 'to get in touch with her myself tomorrow. Oh, she'll give us the three hundred,

I'm quite sure. If you want I'll go and see her myself, even if she flies into a rage. That way you could start another venture.'

'With three hundred francs?' he said more irritated still, 'and what am I supposed to do with that, woman! Perhaps she might give me the six hundred I requested, but first she wants to see us married. Marriage be hanged! Never, by the holy cross! I won't marry you unless she forks out the thousand francs I need.' And he traced the figure on the table with his finger.

'A thousand!' she exclaimed, again going pale, 'where's the poor woman going to find it? D'you want the rest of my family to starve?'

'She has it, your father said so too. And if she doesn't deliver it . . . you've been warned. Six hundred for the house, four hundred for the caique. Then I can find work again.'

'Is that how honourable people behave? Ah, woe is me. How I've been deceived!'

'Shall I tell you what my uncle says?' he replied spitefully, as if he enjoyed making her suffer: 'Since it's all your fault, I ought to kick you out.'

'He says kick me out, does he!' she cried. And a moment later, becoming furious herself and finding a courage she scarcely knew she had, she went on, 'You say that because you've discovered our weakness, because I don't have brothers, because my father is elderly and sick, because my mother has to shoulder the responsibility for our family alone! You say it because you've landed me in this predicament and no one else will give me a second glance, now I've passed through your hands. I'm to blame for trusting you. I took you for an honourable man. Instead I have been cheated. If I'm doomed, so be it! What more can my poor mother do for you? She's willing, I hear, to give you what you asked for. You'll clear your house of debt. So now go out and work. Why are you demanding more?'

'He says,' Andreas broke in casually, 'that I should kick you out and marry the Savvas woman's daughter, who has fifteen hundred. And it's good advice. If I'd listened to him in the first place, today that money would be mine, and I'd have the caique too. But better late than never. If I don't, I'll have to work for others.'

'Go ahead and marry her then,' she answered, suddenly calming down, determined to defend her turf, 'but I'm not leaving this house, even if you kill me. We'll go through good times and bad together.'

And at once she felt a pang of jealousy, like a venomous snakebite, in the corner of her heart. Just then she heard the uncle coming up the stairs, and without greeting him she said with a severe look, 'Honourable advice you're giving to your nephew, upstanding elder that you are! Bravo for trying to get rid of me.' Her blood was up and her anger ready to explode. What had she, poor woman, ever done to this man to make him hate her so?

'Who, me, my girl,' he answered, crossing himself. 'Nephew, have I ever said a word against her? Haven't I always given sound advice? Yet the two of you are already quarrelling and bickering. Wasn't I always reminding you, Nephew, that you have pressing needs and debts? Didn't I tell you to leave the Mandouki girl alone and not to snatch her from her mother's bosom, in case you should find yourself unable to make a living and be obliged to send her home again!'

'Pilate!' cried Rini, glaring at him furiously, 'I know the way you talk and I see through you. That's how you put ideas into his head. Unable to, fiddlesticks! He can work if he wants to, and my hands are quite capable of earning a living. Let him get a job as well. What do we want with mansions mortgaged to the hilt?'

'Mortgaged to the hilt!' Andreas shouted, stung to the quick and taking a menacing step towards her.

'Calm down both of you,' said the uncle intervening and pretending not to have understood the insult. 'Didn't I suggest I find work on the fishing boats for you? Didn't I tell you I had found some? Quarrelling is pointless. Like it or not, from now on, or for the time being at least, you'll have to work for others, as Trinkoulos' wife won't give you all the cash you need.'

'Starting with tonight!' declared Andreas spitefully. 'Let's go and find the fishermen. Let her stew here on her own.'

'But make clear before you go, so she doesn't bear me a grudge and I have to bear the brunt of it from tomorrow when you're gone — have I so much as mentioned the Savvas woman's daughter since you brought this poor girl home? You told me to find work for you and I've done so. Am I now to be blamed because you're away from home?'

'I see through your specious talk,' sighed Rini bitterly. 'You're driving us apart because Andreas no longer provides you with a meal ticket since you lost his caique. Let him go out with the fishing boats, but I'm not leaving here. I won't do you that favour.'

'Me?' he sneered, curling his lip. 'My girl, you're out of your mind!' And turning to his nephew he added, 'Let her mother do *her* the favour! Thanks to that woman's perversity, the house will be snapped up just like that tomorrow or the next day. Then let her stay on if she can. Come, let's be going!'

'Ah, that's the sort of people you are!' she said despairingly, bursting into tears as the two men departed.

Andreas, pausing for a moment, replied, 'If you wish, persuade your mother to stump up the cash.'

X

Ah, how could she ever have imagined that things would end like this? He was leaving her alone, unmarried, without food or occupation, in a house which any day now would be sold, hopeless and miserable, and expecting her to find him the money. And who? The man she had loved more than herself, the man to whom she had entrusted her whole being.

'Unbelievable! Unbelievable!' she said to herself deeply dejected. And the same ideas kept revolving in her mind as she lay awake all night, hoping to hear him any minute, first in the street, then on the stairs and at last entering the bedroom. And with every footstep echoing down the lane she would prick up her ears, her heart would beat faster and something would tell her it was him.

Midnight had passed and still he did not come. The dishonourable uncle had been telling her the truth. And perhaps they really would leave her here alone until she got bored and left of her own accord, since it would be out of the question for her to force her mother to give them all they were demanding. How, how could she ask her? What would she say to the woman she felt ashamed to face and feared almost to the point of cowardice? Who could she send to see her? Everything was so contrary, so ugly, so perverse!

And slowly the hours crept by, but still she waited. Doubtless he had gone out with the fishing boats and she wouldn't see him for perhaps fifteen or twenty days, who could tell. And what was she to do alone like this — a weak woman who had never had to fend for herself in her life before? And now all her strength, all her courage all her faith in work, all her hopes and expectations of better times to come forsook her, leaving her heart completely desolate, like a rich meadow that a freak storm has swept through, wreaking havoc. Outside, silence reigned; even the sea that night was quite inaudible. The hours dragged on and the long winter's night seemed quite interminable. Ah, would that it were over soon! The light is a consolation to the wretched — the blessed light of day. Yet nights spent by his side might have been a source of happiness and comfort too. Oh to have him beside her now, the man she had loved and might still love — even though this evening he had exploited her so ruthlessly, so harshly and inhumanly — the man she could cherish as a stay in life and be proud of before all the world. And ah, he was not to blame either. He was not naturally malicious. Circumstances — his misfortunes — had quite changed him. Accustomed from the cradle to patrician ways, he could not at once adjust to such a comedown and resisted with all his might, so that on that first day, when finally obliged to work for someone else, the change was so hard that he had suddenly taken his anger and frustration out on her. He was not to blame. But would he now repent? Who could tell. And again she pricked up her ears, faintly hoping to hear his beloved footsteps, and lay waiting motionless. But even when she realized this was all in vain, fresh hope would kindle in her youthful heart. She flung off the coverlet and in the dim flickering light of the lamp gazed at her own body, her generous white breasts, her long fair hair cascading over her shoulders like a golden rivulet, and all the harmonious contours of her limbs from head to toe, all her youthful ripeness.

'Isn't this body worthy of his love,' she said to herself, 'and can he totally forget how much I love him? Can he really not care about my life, and am I to be for ever a total stranger to him?' And gloomy thoughts again darkened her mind. Alas, even if he did return and embrace her in his powerful arms with all his former passion, what hope was there of restoring the lost harmony between them, now he had shown himself prepared to reject her at a difficult juncture in his life, when regardless of who was to blame he was duty bound to battle on against all odds? And yet she felt tied to him for ever. And what about her daily bread! she reflected with alarm. No, she'd not go short there either, she resolved. In the morning she would brave the world and venture forth to look for work; she would defy ancient custom and proudly appear in public, since with capable hands like hers she knew she could earn a living. And she would wait for him. He needn't return if he did not wish to. If needs must be, let him abandon her for ever. 'For ever?' And suddenly her deep love for him, boundless, terrifying, tender, stirred within her heart — the heart of the woman who had been thrilled by his passionate embraces and remembered nestling her golden head against his manly chest each night! She wanted him. She wanted him for herself alone and was tormented by the idea that another woman might deprive her of him because she had the cash. No, she did not need him to support her, she could make a living with her own two hands. But his love was as necessary to her as her own blood which she could now feel seething within her. No, no other woman was going to take him away from her. She would not allow it. What did it matter if the mortgaged mansion, where she had been tossing all night under the roof, were sold? Good luck doesn't reside exclusively in lofty mansions and mingle only with the rich and noble. Let them lose the house. What the two of them earned together would be enough to live on, since, as she had told him, they had strength, health, youth and, ah! love. If only he'd return.

And again she pricked up her ears at the sound of someone walking down the lane. From the brisk footsteps she could tell it was the lamplighter coming to put out the streetlamps. 'It will soon be dawn,' she said to herself, a little consoled. She looked at the empty half of the bed and shed a tear. But now her heart was more at peace. In the course of all her soul-searching during the night, she had reached a decision: she would resume life's struggle with renewed energy and go on living with fresh hope. Ah, she told herself while dressing, after the first few days her husband would get used to his circumstances, to working for others without feeling ashamed, and would return to her the same person she'd first known that evening when he had cursed wealth.

XI

And that is what she did. She armed herself with patience, fortitude and hope, and that same morning applied for work in the factory she was familiar with, where her mother was still working. And she found this bold step, in defiance of all the time-honoured and irrational customs, much easier than she had imagined, and not one voice was raised condemning her for taking it. She was poor and needed to work. And now her days passed quietly. Yet Andreas did not return.

It was only through the uncle whom she now saw infrequently, as he too was absent the whole day, that she learned her husband was working at sea seven days a week, and only came to town with the boat at dawn each day to bring the fish to market. But Spyros cunningly avoided saying a word to her about their plans.

Days had passed and she was still going off to work alone, but adversity had toughened her and enlarged her heart. Now she understood the world much better. And the whole suburb knew by now that the Xis family had fallen on hard times and were obliged, both men and women, to work for others to survive, even that on Sunday their ancestral home would be put up for auction. Rini had heard this too, but she no longer despaired. She must submit to fate and was willing to rent a room somewhere and await her husband honourably and chastely, if no help were forthcoming from elsewhere. One hope never forsook her. In her heart of hearts she always believed that ultimately her mother would not allow her to go under.

And sure enough one Friday evening, after clocking off work at the factory, Siora Epistimi came round and found her in her bedroom, where usually she sat all evening. She had pulled her headscarf low over her eyes, which thus were not discernible in the flickering lamplight that played over the rest of her features.

On hearing her footsteps Rini had risen, and for a moment the two women had stood there silently, as if each were fearful of the other, as if they were afraid of the bitter words they might exchange, but then suddenly their love prevailed. The daughter threw herself into her mother's arms, tears streamed from their eyes as they calmed down and finally they kissed.

'My poor girl!' murmured the mother weeping.

Rini responded with a convulsive fit of sobbing and said at last, 'What am I to do, Mother?'

'You did what you did,' she replied releasing her and removing her own headscarf. 'You could hardly have acted otherwise, but let's now see if the situation can be remedied.'

Rini listened to her intently as she wiped her eyes. Might her trials be about to end and her virtue receive its just deserts?

'You know,' continued the mother sitting down at the table, now completely at ease, 'that this house will be sold from under you on Sunday?'

'I know, but good riddance to the dreary place. What do I want with mansions mortgaged to the hilt? That's what's ruined them.'

'Don't be hasty,' her mother told her, her eyes more animated. 'What you say is not quite fair. He is fond of his ancestral home.' And a moment later she added bitterly, 'He's walked out on you, has he?'

'He's working on the fishing boats,' she replied embarrassed, confirming her mother's assumption with a nod.

'And will he not be coming back?'

'I don't know, he didn't tell me.'

'Listen,' said her mother thoughtfully, 'tomorrow I'll seek him out in town, about the time they bring in the catch, and have a word with him. I don't want him to lose the house. Let him have the six hundred francs he asked for, but he must marry you as well.'

'Oh Mother,' she said, with tears of gratitude, 'how good you are! But it wasn't my fault either. I am not responsible for the way things have turned out.'

'You did what you did,' she replied closing her eyes, as if to escape an ugly thought that had just flashed through her mind.

But by now her daughter had gone on to say, 'Only who knows if he'll be content with that. The last night they were here, there was talk of a thousand, perhaps thousands. I've no idea how much. And how would one find the kind of money he's after, mother? He may be trying to fleece you.'

'He's not that sort,' she replied seriously. 'He's doing all this to loosen my purse strings and get what he was asking for. He'll come back to your arms the decent man he was before. Don't despair. He'll retrieve his house. I'll work myself to the bone for the other children, bless them. Even if I have less to give each of them, at least I shall have saved the family's honour.'

'Oh, Mother,' she cried in a grateful tender voice, 'how deeply I have grieved you and my dear father!'

'The poor old drunkard! Now he doesn't touch a drop. He is full of remorse. I console him too as best I can. He would give his very soul for you.'

'Alas,' Rini went on, 'if only I weren't pregnant!'

'That too!' exclaimed the mother. 'He's stolen a march on us all right. That was his scheme from the beginning. He's played a nasty trick on us!' Then a moment later, as if regretting her harsh words, she continued, 'But it is very wrong of me to speak ill of him to you. Fate has brought all this about. Whatever he may be, he's yours. You will have to live together. Accept him with good grace and try as best you can to please him. You have my blessing.'

And the two women stood up and again embraced. Then Siora Epistimi covered her face with her scarf and with a lighter heart descended the stairs of Andreas' house, resolved to sort out everything.

XII

It was eight o'clock in the morning. The picturesque marketplace of Spilia* was bustling: tradesmen going about their business, porters lugging sacks or barrels, carts piled high with hides, sacks, boxes, casks and planks, some drawn by horses others hauled by men, all coming and going with a loud clatter that blended with the hubbub of the people. On the marble steps to the market, or *Markas* as it is known to Corfiots, smartly dressed people were continually coming and going — old nobility, nouveaux riches, merchants, lawyers, doctors — for it was the time of day when the affluent went shopping.* Inside, beneath a broad paved arcade meat and fish were on display, and under the glass roof of the courtyard, vegetables, fruit and exotic flowers. The vendors' cries resounded on all sides. Standing behind the stone counter which ran all round the arcade (higher with a raised wooden floor in the meat section, where hunks of red and white meat dangled from large iron hooks), the fishmongers were vociferously commending their fish — silver, red or glossy black, some still twitching as they expired on the stone slab, others stiff and curved like fiddlesticks, others limp, stunned in the nets and dead for hours.

'Fine fish, fresh from the nets, fifty cents!' cried a rich sonorous voice, while at the same time a greengrocer was proclaiming his wares in a singsong voice, sprinkling water on the leafy vegetables displayed in the courtyard in tilted wooden crates. 'White beet, celery, mustard, spinach, parsley, help yourselves!' Further on another man was selling fruit, also in wooden crates and boxes — golden oranges and tangerines, shiny yellow lemons, dried fruit of every kind — he too proclaiming hoarsely, 'Sweet oranges, lemons, tangerines! Come and take your pick!' And all these cries mingled with the monotonous thud of cleavers, as the butchers chopped their meat on their elevated dais, silently smiling into their moustaches, and with the noise of people talking to each other and haggling over their purchases.

The fishmongers knew everyone.

'Come over here, Count, I've got just the fish for your table.'

'Doctor, welcome! I have fresh sea bass in today, or whatever else you wish.'

A strong odour of fish, fresh meat and rotting vegetables pervaded the air, but no one noticed. All those out shopping recognized one another, as they saw each other daily, and would politely exchange greetings. A few, the last of the old nobility, would cordially greet each other in Italian;* the nouveaux riches and merchants, well dressed and dignified, would look one another in the eye, anticipating an acknowledgement; while the doctors and lawyers would extend courtesies each in his own manner according to his character, self-interest and political convictions. And practically all of them were followed by some boy of twelve or fourteen, barefoot, ragged, with a cap or straw hat on his head and carrying a basket — slung across his back on entering the market, supported on his arm while shopping and balanced on his head when leaving.

One of the old nobility, a tall handsome moderately well-dressed old gentleman with a full white beard, was taking his morning constitutional under the arcade, mingling with the crowd that never failed to recognize him, accompanied by his adjutant, likewise elderly but shorter, stouter and more vulgarly attired, with an even longer, whiter beard, who strolled beside him hands in pockets, holding his baton erect, like an officer's sword, from inside his pocket.* For years the pair had been coming to the market at this hour to observe what the well-to-do were buying for their families.

They were conversing in Italian and as they strolled along they overheard a fishmonger proudly bargaining with a customer over an expensive fish.

'*Magna ben questo qua!*' (He eats well, that fellow!) the nobleman remarked to his companion.

'*Che in tochi falio*' (He's heavily in debt), replied the adjutant, standing on tiptoe to see what someone just passing who had greeted them was buying.

'*Adaseno?*' (Really?) the nobleman exclaimed, as he was smiling good morning to a wealthy gentleman, said to be worth five million, who always chose the cheaper goods for his family, pleading poverty and his numerous children, and who was just then asking the vendor for a bonus fish.

'*No el se vergogna, e el gha tanti tesori!*' (He should be ashamed, he's so rich already!) muttered the nobleman.

'*No la ghe pensa,*' said the other, '*el sona ogni giorno tante strapazae dai pescatori!*' (Don't worry, he gets cursed for it daily by the fishermen!)

Just then Andreas too arrived at the market. He was followed by two porters hurrying behind him, balancing large round baskets of fish, like wicker trays, upon their heads, their hats between their teeth, and steadying their loads with both hands. They staggered forward barefoot and in shirtsleeves, their knees bent. Tipping out their catch before the fishmongers, all three men set about sorting the fish and laying them in rows on the slab, while the fishmongers began to call out their latest bargains: 'Red mullet, codfish, fresh from the nets, only forty cents!'

There was a lot of fish on offer in the market now, creating a flurry of interest among the crowd, and all the while the old nobleman went on strolling up and down, talking in Italian to his adjutant.

Soon Siora Epistimi too appeared in the market. It was the first time in her life she had ever set foot there. Tall, lean and willowy, her wrinkled face a little pale, she was wearing a black headscarf. Her lively, still youthful eyes betrayed her nervousness as she looked about for Andreas, who unsuspectingly was going about his task. When she finally caught sight of him, she went over, quietly greeted the others and said to him, 'I want a word with you.'

'I've no time right now,' he replied impatiently, taken aback. 'Can't you see!' And he gestured towards himself, as if to say that if he was there at all at that hour, barefoot, his trousers rolled up to his knees and without a jacket, he had her alone to thank for it.

'It's for your benefit I've come,' she replied annoyed, biting her pale lip, 'for the benefit of both of you!'

This time she was answered by the uncle, who was one of the porters that had carried in the fish: 'He told you, kinswoman, we don't have time right now. Run along with God's blessing and we'll talk some other time. Is this the place for a discussion?'

She looked daggers at him and answered angrily, 'Of course, you always give him such excellent advice!'

A few people passing by looked at them curiously, but the fishmongers continued doing business.

'Come, I must speak to you,' reiterated Siora Epistimi, getting more agitated.

'And I must sell the fish. This is what you've reduced me to!'

'Attend to what you're doing, Andreas, for God's sake,' said the uncle, 'never mind her. She's probably not in her right mind, poor soul. No end of trouble today!'

'Very well,' said the woman jerking her head threateningly, 'I'll speak out now, so what, if people hear.'

A few bystanders started paying attention; the nobleman and his companion stopped at a discreet distance to listen.

'Tomorrow your house is to be sold,' she went on in a worried tone.

'So much the better,' he replied stubbornly, folding his arms. 'That way you'll get your daughter back and I'll be free.'

'After you've wronged her,' she protested, her cheeks flushing with shame and anger, 'you have the heart to say that! Listen, I've brought you the six hundred francs so that you can clear the mortgage, I'm giving you all you asked for.'

'She sounds an honourable soul,' remarked several sympathetic voices in the crowd.

But now the uncle was weighing in again: 'He told you this is not the time for a discussion. What you say is all very fine and noble, but this is not the place, my good woman. Run along and we'll talk later.'

But Siora Epistimi didn't budge. 'I've brought you the cash,' she repeated.

'We don't want your money,' said the uncle. 'Keep it since you need it, and keep your daughter too. We've found a better match elsewhere. To hell with the house, we'll build another!'

'Yes,' said Andreas, 'what can I begin to do with your six hundred? Can't you see the plight I'm in?'

'I don't have any more,' she replied in a low voice, feeling the blood in her veins begin to seethe.

'I won't marry her! I've found three times that amount elsewhere!'

'Oh, if only she'd been interested in me!' exclaimed Andonis, who was the other porter, 'it was her I wanted, not her cash. But I never dared to tell her!'

By now Siora Epistimi was trembling, her eyes blazed and her headscarf slipped down onto her shoulders. 'The dishonourable rogues!' she thought, 'they are trying to fleece us. Otherwise he'll abandon her to secure the extra cash. What dishonest scoundrels!' She felt an urge to throw herself upon them and gouge their eyes out, to fight them tooth and nail and tear them limb from limb. If only she were two people, she'd lay into both of them at once as they deserved — the wily old uncle and the dishonourable lout who had destroyed her daughter's life.

'So you're sending her back,' she cried hoarsely, 'to give birth in my house!'

'We don't want her! That's enough!' the uncle retorted.

'Not right, not right!' exclaimed several bystanders, who were now following the altercation with eager curiosity.

'To give birth to your bastards in my home!' the woman shouted at him, encouraged by the supportive crowd which was now pressing ever closer. 'Your spineless father did the same. That's why you've had it so good.'

Andreas was enraged and tried to shove her away.

'Clear off, go to the devil!' he shouted at her.

'What's wrong with the old shrew?' the nobleman asked his companion in Italian, as they stood watching from a distance.

'How am I supposed to know!' replied the other, as if to say, 'Be quiet and let me listen.'

'Don't lose your temper,' the uncle advised his nephew. 'Make yourself scarce and let me handle things, or we'll be here all day.'

Andreas was willing enough to follow this advice, but feeling spiteful as he was, he wanted to hurt her further: 'Even if you give her all the riches in Corfu, I won't marry her.'

The woman realised that he was indeed about to give her the slip. She reflected that her daughter was now ruined and her family obliged to live with the shame. Andreas' trials and humiliation had hardened his heart and driven him to this dishonourable conduct, and it was clear that to regain his social standing he had now resolved to marry the richer woman and abandon Rini for good. Was she to let him walk away like this unpunished? The mother's eyes flashed with fury. She flung herself upon Andreas, grabbed him by the shoulder and tightening her grip held him back with all her might.

'Come to your senses,' she said desperately. 'Do you intend to be dishonourable to the last? I can't give you any more.'

Andreas shoved her roughly trying to break free, but she felt a surge in her own strength, her heart telling her she was a match for ten Andreases, though they might be all strong men and she a woman. Looking round the crowd, she noticed they were all watching her with sympathy. And as she did so, she caught sight of a small knife the fishermen kept handy to descale the fish. And while Andreas, still trying to shake her off, was angrily repeating, 'I've told you I won't have her, what more do you want?', suddenly, without quite knowing what she was doing, she grabbed the knife from the wet slab and, closing her eyes so as not to see her crime, lunged at him and stabbed him in the arm. The crowd intervened at once and parted them. Blood poured from the wound. Scared out of her wits, Siora Epistimi looked dumbly at the bloodstained blade and flung it to the ground in horror. Her rage had suddenly abated and she prayed she had only inflicted a slight wound, and was relieved to hear those gathering round Andreas to inspect his arm declare, 'It's nothing, the knife did not go deep.' She was white with shock. Two constables now seized her by the wrists. 'Serves him right,' shouted the crowd.

'Horrendous stuff!' exclaimed the nobleman in Italian to his adjutant.

'What have we come to, Master!' replied the wealthy man who always bought cheap fish, also in Italian, happening to be close by and very anxious to be off. 'Ah for Britiain!'

'We had no such spectacles in those days,' observed the nobleman's companion in Greek.

By now the wretched woman was in tears. Distractedly she was assessing the likely consequences: her lovely daughter abandoned for ever; she herself in jail for months; her house deserted possibly for years; her children as good as orphans left in the hands of her weak husband, especially her two young fillies who were growing up apace, and above all her second daughter who was quite a big girl now and might make the same mistakes.

Meanwhile the constables were hauling her off to take her into custody. The wretched woman looked round a moment at Andreas, who was now rejoicing in his lucky escape, and pleaded with him, saying, 'Don't destroy my family. Here, take the key to my chest. Get my husband to give you all I have. It's deposited in the bank under his name. All, all of it, but please speak in my defence in court. Oh, confound the money!'

'That's the way,' remarked the uncle with a smile. 'At least she's paying for the stabbing.'

'It's a mere scratch,' exclaimed the victim, his eyes sparkling. 'I'll no longer be poor. Leave me be, I'm off to marry her.'

One fisherman who was standing behind his catch, a tall strong red-faced old man, the only one still wearing white baggy trousers and a fez, shouted haughtily, 'You deserve all you get, you Mandoukiots and your daily brawls down here at the market. Just the other day one of you killed the judge — what a bloody mess that was! And Trinkoulos' wife today. It just goes to show!'

'*Cosa ha dito?*' (What did he say?) the nobleman asked his adjutant.

'*Ha parlà de la onfeganda del judice.*' (He was referring to the murder of the judge.)

XIII

Andreas' wound was not serious. After they had washed and bandaged it for him at a nearby chemist, he set out for the suburb. He was going to find Rini, secure the money and pay off his debts, intending to arrange their wedding for the following Sunday. Liberated from poverty, he was rediscovering himself, becoming a decent man again, and love was reawakening in his heart.

Everyone along the way congratulated him on his lucky escape, and in the suburb where the news had spread like wildfire, people crowded round him, eager to hear from his own lips exactly what had happened. All were delighted with the outcome and wished him every happiness.

He went straight home, but not finding Rini there, continued without a moment's delay to his mother-in-law's house.

There he found everyone in tears — Rini, her two sisters and the lad.

He went up to her and kissed her.

She looked at him plaintively, as if reproaching him for all he had put her through, but she did not resist his warm embrace. Would she at last discover some measure of courage in his heart?

Joyfully he announced to her, as if instantly forgetting how he had behaved for so many days, 'On Sunday we'll get married!'

She smiled at him.

'No more poverty,' he went on, 'we can kiss goodbye to all that! Your mother was beside herself and stabbed me, but never mind. She's willing to give everything she has. I won't take more than the thousand that are needed.'

She looked at her brother and sisters in distress, then lowering her eyes said nothing.

'Why, aren't you pleased?' he asked her.

Just then old Trinkoulos entered the house. He was pale, thin, anxious, his whole body shaking, his eyes dull from the many years of tippling. But now he was fairly sober and there were tears in his eyes. He had heard Andreas' last words and lovingly embraced his daughter. Then he could no longer contain himself. A deep sob convulsed his chest and he groaned to prevent himself from bursting into tears.

Andreas looked with concern at these two people who loved each other, were suffering because of him and now seemed affected beyond words.

Eventually the father, clasping her more tightly, cried, 'You've been made so unhappy!'

He didn't say by whom. Possibly he was thinking of his wife, but Andreas assumed these words were aimed at him and said, 'I was to blame, but now all has been put right. On Sunday we'll get married. Here are the keys to her chest. She said you were to give me the thousand francs.'

'And d'you think you can buy back my love as well?' Rini asked him bitterly, 'Oh, what have you done!' And she burst into tears.

'Your love?' he asked her going pale. 'Do I not have it then?'

'No!' she replied. 'No! you were prepared to barter me for a little extra cash and wouldn't marry me without it. Our love is over. The bird has flown!'

'It will return to its warm nest,' he answered crestfallen. 'Our life together will be a true paradise.'

'No!' she said firmly. 'Not after what you've done! And even if I did still love you I wouldn't come with you. I am a worker. Who else need I rely on?' And a moment later she continued, 'Why should my brother and sisters be unfairly treated?'

'You've been made so unhappy!' her father said again, by now completely sober. 'Why couldn't she have let him have it in the first place, as I told her? Confound the money!'

'Let's go!' said Andreas.

'No!' she said resolutely, 'this is where we part. I shall go away and live among strangers in some other town. I'll work to support myself and raise the child I am expecting. My mother will obtain testimonials for me from her factory friends, so I can find work elsewhere. No, I won't come! I'm a worker, who else need I rely on?' And a moment later, as if in response to some private thought, she shouted, 'I won't come. I won't come!'

Andreas looked at her searchingly and realized that nothing he said would change her mind.

'Confound the money!' he too shouted out despairingly. 'My happiness is over!'

And he stepped out into the street.

The convict

I

It was March. Noon had come and gone two hours ago and the sun was still warm and shining brightly in the clear blue sky, where a few gray and white clouds were sailing gently past. The villagers were all down in the valley working in the fields — digging over the earth, rooting out weeds, sowing late seed — indeed just then the work was proceeding briskly, as if everyone were in a hurry to complete his task that afternoon, or anxious to leave less work for the following day.

Yoryis Arathymos was overseeing the ploughing of his field. He had worked all day himself and was now sitting in the shade of his straw hut on a long thick log beside the little door. He was a lean man of medium height in his mid-forties, with blue eyes, unshaven cheeks and a flaxen moustache that curled down round his chin. He was wearing a straw hat, his jacket was draped over his shoulders, and he sat barefoot smoking a thick cigarette. An ugly black-and-white dog was curled up at his feet.

The large field he owned extended before him, three acres of level cultivated land bordered by fruit trees, with a huge fig tree beside the hut; and as he smoked, Arathymos surveyed his plot complacently, calculating in his mind the yield he might expect from it once sown. 'Tourkoyannis,' he shouted with a smile, 'work is never ending but a man must rest ... His oxen too! ... Don't hurry them.'

'We'll soon be done,' replied a stout voice from the field. 'Brrrh, Perdiki, brrrh!' It was the voice of Tourkoyannis at the plough, who was encouraging the oxen with this curious cry as they turned over the heavy clods.

The two huge beasts, one russet the other glistening black, their heads bowed almost to the ground beneath the heavy yoke, one leaning against the other, remained poised for a moment, thrusting forward with their whole massive weight, standing on three legs ready to move forward on the fourth when the clod detached itself, their bulging muscles indicating they were doing their utmost; then, just as Tourkoyannis shouted back, they made one final effort and suddenly lurched forward, taking two or three rapid steps as if about to stumble under their own momentum, while behind them the ploughshare, slicing deep into the soil, turned over a thick gleaming black clod riddled with white roots, and finally came to a halt, the ploughshare gleaming, only to brace themselves almost immediately for a renewed attempt.

Behind them Tourkoyannis, leaning towards the right, steered the plough with both hands, the ropes attached to the oxen's horns running through his fingers, the goad, a long stick spiked with a nail, gripped in his left hand. And every so often he would lean heavily on the plough-tail, or raise it with both hands, or let go of it to guide or prod the animals, praising them by name and encouraging them at their onerous task: one was called Perdiki, being russet brown, the other Paraskevas, as he had been born on a Friday.*

Tourkoyannis was a swarthy man, likewise in his forties. He too was lean and of average height, with small slightly sleepy eyes, a little moustache and scanty beard, his long hair falling to his nape in thick taper-like strands,* while his oval face expressed his kind-heartedness and serenity of soul. He was lightly clad in an open shirt which left his hairy chest exposed, and elaborately patched old trousers* rolled up to the knees; and he too was barefoot and wearing a straw hat.

'Good for you, Paraskevas, keep it up!' he shouted, 'Brrrh!' as he leaned on the plough-tail, plunging the blade deep into the earth. And as the beasts renewed their efforts another clod came loose and now lay waiting to be shaken free of weeds. He looked back over his shoulder. A boy of eight following him and sowing the maize, seed by seed, into the fresh furrow was lagging behind just then, having stopped to watch a bird alight close by. 'Come on, Thanasoulis, don't dawdle!' Tourkoyannis told him. Then glancing further back, where a man and a woman were briskly breaking up the clods with their hoes and bending to shake out the weeds, he shouted anxiously, 'Don't fall too far behind! And keep it fine, any clods will suffocate the shoots.'

The woman was Yoryis Arathymos' wife and the man Petros Pepponas, their neighbour. He had come to lend a hand in their field today, as they had sent Tourkoyannis over to help with his for a whole day. The woman was a beauty. Her radiant dark eyes stood out in her small face even at a distance. Over her white headscarf she wore a scarlet band. She was not too tall and her features were attractive, especially her mouth. The sleeves of her dusty smock were rolled up, and her old black woollen skirt with its fraying hem was tucked up too. Her movements were vigorous, as she hacked at the clods and bent to shake out the roots. Her name was Margarita.

Her companion was a tall broad-chested man, still youthful-looking in his mid-thirties, with a handsome clean-shaven face, a twirling black moustache and flashing dark eyes. He too was lightly clad. Frequently his lively eye would linger on the woman, and with a secret sigh he would address her in an undertone to avoid being overheard.

Just then Margarita had her back to him and was bending low, leaning on the handle of her hoe as she shook out the gleaming white roots from an upturned clod. Pepponas watched her. His eyes expressed boundless insatiable desire, while a sardonic smile played on his lips.

Softly, almost murmuring, he said to her, 'Are things always going to be like this, Margarita?'

'How d'you mean, like this?' she replied without looking at him. 'There's so much going on.'

'I must find myself another woman,' he told her resolutely, 'one who'll be mine and mine alone.'

'Good luck with that,' she replied, perturbed. Involuntarily she straightened up and found herself quite close to him. And to disguise her abrupt movement, she flung a half-shaken clump of weed away. But Petros noticed that her eyes were flashing and her perspiring face had changed colour slightly. 'Is that so, eh?' she continued in a low voice after a pause. 'And when? And who?'

He made no reply. Briskly hacking at the earth two or three times with his hoe, he levelled out the soil and moved forward a pace.

'Ah, so my fancy man won't answer!' Margarita added to annoy him. 'So we're making threats! Yes, threats! When, Petros, and who?'

'Lady Luck,' he replied irritably. 'D'you call mine a life? We've been carrying on like this for five years now and I've become enslaved! You've no idea how much suffering you've caused me. And things seem set to go on like this for ever! Once in a blue moon you remember me, the rest of the time . . . you're his! . . .'

'Keep up!' shouted Tourkoyannis glancing back at them anxiously every so often, 'otherwise you'll have too much to do on the return! — Brrrh, Perdiki! Brrrh, Paraskevas!'

'We'll call it a day on the return!' Arathymos yelled back from where he was sitting. 'Why exhaust the beasts? They've been at it since dawn. We'll finish the job inwo or three hours tomorrow !'

At the sound of its master's voice, the dog woke up, yawned, shook itself and settled down again, its head erect and front paws outstretched. The setting sun had started to turn crimson.

Speaking rapidly without raising her head, Margarita said to Petros, 'I'm tied to him and have to live with him. I'm stretching things already as it is. Do you want to cause a scandal, set people's tongues a-wagging, risk us both being doomed, my children too? . . .' She looked round apprehensively in the direction of her husband, who seemed to be watching from afar. 'Don't ruin me!' she whispered fearfully. 'Have you no sense at all!'

'I've got my back to him, he can't see me!' he replied calmly.

'Enough of this!' she said impatiently, 'I'll come to the hut tomorrow evening if I can, but I can't promise because now Tourkoyannis too is watching me.'

'Tourkoyannis!' he replied taken aback. 'But what's he after? . . . Ah, things can't just go on like this . . . Listen! . . .'

She did not reply and moved further away from him.

'I too need a little freedom!' Petros went on. 'I'll fix things so your husband has to leave the village! Then I'll have you to myself!

I'll get him sent to jail! Yes, to jail!'

Margarita, bent over and looking at him upside down, gave him an anxious glance. 'That way,' he persisted, 'he won't always be around you!'

Arathymos' voice rang out instructing Tourkoyannis, 'Unyoke the team! It's getting late!'

The oxen had reached the end of the field, where the ditch was choked with brambles and wild shrubs, and were about to turn and start a new furrow, but there was no longer time for this. In compliance with his master's orders, Tourkoyannis plunged the ploughshare deep into the earth, and tugging sharply on the ropes brought the oxen to a halt, crossing himself at once. And taking a deep breath, he looked at his two beasts with a sympathetic smile as they stood panting and perspiring, then turned to survey the results of the day's labour. All the ploughed land was now level, black and gleaming. He smiled again complacently. Taking the bag of seed from the boy, he tied it securely and gave it back to him to deliver to the hut, then at once proceeded to unyoke the team, while Petros and Margarita, who had now stopped talking, steadily approached, hacking away with their hoes at the last few clods the plough had turned.

Once unyoked, the oxen ponderously plodded off of their own accord one behind the other towards the hut, not stopping until they reached their customary tree. Tourkoyannis followed them and tethered them next to one another. By this time they had begun to relax and stood waiting for their evening fodder. Paraskevas, the jet black ox, rested its large head on its companion's neck and both emitted a loud bellow, which reverberated all around the hills and down to the sea. Tourkoyannis brought them their fodder in his arms, again crossing himself, then came and sat down next to Arathymos, satisfied with the day's work.

Almost at once they were joined by Petros and Margarita, who had meanwhile completed their task, and now settled on the ground to have their evening meal.

II

It was late afternoon the following day. The sun was about to set and crimson light pervaded everything, like a golden haze of dust in the air, penetrating even the thickest clumps of olive trees, spreading like a mist across the budding vineyards above the freshly ploughed fields, each with its own distinctive colour, and turning all the dells and slopes and hills a rosy hue, leaving nothing pallid, neither tree nor human face. Just then Petros, absorbed in thought, was descending the rough road from the village and heading for the secluded hut where Margarita would sometimes come to meet him. That evening he was wearing his jacket slung over one shoulder and his broad straw hat pulled down over his eyes. He took no notice of anything, his gaze focused on the ground, oblivious to the radiant beauty all around him. It had been months now since they were last alone together. And as he descended the steep slope he kept asking himself, 'Will she come?' And in response he dug his nails into his palms. He quickened his step as if hurrying to reach the deserted hut before her, even though he knew full well that, were she to come at all, he would still have to wait for hours until late in the evening when things had quietened down. Suddenly, on what grounds he scarcely dared ask, a ray of hope, golden as the setting sun, lightened his mood: perhaps tonight she would actually come. And this brought back the boundless joy of their last meeting, which had brought relief to his dejected soul and tears to his eyes, moistening her pretty face. He remembered the glowing expression of the woman he loved so ardently when, disregarding the sinfulness and danger, she had willingly surrendered to him in a moment of rapture that had eclipsed all rational considerations. And closing his eyes for an instant, he pictured her coming to meet him now, walking lightly and proudly down the path and then ascending the familiar slope to the deserted hut, opening the door and glancing round fearfully, then gazing at him from the threshold with a look that gave him new life, revitalized his soul, a look so full of love that it kindled an irrepressible urge within him, a feeling of infinite desire.

Meanwhile he had descended the hill and found himself on level ground between two clumps of brambles covered with blackberries and blossoms. Women were coming up the hill, returning to the village with their goats and lambs, talking cheerfully amongst themselves and spinning with their distaffs as they came. They all greeted him, and their flocks which took up the whole road parted to let him through; he acknowledged their greetings with a smile and wave, but neither recognized nor stopped to talk to any of them, his mind absorbed in pleasurable memories holding tantalizing promise that the paradise he had long dreamed of would soon be a reality. 'Ah, and if she comes!' he murmured to himself, 'what transports of delight!' He noticed how cold and sweaty his hands were and marvelling how this woman could rouse him so intensely that he became indifferent to the charms of all the others, he shook his head sadly.

Now he struck up a narrow path and began ascending a steep hill dotted here and there with tenacious scrawny olive trees. Myrtle bushes clung to the poor soil and the more open ground was overgrown with thorny brambles, gorse and bracken. The tiller of the earth in him awoke and he said to himself, 'What a shame that all this land should be lying here unused. Were it not part of a nobleman's estate it could be cultivated and feed an entire family!' But this reflection lasted no more than a few seconds and his thoughts returned to the meeting at the hut with Margarita, she again taking exclusive possession of his mind. Ah, Margarita! She was his whole life, his boundless joy, his cruel intolerable torment, it was she who cut him off from life and yet was life itself. How he adored her! How he loved her every fault, even the pain she made him suffer. He acknowledged that she was contrary, quarrelsome and timid, knew that the slightest thing made her bad-tempered, that all her trepidation over their affair infuriated him, that she expected him to be patient, uncomplaining, submissive to her will, wanted to see him continually thirsting and suffering from unsatisfied desire. And yet he loved her!

At last he had reached the top of the hill and was now approaching the hut. He stopped a moment to survey the scene. A profound stillness reigned. His ears took in the sublime quiet of the valley extending all around. The occasional lowing of an ox, the distant barking of a dog or the sound of some woman's voice lasted but a few brief seconds, not long enough to disturb the universal mystery. The little houses dotted here and there and the villages gleaming white among the verdant hills lay silent. Further off the sea, pale blue, opalescent, flecked with gold, exuded a light mist which itself turned golden, and the whole scene was lambent, peaceful, infinite. There was not the faintest breeze. The sun like a large crimson disc was descending towards the golden horizon, the radiance from its rippling surface changing by the minute, and as it prepared to plunge into the sea, it ceased to dazzle the eye. And the mysterious quiet and radiant splendour weighed heavily on Petros' soul, infusing it with black despair: he felt small, weak and insignificant, subject to implacable and unchanging laws which governed everything and were not swayed by human will; and apparently the sublime sunset made the same impression on all other human beings, beasts and plants, as at that exalted moment the villages, fields and paddocks were also silent as if themselves in awe.

'Ah!' sighed Petros as he reached the door of the hut, 'Will she come? Won't she? — now that Turkoyannis is watching her as well.'

His mouth was dry and his cold hands more sweaty. Why had the fellow returned from abroad? And why had he sought work in Arathymos' household? This thought vividly revived the image of Margarita's husband yesterday, that thrice-blessed man sitting smoking outside his hut, and he imagined his beloved Margarita now at that very moment by his side, surrounded by their children, reminding him that Yoryis could enjoy her whenever he desired, that she was the inseparable companion of his life.

Petros then went on to brood over the way Margarita had brought Arathymos every imaginable happiness. Nothing was wanting in that blessed family, adorned and enlivened by her refreshing presence. Arathymos now owned his own field, but when he had married her twelve years ago his affairs were floundering. The whole village knew about this. He had even had to borrow the five hundred it cost to put on the wedding feast. His lazy and uneducated father had neglected the land, leaving it fallow, uncultivated and overgrown with weeds. With the earth yielding no returns, he accumulated debts year after year which consumed his entire income when the olive oil was harvested. But then, after Yoryis married Margarita, suddenly things started to improve. Everyone began working hard. Soon they acquired a pair of oxen and some sheep, they paid off their debts, the seed they planted in the earth grew golden, the olive trees sagged under their bounty, the field turned into a sea of crops, the fruit trees became ever more prolific over the summer, and from then on there was nothing the Arathymos family went without.

She had even presented him with three children, each finer than the last: a girl already growing up, who accompanied the sheep down into the valley and did other household chores and errands, and two little boys who went to school each morning and were learning to read and write. Everything in the Arathymos household was progressing splendidly.

All these reflections had come to him instantly, passing through his mind with lightning speed. Suddenly he could see everything at once, just as the eye of someone who has climbed a high mountain peak takes in the entire surrounding scene. But then all at once his mind stopped functioning and he felt dizzy.

Now the sun had set and from the sparse trees on the rugged hillside came the sound of birds resuming their melodious song. The golden haze had vanished from the air and only the coursing clouds tinted the pale sky a rosy pink. Petros opened the door of the hut and peered into the darkness, then he smiled wryly at the way his desires had fuelled his expectations: 'You even imagined she would be waiting for you!' he thought. 'How could she be here already, with all that way to come?'

Entering, he sat down in the corner where they always sat together and closed his eyes a moment, attempting to imagine her beside him just like last time, but try as he might he could not recall her features — something he now found happening quite frequently. He would see her in his mind's eye briefly, but as soon as he tried to picture her beautiful dark eyes, her small red mouth, or some feature of her lovely body, her whole image would vanish like a pallid ghost; he could remember distinctly neither her radiant complexion, nor her fluttering eyes which he had so often gazed into with ardour, nor the contours of her sensuous lips, nor the sweetness of her smile; he could no longer recapture the way those lips would press against his own, then explore further, nor the way he would inhale their fragrance . . . And again he said passionately, 'If only she'd come now, this very instant!' He got to his feet, half opened the door, put his head out and looked about outside. But he did not yet lose patience. Going back inside he strode restlessly up and down the room, head bowed. Again he recalled her saying, 'Now Tourkoyannis is watching too.' Why was he watching, he pondered uneasily, why did he have to return from abroad and become a servant in Arathymos' household? And he pictured him as he had seen him ploughing yesterday, lean and wiry with his sparse beard and dark taper-like strands of hair falling to his nape; he recalled the man's innocent childlike eyes and the sweet smile on his lips that no amount of sorrow or hard work erased. The man served Arathymos' family faithfully, working from dawn till dusk to honour, as he put it, the daily bread that they provided. But Petros also remembered how his soft voice would tremble when he spoke to Margarita, how he would lower his gaze in her presence, as if afraid to look her in the eye, and how he would respond to her beauty reverentially, as if standing before one of the icons adorning their rich and pretty village church. And in some corner of his heart the suspicion gnawed at him that Tourkoyannis too loved Margarita. Ah, and besides he could be with her as often as he wanted, talk to her whenever he felt like it, ogle her any minute of the day, because

he was living in her house! . . . And if Margarita were willing . . .
he could . . . But he dismissed this suspicion with a shudder. Yet
the idea wouldn't leave him alone and tormented him for quite
some time. Involuntarily, a disgusting and alarming image arose in
his mind. Tourkoyannis, pale tearful and speechless, scared by his
own happiness and trembling all over, was holding Margarita in
his arms. He shuddered, broke into a cold sweat and mopped his
brow, as the madness of passion took possession of him. 'That,'
he told himself, 'must be why he's watching her.' Again he began
striding up and down inside the hut, then went to the door and
took a look outside. 'She's not coming, nor will she ever,' he
thought despairingly. Re-entering the hut, he stood with his head
thrust back, staring at the light entering through a chink in the
roof. Then he scratched his head and wryly twisted his dry lips.
'Don't be absurd,' he told himself. 'What, Tourkoyannis!' But he
couldn't allay his suspicions. 'We men are all such cunning
devils . . . but then so are women! Everyone seeks self-gratifica-
tion. And Margarita is that sort of woman.' A moment later he
reflected, 'But no, no, no! . . . She's not carrying on with
Tourkoyannis! . . . If only she'd hurry up! . . . If only she were
here! . . . But why in that case, why should he speak to her so
bashfully, why should he gaze at her as if she were a holy icon, the
way I used to in the early days? Nothing's going on between
them . . . But then again, who knows? No, nothing! And yet . . .
And yet, there's no doubt he loves her! Ah, if only she were here,
ah, if only she would come! . . .'

He went to the door and looked out again. Jealousy was
tormenting him; he was consumed with impatience. His lips felt
more and more parched and there was no water to refresh them,
but he wouldn't for the world leave the hut and go down to the
little trickling spring near the bottom of the hill below the road.
He felt an unpleasant lump in his throat, preventing him from
swallowing. 'With her husband, fair enough,' he went on
brooding. 'Patience! But with this fellow too! Just like with me in
the early days . . . Could it be possible? . . . No, no, no!'

And immediately he recalled those earlier times, five years or more ago now. When, where and how it had all begun he no longer rightly knew himself. He had often worked for Arathymos, his neighbour, and saw her frequently and noticed her husband's respect for and subservience to her. Her opinion always prevailed; what she said was always right; Arathymos never forgot that Margarita had rescued him from the worries and disasters threatening his family. And Petros felt at ease with her, because they had been born in the same village and known each other all their lives. So all their discussions were frank, as if he were not a stranger, and they collaborated and talked openly like workmates, not like man and woman. No, never. Petros was still unmarried and she would often counsel him to take a wife. And at some point Petros had realized that in her presence his mind would suddenly stop functioning, he would look at her and fancy he was living in a dream, and if she or someone else addressed him he would find himself at a loss for words. And he would take great delight in listening to her voice, whatever she was saying. Often when Margarita was talking, whether to him or someone else, he no longer attended to the meaning, instead listening spellbound to the tone of her sweet voice, as if it were an enchanted instrument playing angelic hymns; and he could have sat for hours delighting in that voice without trying to make sense of it. How much time had gone by like this he did not know. Even now he was not sure if Margarita had sensed his deep enchantment in her presence. All he knew was that one day, early in summer, they were at work together and found themselves alone in the tall grass they were engaged in cutting. It was the middle of the day and the sun was scorching. And all of a sudden reason had utterly forsaken him, and as if living in a dream all he could see in front of him was Margarita. They were alone together, in the open air, lightly clad, hot from their exertions. And there was Margarita in all her beauty — young, strong, gloriously tanned, and so close to him that the smell of her sweat lingered in his nostrils, mingling with the fragrance of the freshly mown grass. How that smell intoxicated him. And then he realized he couldn't understand a word Margarita was saying, all he could do was listen, listen. He listened to the cadence of her melodious voice resonating in his ears like strange angelic music, and suddenly the only thing in the world that he was conscious of were Margarita's two lustrous slightly fluttering eyes, the colour and sweetness of which he even now could not recall; and everything outside those eyes became an obscure red blur. Suddenly he was close beside her. He caught her up light as a feather in his broad embrace and tried to kiss her on the lips . . . At first she had turned her face aside to avoid his kiss, gently pushing him away to make him release her, and in a timid, almost beseeching voice had said, 'Go now, go away!' But he sensed that her resistance was at best half-hearted and rapidly diminishing. Before they knew it they found themselves on the ground, on a bed of hay among the tall thick grass that closed over them like a vaulted verdant canopy. The earth exuded fragrant heat and the air they inhaled felt warm and glowing . . . And Petros remembered how when he recovered from the intoxication of sensual delight and was thanking her for making him so happy, she had lowered her head in shame and said, 'How am I to face you in the future? Now I have two husbands in my life!' That's how their affair had started.

And since then his passion had remained constantly frustrated, galling him daily because he was tormented by jealousy and Margarita was only rarely willing to yield to him, concerned for her good name, the tranquillity of her family and her three children. Indeed since Tourkoyannis' return from abroad, she had become even more cautious, insisting the ploughman was now watching her. Petros again asked himself, 'But why? And how does Margarita know he's watching her?'

'I'll ask her the moment she arrives,' he thought. 'But will she come?' It was getting darker. Petros stuck his head out of the door again. The trees had lost their colour and looked gray. The hills had faded and a solitary star had now appeared, twinkling faintly in the darkening sky. He remembered how often before he had resolved to ask her various questions, then had either failed to meet up with her alone, or forgotten to ask her and surrendered to the bliss of the rare moment, eager to drink his fill of love. And while they were together, all he could think of was admiring her and praising her charms.

But this evening she was very late indeed. She should have been at the hut by now. His agitation steadily increased. He again began to stride about, running his fingers through his hair, chewing his fingernails and dark moustache, closing his eyes and taking rapid shallow breaths; and every so often he would go over to the door, cautiously open it a little, stick his head out and peer along the path to where it disappeared over the brow. Still no sign of her! And he went on worrying and fretting, 'So she wasn't coming after all! . . .'

And along with his impatience that mounted by the minute, he was tormented by the insane jealousy that gripped his heart; and he kept trying to imagine what Margarita could be up to, since she should surely have arrived by now. Ah, how different these moments would be if she were here, and how swiftly they would fly. But still there was no sign of her! Still she didn't come!

He sat down in the corner he had occupied with Margarita last time, got up again almost at once, looked out, sat down again, again got up, paced up and down and again looked out. He felt confined by the four walls. Outside it had grown darker and the light was fading faster all the time. If she didn't appear at once, or in a couple of minutes, or in a little while, then she'd not be coming! Ah, she'd not be coming! And he sat waiting like a lunatic, listening intently and plucking hairs from his eyebrows and his hairy chest. She'd not be coming! And he pricked up his ears at the slightest sound, at every leaf fluttering from some olive tree onto the roof, at every creak, every twig snapping or beetle scurrying in the rafters, and each time his heart would leap, then falter as the hope it might be her footsteps faded; and then he would again hold his breath, close his eyes and, craning his neck, hear her approaching, drawing nearer, and arriving . . . But a moment later the sound would fade and hope would again take flight. It wasn't her! She wasn't coming! No, she'd not be coming!

And the darker it became, he realized, the slimmer were the chances. Margarita never went out walking late at night, and her husband came home early every evening. By now Petros was exhausted by the protracted wait, his whole body drenched in sweat from dejection and anxiety, unable to find any consolation in the black despair of the moment. Resolutely he said to himself, 'That's it, she isn't coming!'

Now from the ditches surrounding the fields and the spring at the bottom of the hill came the monotonous chirping of the crickets, punctuated by the occasional croaking of a frog heralding the rain. Inside the hut it was pitch dark and only the cracks in the door and one or two chinks in the roof let in any light. 'Ah, of course she won't be coming now,' he told himself. 'I might as well leave! No, perhaps I'll wait another couple of minutes. Or maybe longer! Might as well stay a little longer, since I've waited all this time already, just in case she should come and then not find me.' And he spent another quarter of an hour fretfully waiting. But in the end he gave up. Now he was positive she wouldn't come. And though deeply saddened, he felt certainty was more tolerable than anxiety and suspense. The disappointment was bitter but the suspense was over.

'What an ordeal I've had of it all evening!' he thought as he lay down in the darkness. He had a crashing headache, so bad that he couldn't just ignore it. And the pain distracted him a little. Brooding, he said to himself, 'I can't go on like this, I must do something, find some solution! . . . If only Yoryis weren't in the way! — Oh, my head! . . .'

His conscience urged him to emigrate, to find a remedy for his passion in the very sorrow of a cruel separation, and thereby escape so many other woes. And spitefully he reflected that by doing so he would also be hurting Margarita, that pitiless woman who was unwilling to sacrifice anything, anything at all, for love of him. But on the other hand he became obsessed with the idea that he would then be liberating her, leaving her in the clutches of her husband and that cursed Tourkoyannis, who was now the cause of all his misery. He was the reason she'd not come. Petros became incensed. For a moment he forgot about his headache, as another ugly suspicion crossed his mind. Margarita had deliberately pinned him down there in the hut all evening, so she could feel free and not be worrying that he might suddenly show up. She had better things to do. But his headache drowned out this worry too.

'If only, if only Yoryis weren't there!' he thought to himself again. And he sensed that passion was trying to drag him down a hitherto untrodden path. His heart thumped violently. He remembered what he had said to Margarita the day before: he could get him sent to jail and knew how to go about it. Yes, he knew how alright. He would stay awake all night tonight and work out a plan. Never mind about his headache!

His erotic obsession was pushing him down a slippery slope he would be unable to draw back from, and he was well aware of this. And yet he could no longer go on struggling with himself, just as at the beginning he had been unable to escape the toils of his regrettable infatuation. And he thought of the glorious sunset he had witnessed on his way up to the hut that evening, which had brought home to him the weakness and triviality of all human schemes. All of nature was subject to iron laws of necessity and one of the laws governing human beings was erotic love!

With this thought he left the hut. Night had fallen.

III

Arathymos' house stood on the outskirts of the village, the first on the main road that climbed up to the village. It was built on a raised plot of level land four meters above the road at the point where it began to climb. All around, dry-stone walls overgrown with weeds held the soil in place. It was a two-storey house, with four small windows at the front and two more in the shorter end-walls. Three rough-hewn uneven steps led up to the large front door, the only opening in the ground floor wall. The door and shutters were old, dilapidated and unpainted, dried out by the sun and darkened by the rain; the walls had not seen fresh plaster since they were built. Behind the house, invisible from the road, was a large allotment where Arathymos grew vegetables, onions, garlic. Within the allotment, attached to the house at one end, was a large shed with its own fifteen-hundred-tile roof, the stable for Arathymos' two oxen, sheep, a goat and a pig. Inside, the house had no partition walls. The entire ground floor was one large storeroom. In one corner stood an ancient narrow chest, its coloured carving faded, on which Tourkoyannis slept, spreading his straw mattress out each night and stowing it away at dawn. Adjacent to the chest was a steep narrow staircase with no handrail, leading to the upper storey. On the other side of the room, to the right of the front door and propped on some old joists, were three casks of wine, an upturned vat for treading grapes, two sealed jars with cheese and olives and a stone vessel with a wooden lid, likewise sealed but containing oil. Under the stairs, directly opposite the front door, was a little door leading to the kitchen, a small single-storey room attached to the rear of the house with a tiny square window. The upper floor was all one open room, with no ceiling and no glass in the windows. Hanging from the rafters were platted bundles of yellow maize preserved for planting out the fields. To the right near two of the windows was a large clean double bed, with a brightly coloured quilt, the Arathymos family bed. There the master of the house, Margarita, their daughter and the two boys all slept together. In the other half of the room stood a wooden table flanked by two long benches and covered with a red-white-and-blue-striped tablecloth; while next to the bed were another trunk like the one Tourkoyannis slept on but more recent — Margarita's dowry chest with all her clothes — and three locked wooden coffers containing maize and beans, the family's entire food supply until the following harvest. Between the windows near the bed hung four smoke-blackened icons with a glass-shaded oil-lamp below, and an ancient hunting gun with a long barrel, always kept loaded. This was all the furniture the Arathymos family possessed.

It was still dark. Dawn was two hours away and though not cold it was raining. At this early hour Tourkoyannis leaped out of bed fully clothed, crossed himself and murmured a brief private prayer, lit the lamp, opened the door to check the weather and the time by the stars, went into the kitchen, kindled a fire and put some water on to boil, came back and stowed away his mattress, then, still unwashed, grabbed a blackened lantern and lit it from the main lamp, tucked a bundle of hay brought home the previous evening under his arm, and, as every morning, went out to the stable to feed the oxen. A fine rain was falling and the moon shone faintly from behind the clouds.

As Tourkoyannis opened the stable door there was a rush of warm air and a pungent odour from the animals inside. The two huge oxen were lying on the damp straw amid their droppings, quietly chewing the cud. Smiling at them affectionately, he doled out the hay, saying, 'Here you are, Perdiki. Here Paraskevas!' Then he looked over the other animals, the four sheep huddled close together and still fast asleep, the wakeful nanny goat which bleated when it saw him, and the pig tethered by its leg and grunting as it rooted in the dirt, and having satisfied himself that all was well, he returned to the house. After his ablutions, he went into the little smoke-filled kitchen and sat down by the fire to await the dawn. The house tomcat, an ugly little tortoiseshell, sprang onto his shoulder, caressed his head as it settled down, and began to purr.

Sometime later he heard the family upstairs beginning to wake up one after the other. First Margarita turned over in bed and a moment later yawned. Immediately her two little boys jumped to the floor and he listened to them scampering around in their bare feet and chirping. Then he heard Margarita getting up, followed shortly by her daughter and finally by Arathymos himself. He listened to them talking quietly as they dressed, and soon could hear them coming down the narrow wooden stairs, and as they appeared in the store room he greeted them. Only the daughter still remained upstairs. The two boys were the first to join him in the kitchen and he smilingly caressed their heads, but when he saw Margarita enter he made way for her, lowering his eyes, and let her make the coffee without speaking to her.

The cat leaped from his shoulders and the boys grabbed hold of it with shrieks of laughter. But the creature started miaowing and protesting. By now the day had dawned.

'Don't torment it, boys,' Tourkoyannis told them gently. 'Let it be!'

'We're going to feed it,' they cried together.

'Don't go running off now!' the adults both replied.

'Don't go running off!' reiterated Tourkoyannis.

'Are we going to dance again today?' asked Thanasoulis, the older boy, and letting go of the cat which swiftly escaped through its hole, he rushed up to Tourkoyannis' knees. His little brother followed, giggling. Tourkoyannis lifted them onto his knees and started bouncing them up and down, humming a little tune.

'No, no,' said Yannoulis, the younger boy, a moment later, sliding abruptly to the floor, 'we want you to dance!'

Tourkoyannis laughed.

'Now, now,' said Margarita, 'Don't crucify the poor man!'

Glancing at her appreciatively, Tourkoyannis got to his feet and led the children into the middle of the room. There he lined them up, made them join hands and taking the elder boy's hand clumsily began a village dance, mimicking the sound of a violin with his lips. The children, laughing their heads off, followed his lead and the adults laughed along with them.

Just then Arathymos' daughter Leni, a girl of ten, came downstairs too and said, 'Good morning.'

Tourkoyannis, rounding off his little dance, laughingly responded, 'So Mistress Leni is the last one down. Late as any countess! She forgot all about the washing, after I'd got the water ready for her.'

'Quite right,' said Margarita, 'why go wandering down the valley like a gadfly in the dark?'

By now they were drinking their black coffee in large mugs and dispersing about the house. Then Leni at once set about sprinkling the washing assembled in her basket the previous evening.

'Girls have to get used to work early in life!' said Tourkoyannis seriously. 'They get married young and move in with their husbands, who will curse their mothers if they haven't been taught properly. With boys it's different.'

Meanwhile the sun had risen behind the clouds and Leni, having got the washing ready, now led the sheep, the goat and the pig out of the stable and, despite the rain, set off for the river with the heavy clothesbasket balanced on her head. The boys got ready for school and Arathymos set out for the village.

'Looks like rain all day,' he remarked to Tourkoyannis as he left. 'No work for the oxen. Do what odd jobs you can find.'

Soon Tourkoyannis and Margarita were left alone together in the house.

IV

It was still pouring. The rain fell steadily in vertical streaks, saturating the air and on hitting the ground exploding into a myriad tiny droplets, churning up the mud. There was no wind and the noise of rushing water as it filled the drains and ditches mingled with the sound of the rain lashing the soil. It was still early, there was not much light as yet and the air was tepid; on the dripping trees the still tender leaves glistened as if silver-coated.

'A day off today!' Tourkoyannis said to Margarita shyly. 'Is Yoryis back yet?' and he looked about.

'No,' she replied from the little kitchen, 'but bring me your plate and I'll serve you first.'

Tourkoyannis looked at her gratefully with his large innocent eyes, stood in the doorway of the little kitchen and glanced around for his plate. Then he went over to a basket suspended from a beam, picked out his thick earthenware plate and wooden spoon and approached Margarita, his eyes downcast.

'The boys,' she remarked as she ladled out his food, 'will have theirs at noon when they get back. Leni took some bread down with her . . . she won't be home till evening . . . Meanwhile you have no work at all!' And as she said this she handed him his meal without raising her eyes.

Tourkoyannis crossed himself, sat down on a thick log and began to eat. 'I'll do whatever you want!' he answered. 'I was thinking I'd fix that broken plough-staff. It deserves it, after all the work it's done! Where's the adze?'

Margarita thought for a while; she stirred the food with the ladle, tapped it a couple of times against the rim, then lifted the pot down from the tripod.

'The adze,' she said, 'isn't it in the chest?' Then choosing her words carefully, as if to avoid saying more than she intended, she continued, 'I'm fed up with keeping oxen, Yannis! I've had them so many years now! They're a lot of work and worry all year round. It's true that where there's livestock, there's a living, as they say, and they've enabled us to kiss goodbye to poverty, but now the children are older I can buy a calf for them to ween. The benefit long term will be the same and we'll avoid the running costs. So I'm thinking of selling the oxen!' And she went to fetch him some bread.

'The oxen!' declared Tourkoyannis in distress, still not looking at her.

'Now all the work's over for this season,' she told him, 'they'll only mean bother and expense! . . . And after all, our marriage agreement did not include a ploughman. Yannis can't say anything if I decide not to keep the oxen!'

'The oxen!' Tourkoyannis reiterated sadly. 'And a splendid pair like yours! The best in all the villages around! . . . Two brave-hearted beasts, my Perdiki and my Paraskevas, who's black as an Arab and his hide gleams in the sun. We call him that because he was born on a Friday. And now you want to go and sell the poor beasts. I can't object as I'm not the owner. You are, and good health to both of you. They're your property, but to let two such fine beasts go under the knife's a shame! . . . Ah well, God gave us them for slaughter! "Sacrifice and eat!" He said Himself.* But it upsets me even so! . . .'

As if aware that they were being discussed inside the house, the oxen in the stable began bellowing and kept it up for quite some time. 'Listen to them!' Tourkoyannis went on. 'They'll have sensed what now awaits them. Animals are very knowing, Margarita. My Paraskevas, ah, he understands everything. All he lacks is speech! . . .'

Margarita looked at him quite touched, but he did not raise his eyes. 'You've taken good care of our animals,' she said, 'but don't worry, you'll not go under!'

'Me?' he said, 'No, I'll not go under, I can make a living anywhere. I've survived time and again. You know me. I've worked since I was a boy. I'll find work alright. People are so good. Wherever I've been I've made a living, always managed to get back on my feet, thanks to people's kindness. My poor mother, God preserve her, used to tell me so! Do you remember my mother, Margarita?' And with a sigh he went on with his meal.

'I remember her alright,' she answered with a little smile. 'She used to wear Albanian costume.'

'She was Albanian,' he replied, 'but like us a Christian,* one of God's creatures too! My father, she would tell me, was a Turk. A man-at-arms and yet God's creature too. But luckily it was my fate to be born here on your island, and to be baptized, so my soul won't have to toss and turn in hell. You've put me in charge here and I love your animals. I also love your children as if they were my own, and you . . . and all of you!' A tear rolled down his cheek.

'You've been a good man and a Christian all your life,' Margarita replied sincerely, 'and to tell the truth, it upsets me to see you leave my home.'

'Then I shan't leave!' he replied, looking at her gratefully with his guileless eyes. 'I'll stay on with you, I'll earn my keep, I won't be a burden to anyone!'

'But will Yoryis want that?' said the woman uneasily, concealing her emotion. 'Will he want that?'

Tourkoyannis heaved a sigh. 'Never mind,' he said. 'I was born fatherless and my mother departed this earth when I was just sixteen. People have said all sorts of things about her. But I don't believe a word of it. May God preserve her soul! . . . And I've been abroad. Many, many places have seen me come and go. I can go abroad again . . . I'd hoped to end my days serving your children, but it was not to be . . .'

They both remained silent for a while. Tourkoyannis finished his food and got up to take a swig of vinegar and water from the flagon.

'D'you remember,' he went on, resuming his seat, 'I was twenty years old and you a little younger. And . . .'

'Are you going to rake over the past again! Don't you ever get bored?' she said impatiently. 'You've brought it up so many times.'

'You were right then! Absolutely right!' he told her.

'Of course I was!' she replied seriously. 'Think what you were proposing!'

'I have thought about it,' he said shamefacedly. 'I thought about it and reproached myself all those years abroad. No one knows how often I regretted it. Youth made me overstep the mark, and I was spellbound by your voice . . . your voice . . .'

'You even tried to kiss me!' she laughed contemptuously.

He looked down, ashamed. 'Yes, I did. Youth is reckless. But you were fond of me. You told me so yourself!'

'But after that, I cursed you! Don't you know whose son you are?'

'You asked me the same question at the time! Remember? The son of an unknown Turk. That's all my mother told me. She was robbed and shamed by a Turk on a mountain in the Crimea. Afterwards she came to your village with some of her compatriots for that season's olive harvest, and it was here the poor girl realized she was pregnant, but she didn't return home with the other women, as she was frightened of her parents and too ashamed to face the villagers back there. And your late father, bless him, Margarita, gave her shelter in a hut of his where she gave birth to me, and instead of killing me, instead of leaving me in an orphanage and sparing herself all the trials I brought her, instead of trying to find a husband, this single mother kept me with her, worked to feed me, was slandered and despised because of me, and remained unmarried till the day she died. To raise me she went begging and rather than leave me alone would take me begging with her, and people fed us with the bread of charity until I was old enough to work and to support her. And then . . . then . . . she gave me her blessing and closed her eyes, her dear eyes, for ever, as if all she'd lived for was to raise me! . . .' Tears welled up in Tourkoyannis' eyes and he remained silent for some time. Then he got to his feet, crossed himself and murmured a prayer.

'How could I have married a beggar!' said Margarita wistfully at last.

'You couldn't!' he replied sadly, 'of course you couldn't! And after behaving as I did, I felt so ashamed before your father, even though I knew you would say nothing, that I left at once. I was a reprobate in those days, worse than many felons. I loved some people, hated others, was envious of everyone, and blamed my poor mother for having had me. Then life abroad taught me a few lessons and set me on a different path. I went determined to succeed, find another Margarita and make a new life somewhere else where no one knew me, but while overseas I met many worthy people, one wise teacher in particular, whom I'd still be with today, had God not called him to his bosom, and through them became so aware of human misery — elderly people, women and children suffering on this bounteous earth, beneath a sun that shines for all — that I forgot my own troubles and began to love mankind . . . I often asked myself why the world is made the way it is, and when I enquired of sage old men and priests, they all told me, "It's a mystery! . . ."'

'How about seeing to the animals,' Margarita told him, getting bored.

'I fed them earlier,' replied Tourkoyannis 'But let me finish, especially now I've got to go abroad again!' And he sighed. 'I'm illiterate' he went on, 'and so as good as blind! But my teacher understood things. He and others told me that only a few people are happy, or relieve another's suffering, or do evil and repent. And they receive salvation . . . Meanwhile I had failed to find another Margarita, nor was I looking any more, and day by day I became less worried about getting ahead and making money, and kept just enough to feed myself, next to nothing, distributing the rest as I saw fit wherever it was most needed. And so to this day I have remained as poor as on the day my hapless mother bore me. And of all the jobs I've done, I prefer the kind I'm doing now. I enjoy working in families with children,* because you see I was raised without a father, and I have loved so many children in so many places! And they loved me a little in return, like your children, Margarita! Ah, children with their innocent souls, a true blessing from the Lord!'

'But they don't love you. You're deceiving yourself!'

'They love me just a little, and rightly so. I'm an outsider and a servant so there are others they're more fond of. What do they stand to gain from me? — But let me finish. — Whenever I began to feel at home in some family and resolved to remain there all my life, becoming acquainted with good people I shall long remember, there was invariably some stumbling block, some vexed situation I was blamed for, and poor Tourkoyannis would gather his few rags in a bundle, tie it to his staff over his shoulder and sadly set forth towards his unknown future... Then somewhere once there was a girl with an innocent and kindly soul and a face like a flower in bud. She had such a sweet voice it always reminded me of your country and your village, Margarita... and at the time there was no evil in her heart and her body was unblemished. But it was hard for any man who set eyes on her not to get crafty ideas, and the unmarried village lads were all mad about her, with her large innocent eyes and sweet angelic voice. Fate had great suffering in store for her, for despite so many young men, rich and poor, being keen to have her, one day she met a married man and fell passionately in love with him, though initially he was quite reluctant. Her name was soon on everybody's lips, very distressing for all who knew her kindly soul and pretty face. Such beauty with such ugliness — a mystery! She became deeply depressed, losing the will to live and came close to death, but no one dared take pity on the woman who had come between man and wife, apart from Tourkoyannis. I offered to marry her, take her away with me and support her with my labour, as I had done with my good mother. And the men in the village laughed at me and mocked me, but Tourkoyannis had decided to save an innocent and grieving soul and paid no attention to their taunts. He turned a deaf ear when they said he'd never find another woman anyway, except one in desperate straits. But all this brought even more shame on the poor creature who had sinned, and it weakened her resolve. Her seducer, unable to extinguish the flame of sinful passion in his heart, still wanted her himself and could not bear either to let her go or let her die. And the Tempter put an abominable idea into his head: he would marry her to his younger brother, still a minor, and thus have her conveniently around for ever, and the hapless girl took his advice and refused the hand of Tourkoyannis, which offered her salvation, because she said marrying an itinerant worker would be a comedown, while doing what her lover urged would also seal the gossips' lips. And so she married the innocent youth whom she and his brother had resolved to hoodwink. But he too fell madly in love with her. And from then on God's curse entered that house like a destructive whirlwind, everything went haywire and one brother wound up six feet under, the other locked away in jail.'

'You've told me all this before,' said Margarita, lowering her eyes shamefacedly.

'Let me finish,' he answered smiling. '. . . And once, after again being discharged from the place where I was working, I was overcome by a desire to see your village, Margarita. I remembered your house and your intoxicating voice, and decided to set foot once more on the soil that nurtured me, to visit the grave of my dear mother and . . . another woman, and then either stay for good and rest my bones here, or set off again towards my unknown future. And your husband took me on as a ploughman in your blessed family. Ah, Margarita! Your animals and you yourselves all came to love me, me a wretched stranger. May God reward you for it. But Fate again has envied me! Tourkoyannis must once more gather his old rags, tie his bundle and depart with his staff over his shoulder. I have worked for my keep honestly. Come and see for yourself, Margarita, I'm not taking anything more than I arrived with. I've honoured my daily bread!'

'Poor Yannis!' she said to him, much affected. Her heart prompted her to change her mind and retain the good man in her service. But then suddenly she thought she simply must be free of his surveillance, as she had another obligation on this earth.

'Your good husband took me in,' Tourkoyannis continued. 'He entrusted me with all his worldly goods. I've honoured his daily bread.'

He sighed and fell silent. And for the first time he raised his eyes and looked Margarita directly in the eyes. She went pale, understanding that look at once. Suddenly she realized that

Tourkoyannis knew her secret and she waited, prepared now to defend herself. And immediately the idea poisoned the tender sympathy she had felt for him only a moment ago.

'So you're going to sell the oxen?' Tourkoyannis asked her seriously. 'But you don't want to send them to the slaughterhouse any more than I do!'

'Animals, they say,' she replied, 'are like humans: eat us or we'll eat you!'

'They don't eat us, they feed us,' Tourkoyannis protested gently. 'I must tell you the truth and unburden myself before I leave, otherwise it would become a serpent gnawing at me! . . . You're selling the oxen because you want to get rid of me, and you don't want to admit it to your husband.'

'What are you talking about?' she said, giving him a fierce look.

'Tourkoyannis doesn't mince his words. He won't leave without revealing what he's been hiding in his heart. This secret, I tell you, is an adder gnawing at the corner of my heart.'

She looked at him again uneasily.

'Don't be afraid,' he told her. 'Tourkoyannis is a person of discretion. Tourkoyannis does not tell tales, he doesn't stir up trouble. He feels upset but is devoted. You're selling the oxen because that's what Petros has advised you!' And he looked round to make sure nobody had overheard him.

Outside the rain was now coming down in torrents. A flash of lightning lit up the room, and seconds later a rolling clap of thunder split the air.

'Explain yourself,' she demanded in a husky voice. 'What's Petros got to do with this?'

'By Him who thunders,' Tourkoyannis replied slowly, as if with trepidation, 'Petros is not behaving well. He wants to drag you into the mire!'

The woman suddenly lost her temper and, removing her headscarf, rolled it up and flung it on the floor.

'Don't be angry!' Tourkoyannis went on gently, 'wrath is a mortal sin. You may not suspect anything, but he wants you, and a woman's a weak vessel!'*

'Why don't you mind your own business, Tourkoyannis?' she smiled sourly. 'Indeed, I'm quite right to sell the oxen and get rid of you. Your tongue, for all its sweetness, is a dagger.'

'Don't shout, your husband might come in and hear you!'

'I shall tell him everything myself!'

'May my head be severed, but I'll speak my mind! . . . Perhaps you don't desire him and have no suspicions, but he wants you and a woman's a weak vessel! Ever since I've lived here in your home, I've watched over you lest you should stray, because I want to revere you like the Blessed Virgin till the day I die. That's why I have brought the matter up.'

'Look to your own nakedness and orphanhood!' she answered angrily. 'Blow me, now a beggar thinks he can advise us! Clear off out of my house, get lost!'

'Ever since I've been here, I've watched over you, I say, and whenever you reproached me for it I played the simpleton. You kept running into me everywhere you went, and I would tell you it was just by chance. Now I'm leaving, Margarita, see that you honour your marriage vows, and if you can't help it, take Petros and clear out. Leave with Petros!'

Margarita was getting more furious by the minute; she had gone red in the face and kept looking round uneasily. 'Why are you telling me all this,' she shouted, 'to have your way with me! Well, you're going to be as frustrated now as you were then!' And she smacked her right index finger against her left palm. 'You're as cunning as a serpent!'

'Not so!'

'It's outrageous!' she went on, shouting, 'The very idea this nincompoop, this Tourkoyannis, has got into his head! The devil must have put it there! What, me become his mistress?' And she laughed out loud. 'Be off, and make it snappy. The cat won't drink the gravy.' And leaning towards him with hand on hip, she wagged the fingers of her other hand under her chin.

'It never entered my mind!' he told her, turning pale and smiling gently.

'I know you, I know you! You think by using threats you'll

have your way with me, ay? If you knew what stock I come from, Tourkoyannis, and what blood runs in my veins! This is what I think of all your calumnies!' And cocking her leg, she slapped the soul of her foot. 'I shall tell that numbskull husband of mine everything, and you'll see what happens to you. I want you out of here, come hell or high water.'

'I've honoured my daily bread.'

'Go on, Tourkoyannis, pretend to be a simpleton! I was right when I told Yoryis not to take you on here! But no way, he wouldn't listen. You cast a spell on him! You sly fox! Serve him right! And he enthroned you in here to bear witness to everything we do. Anyway, go to the devil now and get off our back! You're as sharp as a needle, cunning, stupid and evil! . . .'

'I brought the matter up,' he told her in the same gentle voice, 'because I felt it was my duty. Do what you like, Margarita!' He rummaged inside the trunk he slept on, found the adze and went out to fix the broken plough-staff. Even on his last day he wished to earn his keep.

Inside the house the woman went on cursing him. The rain had now stopped and for a few moments the sun appeared in the sky. Tourkoyannis raised his eyes and watched the dark rainclouds passing overhead. 'What,' he asked himself with a sigh, 'will the unknown future bring?' And he went into the yard and set to work.

Soon Margarita appeared at the door and sat down without noticing how wet the sill was. She was very pale, restless and preoccupied. Her head propped in her hand, she tapped her foot rhythmically on the worn steps. After a little while Petros came by and greeted her with a sour smile; then with a quick look round he stopped in front of her.

'What's up?' he asked uneasily, lowering his voice. 'Did you get rid of him, eh?'

'We're doomed,' she replied shaking her head despairingly. 'Tourkoyannis knows everything and of course he'll spill the beans. We had a row. Did you hear us? And I dismissed him. We'll be the talk of the town!'

'I doubt it!' he said calmly. 'Let the waters in the ditches settle for a while!'

'What have you to lose!' she replied with hatred. 'But me? Be off in case they see us! Go, now!'

Petros smiled and asked her, 'Where's your husband?'

'He went into the village at dawn,' she replied.

He said goodbye and left, feeling elated.

V

He found him in Savvas Ayeris' wine store in the village square. He was playing cards with three other villagers. The wine store was dark and cramped, with smoke-blackened beams and an unpaved floor caked with mud brought in on people's feet. The proprietor, a short stout middle aged man, wearing a straw hat and wide baggy trousers, was standing behind the counter selling his wares and scrawling a note of each sale in his grubby account book. Arrayed on shelves along the wall behind him were a number of dusty and for the most part empty bottles, while lined up on the counter were a basin of water for rinsing glasses, two flagons of wine, a pitcher of drinking water and an old brass tray with several glasses. Beside the counter were two barrels of salt fish.

Petros as he entered greeted everyone, ordered coffee and came and sat down near the table where the others were playing cards.

'Enjoying your game,' he said. 'What are you playing?'

'Whist,' replied one of the players opposite him, a rawboned unshaven man.

'What are the stakes?' asked Petros casually.

'Five cents a trick,' they replied as if proud of themselves.

'Santa Claus must have come early!' laughed Petros.

'It helps me relax!' replied Yoryis Arathymos. 'My wife, you see, no longer wants to keep an ox-team. The marriage contract, she says, did not include a ploughman. She wants to sell the oxen, and you know my team, two brave-hearted beasts — Tourko-yannis says so too — five years old, still no more than calves! What am I supposed to do, since she doesn't want them? I told her to tell Tourkoyannis herself.'

'King of hearts,' said one of the players, tossing his last card, so worn the image could scarcely be made out, into the middle of the table. 'The last trick's ours!' And at once he started counting the winning cards and totting up the score.

'Margarita is right,' Petros responded.

'How d'you mean?' asked Arathymos, looking at him.

'Yet another ox-team leaving our village!' someone else observed.

'Are we going to play or are you going to talk?' snapped a third player, who had already shuffled the cards and was dealing them out four at a time.

'She's right,' Petros continued. 'Oxen mean work, expense, worries, the risk that they might die. They also require an extra hand.'

'That's what my wife thinks,' said Arathymos. 'She says she wants a calf for the children to raise, that way, she says, the cost will be much the same and we'll avoid the bother.'

'Three of hearts,' cried one of the players. 'I'll go for broke!' And he rapped the table with his knuckles as he played the card. 'Yoryis, your turn!'

'I don't want you peeping at my cards, Petros,' said the player sitting closest to him. 'You'll give my hand away!' He looked at each of his cards complacently, having cleverly contrived to deal the best ones to himself.

'You'd also be rid of the hired hand,' said Petros.

'But he earns his keep,' said Arathymos. 'He works like a dog all day!'

'There have been quarrels in your absence, though,' said Petros casually.

'Quarrels?' he exclaimed. 'And how do you know?'

'How can you play like this,' Arathymos' partner declared irritably. 'Pay attention, if you please. You're ruining the game for me! . . . Leave us alone, Petros, there's a good fellow. There, you see, we've lost!' And he cursed, angrily flicking his splayed cards with the back of his right hand.

They all stopped talking for a while until the round was finished.

'You should have played spades when I tipped you the wink!' the same man said to Arathymos. 'See what you've done? We've not won a single trick! We've lost twelve tokens. I'm not playing any more. Let Petros take over if he wants.' He got to his feet, totted up his score and paid.

'How do you know?' Arathymos asked Petros again, going back to the earlier conversation. 'Margarita didn't mention anything to me.'

'Like a virtuous woman,' he replied lowering his voice and secretly observing him. 'Still, only today as I went past I heard them. Now Margarita shouting, now Tourkoyannis. They were having a row.'

'You'd do well to rid your family of that gypsy!' said the rawboned old man seriously, having realized what Petros was driving at. 'You all know whose son he is! Don't you remember his mother? Of course you do. You'd ask her, "What's your name?" and she'd answer, "Areti, number one whore!"* Just like that, no shame. God forgive her, she'd let anybody straddle her, Turks, Jews, Westerners, she wasn't squeamish!'

Everybody laughed, Yoryis alone remaining thoughtful.

'And who's her son going to take after?' remarked someone else, eager to side with the view of the majority. 'Ah, and what a hypocrite, God preserve us! You'd think he were serving you Communion. And he speaks such honeyed words! . . . But still waters run deep! . . .'

'Feed a stranger, feed a snake!' said the rawboned old man maliciously.

'What's the poor orphan done to deserve your condemnation?' said the proprietor from behind the counter. 'As far as I know he's always been well-behaved — not the slightest rumour of any thefts or quarrelling or anything like that! He's not in debt to anyone. He was raised an orphan. He always comes here to do his shopping and pays on the nail. He's humble and . . .'

'Very soon he'll be a saint!' said Petros spitefully. 'I tell you, I know what I'm talking about. Anyway, Margarita is the most virtuous woman in the village!'

'Why virtuous?' asked Arathymos, uneasy and perplexed.

'Something must be going on,' said Petros.

'Of course!' said someone else.

'Going on?' asked Arathymos, frowning. 'What?'

'You're stirring up trouble!' the proprietor told Petros, 'It's sinful, Petros! Why can't you let a poor fellow work to earn his keep?'

'So we're supposed to let Tourkoyannis do anything he fancies! Is that it?' replied Petros obstinately.

'Well of course!' laughed the rawboned old man, 'that's what he'll do in the end anyway! Natter, natter from the lad, soon the old lady wants it bad!'

'What did you say?' cried Arathymos flushing red, his eyes bulging. He stood up behind the table.

'Shush!' said Petros, raising his finger to his lips, 'Shush! Margarita gave him a flea in the ear, as he deserved!'

'Does that sound like an honest fellow?' the old man said to the proprietor.

'What did she say to him?' asked Arathymos, trying to get out from his tight corner. 'What did she say to him?'

'I didn't hear everything,' replied Petros. 'I was just passing by, you see. I didn't stop for long, but she was cursing him, she called him a gypsy, she told him the cat wouldn't drink the gravy! She went on and on! She told him you yourself would soon show him! . . .'

'And how come she didn't slap his face?' asked the old man maliciously.

'Oh, don't believe it!' the proprietor told Arathymos. 'A fine soul you'll be delivering up to God!' he added, addressing the old man.

Arathymos was by now in a rage. He'd finally grasped what they were telling him. So Tourkoyannis had assaulted his wife! 'So that's it, ay?' he said, 'Areti's son entered my home to cuckold me! That was his intention! And I didn't know a thing! And the whole village knew about it! The sponger, the deceitful mongrel! Tell me what I should do to him!'

'Don't land yourself in jail!' someone warned him.

'It's not worth it over such low trash,' said another.

The proprietor expressed his disapproval with a dismissive gesture.

'Will you say all this to his face?' Yoryis then asked Petros. And on Petros nodding his consent, he at once continued, 'I have two witnesses, my wife and Petros. I'm acting within the law. Come, Petros, let's go! He must leave my house right now, immediately! . . .'

'He'll come up with a thousand explanations, cunning fellow that he is!' said Petros. 'But anyway let's go!'

As the two of them set off, Arathymos getting even more irate declared, 'He certainly picked the right man to trust him!'

And though they were already on the road, the proprietor shouted after them, 'Say what you like, I still believe that Tourkoyannis is a man of God!'

VI

The two of them were now descending the hill to Arathymos' house in silence; in his heart Petros secretly rejoiced. Soon most of the obstacles in his path would be removed. Tourkoyannis, once expelled from Arathymos' home, would naturally disappear and with him his surveillance, indeed Arathymos himself would perhaps end up in jail and then he'd have access to Margarita when he felt like it! Passion blinded him to the evil he was unleashing. In a low voice he said to Yoryis, 'Tourkoyannis has strong arms, you know. He's descended from the Turks! Don't lay into him!'

'Don't lay into him? You must be joking! If I don't kill him, it's only because I don't want his soul on my conscience, but I'll give him a hiding he'll remember all his life. I'm within the law!'

'Well, be prepared!'

'But there are two of us!'

'Ah, I'm not getting involved. He's done me no harm. My advice is, be prepared. You have the weapons.'

Arathymos looked at him, alarmed, and his companion added, 'Otherwise don't do anything except dismiss him.'

He made no reply and meanwhile they had reached the house. Margarita was still sitting on the doorstep looking pale and preoccupied, but when she caught sight of them she got up and went inside. Her heart was pounding. She realized with trepidation that the moment was critical and would decide the remainder of her life. Following her in, the two men confronted her.

'What was the quarrel about?' Yoryis asked her apprehensively.

'Oh, nothing really!' she replied frowning. 'He's leaving now, so we'll have no more bother.'

'Why did you swear at him?' he persisted. 'What are you hiding from me?'

'I have nothing to hide,' she answered sullenly.

'Was there a quarrel? Did she swear at him?' Arathymos asked Petros.

'Yes!' he replied firmly, trying at the same time to reassure her too. 'But Margarita is a virtuous woman and doesn't want recriminations, that's why she's not saying anything. Am I not right?' he asked her.

'What did he say to you?' Arathymos demanded.

'Let's forget about it,' she replied. 'He's leaving now. I don't want another stranger living in our house.'

'What did you hear?' he asked Petros. 'Margarita doesn't want to tell me. Why?'

'Perhaps because I am present,' suggested Petros. 'I heard her call him a gypsy Turk. I heard her say the cat wouldn't drink the gravy, that she, Margarita, was not like his mother, that he'd have to put up with his frustration . . . and I don't recall what else.'

Margarita looked at Petros and shuddered. Fearfully she contemplated the path she was being dragged down by his illicit ardour. She pitied him with all her heart and gave him a reproachful look, which he however failed to comprehend. For a moment or two she remained silent. Aware that she must reply, she wondered whether to follow him down that slippery slope, but before she could decide, and feeling the pressure to say something, she finally with beating heart and downcast eyes admitted, 'Yes, I said all that!'

'And why?' asked Yoryis, turning white.

'We're in the presence of a stranger!' she said evasively. 'Don't you understand, I can't just tell you everything?' And in alarm she realized that these words had produced the opposite effect, providing firmer grounds for her husband's suspicions. And she thought to herself, 'How can I calumniate a good man like this?'

But meanwhile her husband was saying, 'He'll get what he deserves!'

'Oh, don't kill him!' she cried out in alarm, and was on the point of giving herself away.

But Arathymos' next words reassured her: 'I don't want his gypsy soul on my conscience!' he declared. And he cast an eye round the room for his crook, which he sometimes took with him at night to ward off wild dogs,* and for the large rusty knife hanging on the wall above the trunk where Tourkoyannis slept. Taking this down, he said to Petros, 'Let's go!'

'Where are you going?' she asked fearfully. 'What are you going to do?'

'Don't worry,' he told her, 'we'll find Tourkoyannis.'

'But he's here! Listen, that's him hammering in the yard outside. He's mending the plough-staff.'

'Summon him!' he ordered her, frowning.

Her anxiety increased. 'Tourkoyannis, Yannis!' she yelled out, trembling.

A moment later the man entered the house. He gazed with his innocent eyes at each of them in turn, then lowered them sadly and, still standing near the door with his head bowed and a tear in his eye, said humbly, 'Here I am! What do you want me for?'

'What d'you mean by quarrelling under my roof?' Yoryis at once demanded angrily. 'I'm the master here! And like it or not, I'm selling the oxen today and you are leaving!'

'I know!' he replied dejectedly. 'My Perdiki and my Paraskevas — we call him that as he was born on a Friday — are going to the slaughterhouse! . . . That's what God has ordained! . . . But why? . . . A mystery!'

Arathymos was conscious that these words were mollifying him and his ire abating, and this displeased him. What? Had he no sense of honour? He looked at Petros and then at his wife and thought for a moment, asking himself why they were stirring up all this trouble for him. He noticed that Margarita was very pale and trembling from head to foot.

Petros quickly said to Tourkoyannis, 'So you're weeping, eh? Because you have to leave this house!'

'Because of that too,' replied Tourkoyannis in a sad gentle voice. 'Their children are like my own. I love them and have shared their bread . . .'

And for several moments he gazed tenderly at Margarita and murmured something with his lips. Their eyes met. Seeing this,

Yoryis flew into a rage, his suspicions roused. He went red in the face and clenched his teeth.

'So what's the meaning of all this?' he demanded, glowering from Tourkoyannis to Margarita and then Petros.

'You gypsy, you, how dare you shame me in my own home!'

'Me?'

'That's what the woman says. So does this fellow here who heard you!'

'Yes, I heard him!' confirmed Petros.

'Why,' replied Tourkoyannis calmly, 'are you slandering an orphaned human being who has nowhere to lay his head and who, as you well know, is innocent? How can you commit such a sin?'

Margarita turned even paler. Her lips began to quiver, her heart prompted her to speak, but no sound issued from her throat. She felt her knees buckle and sat down on the floor. With dread she realized that if Tourkoyannis were to speak out, she was a doomed woman. She threw him a beseeching glance and Tourkoyannis gazed at her tenderly, as if he had understood what she was asking.

'Why are you looking at her like that?' Arathymos shouted at him furiousl. 'I've had enough of this!' And he rushed towards him. 'So it's true, then, it's true!' And he felt his rage mounting by the second. 'Clear out of here, you Turkish bastard, Turkish gypsy!' And seizing him by the shoulders, he shook him violently and tried to throw him out.

'An orphaned human being!' repeated Tourkoyannis plaintively.

'Dishonourable scoundrel!' Yoryis cursed him. 'Sponger, serpent!' Just then he caught sight of the crook within his reach. He quickly grabbed it and dealt him a hefty blow to the right shoulder.

'Ah!' Tourkoyannis cried out in pain. And for the first time in years he realized that he was getting angry, not prepared to tolerate such insults. He also sensed that Yoryis in his towering rage would put paid to him, and instinct prompted him to defend himself at once. He clenched his fists and confronted Yoryis, getting up close to prevent him swinging at him with the crook. And before

Arathymos had time to step back and deliver him a second blow, Tourkoyannis took hold of him, pinning his arms down and clasping him tightly to his own body. The two men wrestled for a few moments, but neither managed to shake the other off.

'Oh, they'll kill each other!' cried Margarita clutching her head, and fainted away.

Petros joined the fray shouting, 'What are you doing! What are you doing! What are you doing!' And he pretended to try and separate them, but did not put his back into it as he wanted one of them to win. Finally Yoryis managed to free one of his arms and dragged Tourkoyannis towards the chest where he had left the rusty knife. He was red in the face, panting and perspiring. Tourkoyannis felt that his last moment had arrived.

'Don't kill me, brother,' he cried out to him, 'don't shed innocent blood!'

But Arathymos did not listen. He had made up his mind and was about to strike. Suddenly Tourkoyannis seized him by the neck, shook him violently for several seconds and brought him sprawling to the ground, still gripping him tightly round the throat. Yoryis was unable even to cry out. His eyes bulged from their sockets, his face went black.

'You've finished him!' cried Petros with a malicious smile.

The sound of Petros' voice brought Tourkoyannis to his senses, he let go of Yoryis' neck and looked at him closely, terrified lest what the other had pronounced turned out to be true.

'Ah, Judas!' he said to Petros, 'You've done this!'

But Yoryis was not dead, he had merely become dizzy and exhausted. He raised himself into a sitting position on the floor and glared savagely at Tourkoyannis. But the knife had fallen from his grasp and was out of reach. Tourkoyannis kneeled down before him and with tears in his eyes cried, 'Oh, forgive me, brother, forgive me! Kill me! What was I about to do! Put me to death if you wish, I will not resist!' And turning towards Petros he repeated, 'Ah, Judas! To push me, an orphaned human being, to the brink like this! May God in His greatness have mercy on you and bring you to repentance.' He got up and with a final glance at

Margarita, who was still lying there unconscious, walked out of the door.

By now Yoryis too had staggered to his feet. His head was lowered, but his anger had subsided.

'Are you going to let him get away!' cried Petros, who saw his entire scheme evaporating.

'I haven't the heart to kill him,' he replied. 'He's gone now!'

A moment later Tourkoyannis was standing outside the door and with a serene smile bade them goodbye. 'Oh, forgive me,' he said to them. 'Long life and a kind heart to you!'

The rain had taken hold again and it was afternoon. Tourkoyannis, an orphaned human being, with his little bundle on his staff, headed off down the road towards the unknown future.

VII

The next day Yoryis Arathymos drove his two oxen into town to sell them. And the following day people in the village learned how on his way home that night he had been robbed and murdered, and that they would be bringing his body back in the cart the next day to bury him in the cemetery of his church.

VIII

It was a cheerful sun-drenched winter morning, towards Christmas. The court was in session. Light streamed through all the windows into the courtroom, which was packed with people — townsfolk, villagers, rich and poor — so that inside they were not conscious of the cold. On a broad dais elevated above the public at the far end of the courtroom were the three judges seated beneath a red satin canopy, in the centre the presiding judge, a still youngish gentleman in a dark suit with lively eyes and a trim moustache, flanked by a fat middle aged man who appeared to be snoozing behind his spectacles and a genial spry old man. On the left side of the dais, seated in two rows were the twelve jurors, people of all ages, physiognomies and styles of clothing. Opposite them on the right sat the public prosecutor, a tall thin elderly man in a long black gown with a pale ugly face, glittering eyes and a short dark beard, his expression thoughtful and unsmiling. Seated next to him were several lawyers and two or three ladies who had come to observe the trial. The dais was in the form of a semicircle, its two ends connected by a low iron balustrade, and within the space thus formed were two tables, one for the defending lawyers, the other for the clerk of the court and the minute-takers. In front of these tables close to the balustrade, under the stern eye of the public prosecutor, and seated on a wooden bench between two boorish ill-clad policemen with fixed bayonets, with several more policemen standing guard, was Yannis, known as Tourkoyannis, paternity unknown, who today was being tried for robbery and murder.

He had grown thinner while in jail. His innocent blue eyes had receded into their wide sockets, and he was very pale, as if recovering from a protracted illness. His dark beard, scrawny and unkempt, was now longer, covering half his throat. His hair had grown in thick taper-like strands over his ears and neck, while his expression was one of serenity tinged with quiet sorrow, like the expression of a handsome corpse. He was wearing his best clothes that day, acquired during his time abroad: a full-length brown woollen overcoat, its wide sleeves reaching to his fingertips, a low-cut waistcoat buttoned at the side and leaving his white shirt exposed, a black sash about his waist, brown woollen breeches with white stockings and pointed red *tsarouchia*.* Only his hands seemed restless; he was breathing rapidly and held his head elevated slightly, gazing at the ceiling.

The trial had begun. The clerk of the court had read out the indictment, and after the usual preliminary questions, the presiding judge addressed the accused: 'The charge is that on the thirtieth of March this year, on the road near the ruined church of the Holy Virgin, you did with malice aforethought murder and then rob Yoryis Arathymos . . .'

'I did not,' Tourkoyannis interrupted him.

'First pay attention to the proceedings and the witnesses,' the presiding judge continued, 'and answer the charges at the end.'

Then, shuffling some papers, he said, 'Let the first witness for the prosecution, Margarita, the widow of the said Yoryis Arathymos, come forward.'

In a sonorous voice the sergeant-at-law shouted out her name two or three times.

A moment later the woman appeared, emerging from a door at the back of the courtroom, and made her way forward through the audience.

All eyes were turned towards her. She was still dressed in mourning, with a dark headscarf and blue ribbons in her hair and sash* (worn inside out to leave no white showing), her blouse was fastened with a little black bow, and the ribbons on her coat were also black; she was looking pale and her dark beauty was enhanced by the blue trimmings.

Catching sight of her from where he was sitting, Tourkoyannis flushed and then turned pale repeatedly. He had not seen her for eight months now, but had spent most of his time thinking about her. His eyes became animated and he immediately attempted to get to his feet and move towards her. The policemen however at once restrained him. The woman looked at him and he thought he saw a faint smile cross her lips. This set his heart pounding and a sweet joy suffused his soul.

'Margarita,' he said to himself, 'doesn't believe I am a murderer!' And his joy and the presence of the woman made him feel light-headed.

After the usual questions the presiding judge asked her, 'Do you know who killed your husband?'

'Everybody says,' she replied with a sigh, 'that Tourkoyannis killed him. I don't wish to have him on my conscience. But nor can I say he didn't kill him, because then people would malign me.'

'Do you recognize this knife?'

'It belongs to Tourkoyannis.'

'Tourkoyannis was a servant in your household for some time. Were you satisfied with him?'

He was always satisfactory. He cared for the children, our whole family and the animals as if they were his own.'

Tourkoyannis looked at her gratefully, his whole face glowing. The poor man recalled the many happy days he had spent under Arathymos' roof and two tears trickled down his cheeks. By now no longer conscious of what was being said around him, or of the meaning of Margarita's words, he was simply listening spellbound to her enchanting voice, just as on that day when he was twenty and had tried to take her in his arms, before setting off for distant parts. Now all he could think of was that Margarita did not want to see him convicted. How good she was!

'Why did you dismiss him?' the presiding judge was asking meanwhile.

'We wanted to sell our oxen and there was no more work for him.'

'During the investigation you stated, and another witness confirmed, that you had a quarrel with Tourkoyannis on the day he left.'

Lowering her head shamefacedly, Margarita replied in a subdued voice, 'I got the idea that he was following me and I didn't know what for. But whether he really had designs on me, I cannot swear!'

'You, the accused,' said the presiding judge, 'why were you following her?'

Margarita looked at Tourkoyannis fearfully. Would he now speak out? Would he now say what he had said to her at home before the court, before all those people, to mitigate his own position? But when she saw that he was lost in his own happy reverie, his head held high, his gaze quite steady, she relaxed. He was no longer listening to anything, indifferent to what was going on around him, as if he were not himself on trial. 'Margarita,' he was saying to himself, 'does not believe me to be guilty, and when she spoke she spoke so sweetly! And she gazed at me with such compassion!'

And so he did not answer, not having taken in the question.

The presiding judge was about to dismiss Margarita, when one of the jurymen asked to put a question to her. He was a small middle aged man with an ugly face, shabbily dressed but well built and strong. He was a doctor. 'One query, your Honour,' he said.

Everyone looked at him.

'Were you in a relationship with the accused?' he went on, addressing Margarita.

'What relationship, Sir,' she asked flushing.

'A relationship, we all know what — as man and woman.'

'You're insulting me, Sir!' said Margarita pretending to be angry.

'Ah, no!' he replied with a smile that seemed at odds with his ugly face, 'but women . . . well, we all know . . .'

The presiding judge smiled too and rang the bell. The public prosecutor asked him sternly to respect the woman's reputation. But the doctor shrugged his shoulders as if he had not understood and continued, 'Or with any other man? . . . Not with anyone? . . . Can you swear to it?'

'What are you suggesting, Sir?' she cried out with beating heart before she had time to think what she was saying. But the doctor noticed that her face had gone white and her lips were trembling.

'Let the accused be asked again,' said the doctor.

But Tourkoyannis had not heard, absorbed in his rapturous daydream. The presiding judge was obliged to repeat the question and the policemen gave him a nudge to rouse him. He looked about, gazed fondly across at Margarita and thought she too was looking at him out of the corner of her eye and pleading with him, begging him to say nothing. Then he replied with all the passion of his soul, 'Ah, Margarita. Margarita is like a dove, she is as innocent as a little child! Whatever sin she commits as a human being, she at once repents, and her contrition renders her pure and without sin. Don't you see, she doesn't want to send me to the gallows, because she knows she too has wronged me?'

The doctor shrugged his shoulders in despair. 'At the inquest,' said the presiding judge, 'the accused insisted he spent the two days after his dismissal from your home sheltering in a deserted hut you own. Did you go down to the hut during that time and see him?'

'No!' said Margarita after a moment, pale and frightened, turning towards Tourkoyannis and looking him in the eye.

'Let the accused be asked as well,' said the doctor.

'Answer!' the presiding judge directed him.

'No!' said Tourkoyannis, sighing and shyly lowering his eyes.

'You've lost, doctor!' said another member of the jury, a thin young man with glasses and a childish, meticulously shaven face.

'He doesn't want to speak!' replied the doctor giving up. 'Who knows what he's concealing in his heart!'

They went on to ask Margarita about the row her husband had had with Tourkoyannis and his expulsion from their home, and finally they let her go.

She left with a sigh of relief, as if released from a terrifying nightmare, but Tourkoyannis' sad eyes followed her until she left the courtroom.

The second witness, Petros Pepponas, was now called. He did not recognize the knife, but he had much else to say. He had known Tourkoyannis since he was a child. Tourkoyannis was older than him and had grown up in evil company. From the cradle he had been a thief and would steal alongside his mother, the Albanian Areti, who had taught him how to. He also was a beggar. And the whole village knew he was a hypocrite, everyone distrusted him. He himself was convinced that Tourkoyannis had ruthlessly murdered and then robbed his master for revenge. That's what the whole village believed, and that was Tourkoyannis' reputation — a hypocrite, a notorious hypocrite!

Tourkoyannis listened to Petros' testimony unmoved, indeed he tried not to pay attention to his malicious tirade. But the presiding judge asked the witness, 'Do you know whether the accused had a row with Margarita!'

'I was passing by Arathymos' house and heard them,' he replied. 'I informed her husband.'

'Do you know why they were quarrelling?'

'He had become a burden to her. He followed her everywhere she went. It was hell for her. She had every reason to curse him and get rid of him!'

'Ah, Judas!' Tourkoyannis said to him. 'God has still not graced you with repentance and you're still hounding me, an orphaned human being, lost soul that you are! . . . But no!' he added reflectively, 'no soul is ever lost because it may still repent, be it in the hour of death or in the next world, and a person who repents becomes a friend of God. The proof is that the souls of those who die in sin, burdened with their crime, become vampires and terrify the living, until God graces them with penitence, then they depart in peace and vanish from the face of the earth!'

The whole courtroom laughed and the presiding judge, disconcerted, rang his bell.

'What else do you know?' he then proceeded to ask Petros.

'I know,' he replied, 'that having informed the unfortunate victim, I accompanied him back to his house. He and Tourkoyannis came to blows. Margarita was present, but after a little while she fainted. Arathymos gave Tourkoyannis a good hiding and Tourkoyannis swore on the bones of Areti that he would

make him pay for it. But he had plenty of time to cool down —
two whole days!'

'Ah, Judas!' retorted Tourkoyannis calmly once again.

'Don't abuse the witness,' said the presiding judge, 'or I'll order
you to be removed from the courtroom!'

'You're trying to send an orphaned human being, who's never
done you the slightest harm, to the gallows! Never mind. May God
have compassion on your wickedness, and may I be the instrument for you someday becoming a good man. I did not kill, you
know this!'

The whole court laughed again and the doctor became irritated
by Tourkoyannis and his inane theology. 'Is this what theology
does to you?' he said. 'Ah, religion has a lot to answer for!' Two
or three members of the jury laughed at his annoyance. They knew
the doctor was an atheist and a fanatical enemy of all religion.

But Tourkoyannis began again: 'Wickedness is easy, Petros, it's
goodness that is hard. When I was abroad, that was what my
teacher too would say. I'd still be with him if God had not called
him to a better place. Virtue, he would say, means manliness, and
that's why virtue requires sacrifice!'

'Silence!' ordered the presiding judge. 'You'll be removed if
you show disrespect for the court and abuse the witness. You will
be sentenced without the chance to reply!'

'D'you think you're here to act the preacher?' the doctor said
to him mockingly.

'Bizarre stuff!' remarked another member of the jury.

The doctor, anxious to win him over to his point of view,
responded thoughtfully, 'Can a man like that be a murderer? Judge
for yourself!' And looking at the presiding judge he went on, 'Let
the witness please be asked, whether he went past the deserted hut
during those two days,'

'I go past there every day,' replied Petros promptly. 'I did so
on those two days as well. No one was inside!'

'I was there, Petros,' replied Tourkoyannis. 'You saw me and I
saw you!'

Petros turned crimson, but gritting his teeth and clenching his fists he now played his trump card and with beating heart demanded, 'And was I alone?'

Tourkoyannis started trembling. He looked down and remained silent.

'You see how he's lying,' said the young member of the jury to his colleagues, 'he's been caught out good and proper!' and he laughed.

Finally Tourkoyannis said to the witness, 'Ah, Judas, you would have betrayed our lord Jesus Christ himself!' And his eyes filled with tears as he recalled how on that occasion too he had protected Margarita from sin.

Angered, the presiding judge rang his bell again loudly, but did not follow through his earlier threat. And the doctor in the jury shouted out to Tourkoyannis, 'Enough of your theology and your idiot pronouncements, just tell us, tell us everything! If you're innocent, we are here to see you receive justice!'

Tourkoyannis made no reply.

'Innocent!' exclaimed the young juryman in spectacles with a sarcastic smile. 'If he were innocent, he wouldn't be here!'

'Quite right,' said another member of the jury. 'For him to be here at all means the public prosecutor has found him guilty, and for the public prosecutor to find him guilty means he is guilty!'

The doctor gave him a fierce look. 'You are too judgmental!' he told him with contempt.

'Any juryman worth his salt,' said the young man with the childish face, 'needs to be more judgmental than the public prosecutor!'

The presiding judge rang his bell vigorously .

Then a number of other witnesses, Tourkoyannis' fellow villagers, were questioned, all of whom blamed him: first those who had found the victim by the roadside near the ruined church of the Holy Virgin, then the policemen who had arrested him inside the village church. Finally the coroner's report was read out and because the defence had no witnesses, the public prosecutor invited the accused to answer the charges.

'You've heard what you are accused of. Tell us, did you do this deed?'

'No,' said Tourkoyannis firmly, 'I've been telling you so from the day you put me in jail. I did not do it!'

'Should you wish,' the presiding judge continued, 'to acknowledge your crime, however great it may be, you will significantly lighten your sentence, though the court cannot oblige you to do so!'

'It is written,' he replied calmly, 'thou shalt not kill. And I did not kill! It is written, thou shalt not steal! And I did not steal! Tourkoyannis knows that Death is an angel of the Lord who appears to man with a joyous face if he is innocent, when he comes to fetch his soul. This is why they call him Death the Comforter.* But to the murderer in his last hour he appears as a terrifying figure in the likeness of his victim, and affrights the soul about to leave the body, protracting the terrible ordeal. But all this happens simply and solely so that, even at the very last minute, the sinner may repent and be blessed with seeing the friendly face of his Creator.'

'Your Honour,' said the public prosecutor addressing the presiding judge, 'please oblige the accused to refrain from such theological theories. They have no place on the lips of a criminal!'

'Criminal!' expostulated Tourkoyannis without further comment.

The presiding judge, with a sign to the clerk of the court, proceeded to ask Tourkoyannis, 'Do you recognize this knife?'

'Yes, it's mine. I've been telling you so ever since you locked me up in jail.'

'Yoryis Arathymos was killed with this knife,' the presiding judge went on, 'how come it was found with the victim?'

'I don't know,' he sighed, 'I forgot it when I left Arathymos' house that day. I don't know who took it. I don't know who killed him . . .'

'What did you do,' asked the presiding judge, 'from the time you left Arathymos' house to the moment the police arrested you?'

'When they threw me out,' he replied with feeling, 'I was so upset I made my way to a deserted hut belonging to Arathymos and stayed there for two days and nights, without food or drink, without sleep even, and by the third day I was famished. I went into the village to buy bread and everyone looked at me strangely, muttering as I passed by. It was the hour of the funeral service for the man unjustly murdered, may he bless us as he has now paid for all his sins, and I too went into the church and wept for him, because I had long received my daily bread from him and loved him. I loved his whole family, his animals as well. There the police arrested me and brought me into town in shackles and threw me into jail. I have told you the whole truth.'

'And did no one see you in this hut?' asked the presiding judge.

Tourkoyannis thought for a moment and then looking down nodded and replied, 'On the second day, a man and a woman came there to commit a sin. They got wind of me and left. Did they not testify to this?'

The court laughed. The presiding judge rang the bell and asked, 'Who were they?'

'I will not betray them!' he replied in a firm voice. 'Tourkoyannis knows how to keep a secret, he can hold his tongue, and what he knows in his heart is sealed as in a tomb!'

'Your attitude's perverse,' the presiding judge told him, 'any other defence would be more to your advantage!'

The members of the jury looked at one another and smiled.

'Why,' the presiding judge continued, 'did Arathymos dismiss you?'

'Because he wished to sell the oxen. Two brave-hearted beasts, one we called Perdiki, the other, a black one, we called Paraskevas, because he was born on a . . .'

'None of that is relevant,' the judge interrupted him, 'we'll be here all night with your digressions. During the proceedings it was established, and under interrogation you yourself admitted that before you left his house you and Arathymos had a row. Is that correct?'

'Indeed it is. Petros Pepponas hates me, I don't know why, an orphaned human being like myself! He knows. Ask him! . . .

Petros kindled Arathymos' ire against me and Arathymos swore at me and tried to stab me with the knife. I was obliged to defend my life and I disarmed him. It was just as well for him, as he was saved from such a hellish deed and did not enter the next world a sinner. I did not harm him otherwise. Margarita, Arathymos' wife, was there as well, but she had fainted!'

'During the proceedings it was established that you and Margarita had also quarrelled in the morning. Is that true?'

'Indeed it is, she was the first one to dismiss me.'

'And why?'

'She told you herself. I gave her no cause.'

'She said that you followed her everywhere, that you had designs on her and that for this reason she decided to sell the oxen and dismiss you, before people started gossiping.'

'She wouldn't have said that. If she did, she is mistaken . . . And yet she knew that Tourkoyannis loved her, her and her whole family!' He sighed.

The jury and the court were showing signs of impatience. The attitude of the accused was tiresome. And now one member of the jury, a tall well-dressed gentleman, his ugly face bespectacled, asked the presiding judge with polite solicitude, 'If you'd be so good, your Honour, could you please ask the accused if he ever had erotic relations with the victim's wife?'

'Let the accused respond,' said the presiding judge.

'It is written,' Tourkoyannis answered gravely, 'thou shalt not satisfy thy flesh except with thine own lawful wedded wife. I am not married. Let all the doctors in town examine me. I have never slept with a woman. They say one can tell these things from a person's body.'

The whole courtroom rocked with laughter. The presiding judge finally rang the bell and Tourkoyannis, unperturbed, continued, 'I earned my keep honourably in Arathymos' house. Let Margarita herself bear witness.'

'How many years were you in that house?'

'Not long. I don't remember. A year, maybe two . . . more perhaps.'

After that the presiding judge again asked him about his earlier life and he told the court about his years abroad, his childhood and the circumstances of his birth. Only about his love, his one and only love, he didn't say a word, not even mentioning Margarita's name.

The presiding judge asked first the public prosecutor then the defence whether they had any questions. Only Tourkoyannis' advocate, a tall thin very short-sighted but distinguished criminal lawyer, got to his feet and said, 'Gentlemen of the jury, your attention please! You will note what must be inferred from the absurd and idiosyncratic manner of the unfortunate accused — patently some form of lunacy is involved here. Lombardo* would classify him among the mystics: his self-restraint is clear proof of this. The accused must be considered mad.'

'I'm not!' interrupted Tourkoyannis calmly.

'Has there been a psychiatric examination?' the lawyer went on to ask.

'There is no record of one,' replied the presiding judge.

'I propose,' continued the lawyer, 'that the trial be adjourned and the accused examined by specialist physicians.'

The jury at once showed signs of their delight. This would mean they would get off early and moreover not have to reach a difficult verdict. The presiding judge rang the bell and suspended proceedings for a quarter of an hour. Meanwhile he opened a large volume of the penal code and with his face concealed behind it beckoned his fellow judges towards him; there behind the book the three of them conferred in an undertone for a few minutes and arrived at their decision. After this, one judge got up and went out for a smoke.

Half an hour later the session resumed. The presiding judge read out the decision they had reached. The court did not accept the lawyer's proposal.

'One question, your Honour,' the doctor on the jury asked again impatiently. 'Were any bloodstains noticed on the clothes of the accused?'

'The report,' said the presiding judge somewhat disconcerted,

' doesn't mention anything!'

'Perhaps, Doctor,' suggested the juryman with the childish face, 'he changed his clothes to commit the murder and then got rid of them.'

'And was the money,' the doctor went on to ask, 'ever recovered?'

'The report doesn't mention anything,' the presiding judge reiterated and rang the bell nervously.

'He'd hardly be stupid enough to keep it on him!' said the young juryman.

'Another question, your Honour,' said the doctor. 'Did the investigator look into whether or not anybody really did go past the deserted hut?'

'That all emerged during the proceedings,' said the presiding judge.

'Whose property is the hut?' asked the doctor.

'It belongs to Arathymos, the man unjustly murdered,' Tourkoyannis replied.

'Now look,' said the young juryman, 'are we really going to sit here agonizing over every lie the accused has told? It's too much bother, Doctor!'

The presiding judge rang his bell again and the doctor gave his colleague a black look.

'The public prosecutor may now speak,' said the presiding judge.

At once the celebrated public prosecutor launched forth in a grandiloquent and sonorous voice. Ten times in the course of his speech Tourkoyannis attempted to stand up and interrupt him, but the police guards held him down and whenever he tried to say anything clamped a hand over his mouth. The wild orator, as he ranted on, would point accusingly towards him with his finger and glare at him fiercely, pitilessly, full of hatred. His every word was a curse, a calumny, a jeer: repeatedly he would call him a bandit, a murderer, a thief, a hypocrite, a benighted soul, a monstrous villain and a very dangerous man. Tourkoyannis had by now given up, and deep dejection had overwhelmed his orphan heart. He was drenched in a cold sweat, since he felt ashamed that the assembly should have to listen to so many imprecations, and with tears streaming from his eyes he uttered plaintive sighs. The public prosecutor talked on in this manner for half an hour and finished by requesting the death sentence.

After this the defence council spoke. From the moment he opened his mouth it was clear that even he did not really believe in Tourkoyannis' innocence. He characterized him as unstable and therefore not responsible. Making reference to Lombrozo, to Krafft-Ebing, to Carrara* and other criminologists and scholars, he said the accused was so devout it was impossible to imagine him being a criminal, or at any rate a common criminal. He pointed out that no witness to the murder had been produced, and while praising the public prosecutor's oration as marking an epoch in the annals of legal history, he urged the jury not to accept his proposed verdict and send the man to the guillotine,* since that would manifestly mean putting an innocent to death, but rather, assuming they had formed the conviction that he was guilty, to at least make allowances for his confused mental state and grant him his life, especially since, even if the jury did not accept that Tourkoyannis suffered from insanity, as from his mystical notions clearly appeared to be the case, then he must surely have done the deed while still in a towering rage, as two days earlier Arathymos had beaten him, and the ensuing nervous trauma, according to medical and legal experts, would have lasted two or three days or even longer.

The good lawyer had no way of accounting for, or making the others sensible of the infinite benevolence and love with which the martyr's innocent and childlike heart was overflowing.

The public prosecutor did not take the floor again. The presiding judge cut short the proceedings and the jurymen retired to their chamber to consult. They remained closeted for many hours. And in their final verdict they found the accused guilty of murder as charged, mitigated by a degree of mental confusion, and the court sentenced Tourkoyannis to imprisonment for life.

IX

He could scarcely believe his conviction. He felt like shouting, protesting, telling the court they had been hoodwinked. Had he not plainly shown throughout the trial that his accusers were lying? Wasn't it patently evident that he could not have been the murderer? So why were they imprisoning him for life, and why had God permitted such injustice? Meanwhile however the presiding judge had dismissed the court, the policemen promptly clapped iron handcuffs on his wrists, tied a rope around him and ordered him to come with them. The courtroom was still packed and everyone was staring at him curiously, murmuring as he passed them, evidently satisfied with the justice of the verdict. Then in broad daylight (it was still afternoon), Tourkoyannis was marched in fetters up the street, his eyes downcast as he felt ashamed in the presence of all these people who, seeing him surrounded by policemen, stopped and stared at him. But he trudged on dejectedly without a single word of protest, knowing there was no resisting this misfortune, and eventually some time later they reached the penitentiary outside town . . .

That same evening they immediately cut his hair, shaved off his beard and put him into prison uniform; the warden gave him a long lecture which he failed to understand, and eventually he was handed over to a guard, a young man with a placid expression, who, unlocking a large iron door and then a smaller one, ushered him through a triangular yard* to a small cell and locked him in, drawing the two stout bolts and turning the key with a piercing squeak. The sound aroused him as if from a deep sleep beset by dreams of some other terrifying world, and he looked anxiously round the small dark cell. He was utterly alone. A sense of desolation chilled his heart and his overheated brain could make no sense of what was happening to him; and this bewilderment was accompanied by a vague sense of dread which made him tremble, and every so often Margarita's sorrowful expression at the hearing would flash through his mind, in turn reminding him of Petros Pepponas who wanted him executed and had managed to get him thrown into this jail. There was a buzzing in his ears, his eyes wouldn't focus and his dizziness increased as if he were blind drunk, confusing and darkening his mind, making him forget the present, recalling disjointed fragments of the past. He had understood neither the warden's earnest lecture, nor the violent threats made by the guard with the placid expression. Nor had he noticed the other convicts awaiting him in the prison yard, some with looks of sympathy, others with smiles of admiration for his hideous crime and keen to celebrate his arrival. And he had woken only briefly at the sound of the cell door being bolted from outside and the huge key squeaking in the lock. That squeak went on ringing in his ears and a heavy hand seemed to tighten round his throat and heart. A shudder ran through his whole disoriented frame.

He again looked round the chilly flagstoned cell which was to be his home for the remainder of his life! For ever! . . . It was unfurnished save for a narrow bed without blankets and an icon on the whitewashed wall. He was overcome by black despair. 'For ever a convict!' he suddenly said to himself. And sitting down on the bed, he cradled his head in his hands and groaned aloud in anguish. In his deranged imagination he thought he saw his mother Areti in ragged clothes dancing in the hut that belonged to Margarita's father and had been his childhood home, and there beside her was Petros Pepponas, now her son. Margarita herself had become a man and was taunting his mother, like so many men in villages where they had begged during his untutored youth. Yoryis Arathymos too was there laughing, his massive chest wound a bloody fountain flooding the whole hut, so that the ragged dancer could not find anywhere to put her feet. He returned to his senses thoroughly shaken. 'For ever a convict,' he reiterated to himself. 'Oh, I must be going mad!' And the good man racked his brains as to what errors in his life had brought him to this pass, what had blinded so many people — his fellow villagers, the judges, the jury, the lawyers who had testified against him and condemned him — when he knew well that people were good, merciful and just. Indeed it was thanks to their compassion that he, a vulnerable child, and his mother, a beggar and a foreigner, had managed to earn a living, and hitherto he had always managed to earn his living among strangers and sympathy from their charitable hearts. But looking back over his entire innocent life, he could find no crime, no act of malice, that could account for such appalling punishment. And again his mind became disoriented and for some time he was unable to think clearly. When he recovered, trembling all over, he realized that he had been pacing up and down his narrow cell. It was very cramped and locked securely! He looked out of his tiny window onto the prison yard. At that hour it was deserted. He listened to the absolute silence that reigned throughout the massive building and his anxiety increased. A lump in his throat was almost choking him. In despair he flung himself onto the bed; he was exhausted and felt like weeping. But the tears refused to flow from his dry smarting eyes and suddenly he longed for the release of death. His hair stirred, his eyes started from their sockets and jumping back off the bed he found himself standing in the middle of his cell. For the first time in his life he felt real hatred for his wretched existence, his soul was in revolt against the injustice being done to him, against the verdict of the unjust men who had incarcerated him for the rest of his miserable life, while in the free world outside life was so beautiful, so full of worthwhile tasks and decent honest people! And for the first time in his life he was angry with himself, because he had unmanfully allowed himself to be imprisoned and not chosen to die, resisting neither the police when they arrested him nor the guards who locked him up. Now his soul commanded him to act with resolution and either escape or put an end to his existence. But the bolts of course were strong and wouldn't yield, the prison doors were ironclad, guards and soldiers with fixed bayonets were patrolling everywhere and the thick double prison walls were high. Driven to despair by these reflections, the convict fell to the ground and beat his head violently against the flagstones, trying to split his skull. The pain was intense, but when he felt his brow he realized he had failed to crack it. So he banged it again repeatedly with much greater force. But the pain persisted until eventually he knocked himself unconscious. When he came to it was already dark and he was frozen, his whole body was shivering and his teeth were chattering with cold. Instinctively he got to his feet, groped towards the bed and there curled up to await nightfall. He lay awake shivering for quite some time. Later he again began to dream. He was an emigrant and as in a vision beheld his distant village. It seemed like some beauteous other world, its dells and slopes and ridges covered with venerable olives trees.

Here and there dark cypress trees rose above the olive groves, their tips reaching towards the heavens; the meadows were green and the fields a bounteous sea of crops, man's consoling sustenance . . . Margarita's daughter was leading her favourite ewe out by its rope, the two boys were off to school, one whistling the other singing, each clutching a large slice of bread, the two oxen Perdiki and Paraskevas, so named because he was born on a Friday, had not been slaughtered and were tethered to the tree beside Arathymos' hut, flicking their tails to chase away the flies, Perdiki scratching his neck against the trunk, and Arathymos had not expired but recovered from his massive chest wound and risen from the other world . . .

This image brought back that of the slain Arathymos laid out in the middle of the pretty village church crowded with people, Margarita wailing and lamenting and beating her breast beside the corpse, Petros Pepponas with a sardonic smile upon his lips, and the priests chanting over the mortal remains of the man unjustly murdered . . . Then he saw himself in the church too, his long hair (now shorn) covering his ears and falling down to his nape in thick taper-like strands, his sparse beard (now shaven), and his crooked staff in one hand and his little bundle in the other; and finally he saw the policemen pouncing on him there in the church in front of everyone, as if about to kill him too, throwing him to the ground, tying him up and ordering him to follow them, without his having the least idea where he was being taken or why he had been shackled . . . Then he saw the other penitentiary where he had been held initially, a cheerful place crowded with people. All the prisoners were housed together, mostly quiet decent people who in a moment of anger, drunkenness or need had committed some offence, and some who no doubt had acted in a more calculating manner. Ah, that prison had not been so very different from the normal world. And in his mind's eye he recalled the faces of all the men there with him during those ten months, none of whom he would ever see again . . . He then remembered his own trial today! Oh, how he had been intoxicated by Margarita's voice! How he longed to hear that voice again, wafting to him through the darkness of the prison . . . But all he could hear was protracted silence. By now he felt much warmer. Suddenly he was startled by the harsh cry of the sentry on the third watchtower shouting out at the top of his voice, 'Guards, get moving!' followed again by impenetrable silence! . . .

Now even religion no longer consoled him, since his innocent faith in Justice and the benevolence of divine Providence had been shattered. Why should he be in prison and the man who had really slain Arathymos be enjoying the beautiful world and his ill-gotten gains? And who was the murderer? Tourkoyannis didn't know, no, he didn't know, he didn't even want to suspect him! . . . No, it couldn't be Petros, surely . . . and in any case Margarita wouldn't know anything about it . . . and of course now she had been widowed she would no longer be his mistress . . . and once again he found himself brooding over the overwhelming problem: why was it that so many other criminals were freely roaming the world and enjoying its blessings while sowing discord, pain and hatred everywhere? Why did so much injustice prevail, while innocent creatures suffered — children, honest people, splendid beasts like Arathymos' oxen?

Somewhere deep within his heart a faint consoling voice assured him that this mystery, like so many other mysteries of creation, could only be fathomed by the dead upon entering the realm of Truth, and then he remembered the good teacher overseas whom he would still be with if God had not called him to his side. He heaved a sigh. Again he longed for the release of death. Why didn't God call *him* to his side as well and reunite him at once with his beloved teacher, who by now would have learned the truth about so many other mysteries?

But when he sighed his head ached unbearably and he realized that he would never have the strength to split his skull. He resolved to try an easier way — he would starve himself to death.

Having reached this decision he closed his eyes. Then he wailed aloud and his sobs, emanating from the very depth of his being, shook his whole frame and continued for some time in the silence of the night, bringing him relief. At last sleep overcame him in his dire suffering and with it oblivion till dawn.

X

It was March and spring had returned once more. Noon had come and gone two hours ago and the sun was still warm and shining brightly in the clear blue sky, where a few gray and white clouds were sailing gently past. The villagers were all down in the valley working in the fields — digging over the earth, rooting out weeds, sowing late seed, indeed the work just then was proceeding briskly, as if everyone were in a hurry to complete his task that afternoon, or anxious to leave less work for the following day.

Petros Pepponas was overseeing the ploughing of the murdered man's field. He had worked all day himself and was now sitting in the shade of the straw hut on a long thick log beside its little door. Arathymos' ugly black-and-white dog was curled up at his feet.

He was staring thoughtfully at the pair of oxen as they plodded lazily down the long field, the ploughshare turning over the soil, while the hired ploughman behind urged on his team with his curious cry, cracking his whip to prevent them dozing off. And the two huge beasts, both russet brown, their heads bowed almost to the ground beneath the heavy yoke, leaning one against the other, remained poised a moment, thrusting forward with their whole massive weight, standing on three legs, ready to move forward on the fourth when the clod detached itself from the bowels of the earth, their bulging muscles indicating they were doing their utmost, and just as the ploughman gave out his strange cry, made one final effort and suddenly lurched forward, taking two or three rapid steps, as if about to stumble under their own momentum, while the ploughshare turned over a thick glistening black clod riddled with white roots, and finally came to a halt, the ploughshare gleaming in the sun, and a moment later the animals braced themselves for a renewed attempt.

The plough was followed by the same young lad, Margarita's son Thanasoulis, sowing the maize, seed by seed, into the furrow opened by the oxen, and after him came Margarita and her daughter breaking the clods up with their hoes and bending to shake out the weeds; that afternoon Margarita was dejected and said little. They carried on working like this for another two hours.

'We'll call it a day on the return!' Petros shouted from where he was sitting.

These words resonated strangely in Margarita's soul, as they brought back to her how this time last year Arathymos had issued the same command from that same seat beside the door of the straw hut. She raised her head, as if half expecting to see him there, instead saw Petros and sighed.

'She's remembered him again,' Petros reflected bitterly. A moment later he shouted to the ploughman, 'Unyoke them. We'll finish the job in two or three hours tomorrow!'

The dog woke up, yawned, then settled down again, its front paws stretched out, its head erect. The sun was descending and beginning to turn red. Margarita again was startled and looked in the direction of the hut as if to make sure that this order really had not come from Arathymos' lips.

The ploughman thrust the ploughshare deep into the earth and immediately unyoked the oxen, which then ponderously set out towards the hut, not stopping until they had reached their customary tree, where Tourkoyannis used to tether Perdiki and Paraskevas, now also no longer living. Following behind the ploughman came Margarita with her two children and they all joined Petros outside the door of the hut.

'What's the matter?' he asked her in a low voice, without even looking up.

'He was always so good to me!' she replied . . . 'And he suffered such a brutal death! . . . He'd still be alive if I hadn't made him sell the oxen!'

'It was his fate!' said Petros gloomily.

'Such a brutal death!' Margarita sighed again.

'Life is for the living!' Petros replied in a husky voice.

Margarita stood there motionless in front of him, her arms folded and her gaze averted. She remembered the decent villager with his long flaxen moustache whom she had lived with for so many years, and who had never raised a hand against her. How different he had been from the other husbands! They all beat their wives. But he? — never!

Yet for five whole years she and Petros had deceived the poor man, and his honest heart had never suspected a thing, indeed he had died believing in her virtue, cleverness and housewifely good sense. Because of this, his demise had genuinely grieved her. It had never occurred to her that his death might improve her life, and it had been so cruel, so agonizing that she still could not forget she had been the cause of it. She had not married him for love, nor he her, but God had blessed their family and she would have continued to live happily and peacefully alongside him, had not Petros appeared on the scene . . . Petros who was now her husband! . . .

She glanced at him fondly, admiring his manly features and broad chest, and he smiled up at her.

By now the ploughman had seated himself beside Petros and was chatting to him casually; the two oxen were patiently munching their fodder underneath the tree and the crimson sun was descending towards the west, turning all to gold. It occurred to Margarita that she should be getting her workman's supper and she went inside the hut.

There she went on brooding: 'Petros couldn't know either that events would take such a bloody turn, when he advised him to sell the oxen to get rid of Tourkoyannis, no, no, of course he couldn't! Petros was only to blame in loving her so terribly! . . . He alone had truly loved her. He had fancied her when she was a girl, but then so many other young men in the village had also fallen for her and she was too young to recognize true love. Besides, she was too obedient to her parents, who didn't want him to have her, favouring other suitors, particularly Yoryis Arathymos, who came from a good family . . . Poor Tourkoyannis too had been in love with her! . . . He had been languishing in jail for a year already!

Why had Petros testified against him so severely? Out of jealousy? Merely out of jealousy? . . . Might he have had other reasons? . . .

She came out of the hut again with bread, cheese and olives for the ploughman and sat down by herself a little apart. The two men continued their conversation. Her daughter was mustering her sheep, getting ready to go home, and the boys were eager to accompany her as the three siblings were still very fond of one another.

She again started mulling over things. Petros was the jealous type, yes, very much so, he was jealous of his own shadow. But why? Because he loved her of course. And what a handsome man he was! She could see him in her mind's eye with his broad chest and strong embrace. He could dandle her in his arms like a child, grown woman though she was, and he had fallen so madly in love with her and been devoted to her for so long now. His devotion had stood the test of time. But didn't she love him too herself? Ah, yes, ah, very much of course, very much indeed, but even more so when Yoryis was alive! . . . She corrected herself — no, surely that wasn't true, surely she aught to love him more now! . . . Did she not even now experience ecstatic moments when she would become oblivious to the world? But she also recognized another stronger bond that erotic love could not compare with, her love for her own children. They were more important to her than Petros! But even for Petros what had she not done? She had deceived her husband, she had suffered, lived in fear! Yet although she had often regretted her first lapse from virtue, especially in difficult moments when Tourkoyannis had been watching her . . . she had loved Petros nonetheless. Wasn't that evident from the way she had agreed to sell the oxen, out of compassion for all his fretting and suffering on her account?

But that decision had brought chaos in its wake. Her husband had left the same evening with the two fine oxen, Perdiki and Paraskevas, and had met his unjust and savage end there on the road . . . but she herself had never wished for his demise, all she had thought was that by getting rid of Tourkoyannis she would resolve things, that Petros would finally satisfy his obsessive craving for her and calm down. How could she have foreseen all the ills that had ensued: her children orphaned, the hapless man in prison? . . . And who was the real murderer? Ah, Tourkoyannis, surely not! He had shut himself away in the deserted hut in his despair, she had seen him there the day Arathymos was away in town selling the oxen . . . He was hiding miserably in a corner and she had seen him weeping . . . No, Tourkoyannis was incapable of killing anyone! But then neither had Petros killed anyone! Why did she suddenly think of Petros now? No, no, he wasn't that sort either, how could a man who loved so passionately be a treacherous murderer? . . . She mustn't even think of such a thing! How could Petros be so cruel as to plunge that huge knife into the heart of a man he'd wronged, inflict a wound like that? . . . Ah, she remembered the gaping wound in her husband's chest, like those she'd seen in slaughtered animals . . . That's the way their fine oxen, Perdiki and Paraskevas, would have been butchered too . . . Why did she always keep remembering them? . . . No, no, she mustn't even think of such a thing! How could a man, a few hours before committing murder, preoccupied with plotting murder, surrender with such abandon to the rapture of illicit love? And indeed she had never known him so self-forgetful as on that evening when Arathymos was away in town. Never had his embraces been so ardent, his kisses so insatiable, never had so many tears streamed from his eyes, relieving, he said, his pent up feelings, never had his joy been more ecstatic than that evening! After stumbling across Tourkoyannis grieving over his dismissal in the hut, alerted by his little cough they had retreated and arranged to meet that night at Petros' house. And when darkness fell she had kept her word, creeping through back gardens, her heart in her mouth . . . It had been one of those rare moments of total freedom for them both. He had awaited her as usual with gloomy impatience, but that night he knew she would come for certain . . . She recalled how she had gently pushed open the door to his house . . . The faint light emitted by the oil lamp was engulfed by the yawning darkness. At first the darkness frightened her but it did not deter her, and entering with a sigh she at once found herself in his impetuous embrace . . .

How could a man who loved so passionately kill someone a few hours later? But why did the idea keep tormenting her? . . .

'Everything's the same as last year!' she remarked glumly.

'Everything's the same,' he replied as if in a dream.

'Except that he's not here,' she added with a sigh.

'He's not here,' he answered frowning.

A gloomy silence followed.

'And we have different oxen!'

'Different oxen!'

'And a different ploughman!'

'Different!' he replied, irritated, and looked her in the eyes.

During the year she had often talked to him about Tourkoyannis, about the unjust suffering of this innocent man who had loved her and her family so dearly — the children too would often remember him and his little dances. And now she sensed that she was about to raise the topic again.

'Poor Tourkoyannis!' she said sadly. 'He's in jail for life . . . ah why did you want to see him hanged?'

'Don't you remember everything he put us through?' he asked.

'But since Yoryis was dead, you knew you'd have me. So why testify against him so relentlessly, sealing his fate?'

Again a deep silence followed. Such moments were now frequent, as she often raised the matter of Arathymos' death with him. Now she was waiting for his answer.

'Why, why?' he said finally. 'Because he killed him!'

'Ah, no,' she replied at once, 'it must have been some stranger on the road, someone after his money . . . Don't you think so, Petros? . . .'

Petros got to his feet, deeply perturbed. He wished to end this conversation and to be alone. He walked to the bottom of the field, pretending to be inspecting the day's work. He had a heavy heart that evening and the quiet descending all around him made it heavier. Dark thoughts arose in his mind, stifling all more cheerful reflections and making him indifferent to his task. Why couldn't Margarita too finally forget about the past? Why didn't she start a new life with him, instead of trying to base her present existence on the past and reconcile the two? . . . And involuntarily he thought about the murder . . .

It had been spring then too, a day in March just like today, when he had resolved to commit murder! . . . If Margarita didn't come to the hut that evening, he knew he would have to do something drastic, as passion now held complete sway over him, and he had realized he could not go on living in such insufferable torment! . . . Margarita had followed his advice and they had turned Tourkoyannis out. That same day Arathymos had taken his oxen into town to sell and that evening Margarita had come to the hut, but Tourkoyannis had taken refuge there as well, and on hearing his faint cough Margarita had taken to her heels in panic. It was Tourkoyannis' unexpected appearance that had steeled his heart to make the harsh decision. He now knew that to free himself of all impediments he had to, simply had to, commit murder.

That night Margarita had come home with him and surrendered body and soul to the frenzied joys of love, and for a little while he had quite forgotten what he planned to do. But the hours of rapture too had passed, leaving him with an unquenchable sense of longing. He again found himself alone, and realized that if he allowed matters to follow their customary course, it would be a long time before such rare moments of happiness occurred again . . .

And so he had headed for the main road, not that he had irrevocably made up his mind, but simply to explore whether it might be feasible to kill the man safely as he returned from town that night.

On and on he walked, absorbed in his dark deliberations. It was a moonless night and innumerable stars were twinkling in the sky, shedding a faint light. The air was still cold, his fingers were freezing and every so often a shiver would run down his spine. He felt like returning to his warm bed and resting, but he couldn't stop himself, his legs seemed to propel him forwards. On and on he strode. What would he do if he saw him coming along the road alone and it were an isolated stretch? Instinctively he reached for his belt and realized that he was wearing Tourkoyannis' knife, taken from Arathymos' house that morning. His first impulse was to fling it into the undergrowth beneath the olive trees where he would be unable to retrieve it, then even if he were to come upon the man in some deserted spot he couldn't murder him; yet inexplicably instead of throwing it away he tightened his grip on the hilt, thrusting it more firmly into the sheath. And at once he started imagining what killing someone would entail, picturing himself, almost like some apparition, wielding and stabbing with the knife. He would have to hold his breath and grit his teeth, he thought, then deliver a precise blow to the jugular, or better still the heart, because if he wasn't careful the knife might as it descended injure him instead . . . On and on he strode. Finally he arrived at a lonely spot near a ruined church, that of the Holy Virgin by the Wayside. It was pitch dark. The huge black olive trees with their dense intertwining branches prevented the starlight penetrating, and only the white road gleamed faintly beneath the massive canopy. Utter silence reigned in that godforsaken place. There Petros halted, sat down at the foot of an olive tree and, scared out of his wits, prepared to wait. He found it hard to swallow and asked himself, what was he waiting for? Why didn't he just get up and leave? And in response he did his utmost to deceive himself: he wanted to watch him go past, not of course to kill him, but to relish the thought that if he wished he could pounce on him and dispatch him there and then! . . . He again reached for his belt and with a shudder gripped the knife. Just then a chill breeze swept through the olive trees rustling the leaves, and that whispering sigh was enough to make him tremble. Could Arathymos already be approaching? Straining his eyes, he peered into the darkness and waited. The breeze had passed and silence reigned once more. His conscience urged him to fling the weapon far into the night, since every passing minute made the crime easier to contemplate, but then with a derisive smile he taunted himself: What, was he too weak to control himself? Had he not succeeded all these years in doing just that? And his life, if truth be told, had been neither an easy nor a happy one . . . and would he now find truth, in the hour of darkness, on the road? But he knew he was deceiving himself, because something raging at a deeper level of his consciousness was telling him he would commit the crime that night, come hell or high water! . . . Thrusting his hand into his pocket for his pouch, he mechanically began to roll a cigarette. Then realizing the glow would be visible from a distance, he let the tobacco slip through his fingers to the ground. But why should he care if he were seen? Why so cautious? Ah, so he really was lying in wait for the man, he really did intend to kill him! . . .

And he went on agonizing for some time. He recalled his agitation two days earlier when he had waited in vain for Margarita at the hut; then the blissful moments they had spent this evening flashed through his mind, their sweetness still lingering, and with a sigh he asked himself, where and how and when would he see her again? . . . unless . . . and a moment later the whole crime was again unfolding before his mind's eye. Tomorrow her husband would be back in the village, he reflected with a shudder, able to enjoy her because she belonged to him — yes him! — and Tourkoyannis would find a way to avoid leaving and again be on the watch; both of them had to be removed before he could start living! . . . Ah why had Fate not helped by intervening and restoring Margarita's liberty, as was only fair and just? . . . But he was there at that hour to rectify the injustices of Fate! . . . Well then, he said, frightened of himself, was he going to commit murder? . . . Was that why he was there? . . . No, no! . . .

Now he could hear distant footsteps. His heart started pounding violently; shrinking back against the root of the olive tree where he was sitting, he peered into the dark and listened. The footsteps drew nearer. Why was Arathymos coming back so early? Why wasn't he spending the night in town? And the footsteps came closer still. Clenching his teeth he again reached for his knife but immediately withdrew his hand, as if the hilt had seared his fingers. Meanwhile the footsteps continued to approach and he listened intently. It was more than one person, Arathymos was not alone, and that was natural enough as he would not want to venture forth alone at night with so much money on him. And for a moment he rejoiced from the bottom of his heart. God was protecting him at a difficult juncture in his life, God who ruled the world and did not allow his creatures to lapse into criminal behaviour! . . . But his joy lasted no more than an instant, as he again recalled the life awaiting him in the village from tomorrow. Absolutely alone in life! Separated for ever from his Margarita, from the only woman he loved! And to think that the other fellow would be enjoying every imaginable bliss! . . .

By now the two wayfarers were passing quite close to him, talking in loud carefree voices in the night. Ah, Arathymos wasn't one of them! They were strangers, evidently also coming back from town. They were discussing Arathymos and his oxen. He had sold them for a good price and would be returning to the village laden with cash. They had walked on ahead, but it would not be long before he came past . . . And as they continued on their way, their voices receded slowly into the darkness and quiet of the night, and very soon their steps were no longer audible . . .

Despite himself he lingered on. It occurred to him that if day dawned soon, the light would prevent him from doing the abominable deed. But dawn was still a long way off and he could not bring himself to leave and went on waiting . . . longer and still longer . . .

Again he heard footsteps in the distance and began trembling from head to foot. Now he was certain: Arathymos was coming, Arathymos and none other, no, it could be no one else! Oh, of course he wouldn't kill him! The man was walking briskly and his footsteps were rapidly approaching. With beating heart he caught sight of him in the distance, a dark shape moving along the endless road, and recognized him as he entered the clearing just before the dense clump of trees. He was walking unsuspectingly through the night, keeping to the verge to avoid the stones and shuffling his feet a little as he was wearing *tsarouchia* . . . By now he was getting very close, was practically level with him and in a moment would have passed . . . Without realizing what he was doing, he sprang to his feet and with another bound blocked the wayfarer's path. Then quick as a flash he drew his knife, and with his other hand reached out to seize Arathymos. His palm brushed against the man's forehead, which was bathed in a cold sweat, and he realized that fear must suddenly have chilled him. Arathymos let out a hideous cry that echoed far into the night and staggered back a pace, but as he was already on the verge and the road just there stood proud a little, he lost his footing and fell flat on his back into the soft undergrowth . . . And Petros now recalled how he had pounced on him at once, kneeling on his chest and grabbing hold of his head. The poor man's whole body was shaking uncontrollably and he cried out, 'Take the money, man, but don't kill me!' Just at that moment a beam of starlight coming through the leaves had lit up Arathymos' eyeball, which Petros had noticed was staring in horror at the knife quivering above it. By now he was trying to wrench the man's head towards his shoulder to expose the neck and deliver him a mortal blow; the poor man had resisted with all his might, but eventually he had managed to subdue him; and yet his hand refused to strike; a thousand thoughts flashed through his mind with lightning speed and kept restraining him. Compassion had struggled valiantly within his soul to gain the upper hand. Then suddenly the man had recognized him and in a faint voice cried out in terror, 'Petros, Petros, what are you doing? D'you intend to murder me to take my Margarita from me?' And he again let out a frantic scream. At this point Petros had realized that he would be doomed if he were to let the poor man live, and immediately plunged the knife into his bare neck, with a shudder feeling it sink deep into the flesh and hearing Arathymos' cry turn to a hoarse gurgle as he drowned in his own blood, his whole body writhing convulsively beneath the knee that pinned him down. There was now no question that Arathymos must be dispatched. Pulling the knife from the neck-wound he had just inflicted, he thrust it deep into his heart, and a few moments later, now completely calm and rational, he felt confident that the man was dead. He left the knife in his chest and took all the money from his pocket and his belt.

It had still been night when he reached the village and he himself had no idea how he had found his way back, like a man blind drunk, nor whether he had taken byways and cut across fenced land to reach his home. He now had no recollection of any of this. All he knew was that as day dawned, perspiring and exhausted by the violent struggle and long walk, he had flung himself onto his bed without taking off his bloodstained clothes and immediately fell into a deep sleep, as if his soul had departed for another world.

It was broad daylight, noon already, when he awoke and with horror recalled the unholy deed, yet he couldn't believe he had actually killed the man, persuading himself that in his heavy sleep he had had a hideous nightmare that still lingered, maddening his reason and making an act seem real which of course he hadn't done! Soon he'd see Arathymos in the village, have a chat with him, ask where and when he'd sold the oxen and be able to relax. But as he was thinking this his eye fell upon the bloodstained clothing, and starting back he stared at it with bloodshot eyes, pursing his dry lips and scratching his aching head. But despite this palpable evidence he was still not convinced and tried to persuade himself that, although alert, in reality he was still asleep and in the middle of a hideous dream. He remembered robbing the corpse and put his hand in his pocket to see if the stolen money was actually there. Finding it carefully wrapped in some brown paper, he flung it with revulsion to the floor and then kicked it into the grate, where the fire had long gone out.

He still couldn't believe it, he simply couldn't! And yet the money was there, he was all covered in blood — his clothes, his sticky hands, and probably his face and hair as he had scratched his head. He stared at himself in a small mirror on the wall and noticed that he looked gaunt and pale as a corpse, though there were only a few red stains on his face and hair which would readily wash off. Suddenly he panicked. Someone might see him with his hands and clothing in this state, someone might come by looking for him — was that not the door just opening? What would he do, what would he say? Was the door locked? He glanced across.

Yes, it was securely bolted. He hastily started undressing in the middle of the room, panting with anxiety, and in a moment was completely naked. He had another fright when it occurred to him that perhaps there was no water in the house, and he shook and peered into the water pitcher. It contained only a little water. He would need bucketsful to cleanse himself of so much blood. Meanwhile he began washing his hands, face and head as best he could and managed to clean himself up. Next he put on clothes out of the dirty washing still under the bed, then all that remained was to dispose of the bloodstained ones and he would again be able to believe that he had not committed the crime. He listened attentively, in case the neighbours were at home, and as all was quiet softly opened the door, letting in the brilliant sunlight, and after involuntarily glancing at his hands went out and looked around. All the neighbouring houses at that hour were shut, as everyone was away working in the fields down in the valley. Re-entering the house and bolting the door, he carefully gathered all the bloodstained clothes and flung them into the grate, then, forgetting all about the money, sprinkled them liberally with oil and set them alight. The clothes smouldered for a while at first, the smoke giving off an unpleasant odour, but eventually they blazed up brightly, the flames soaring to the rafters. The smoke and toxic smell drove him out of the house, and he sat down on the doorstep much relieved. Then he realized that the stolen money must be burning with his clothes and decided he should rescue it. Going back inside, he poked about in the fire with a stick and retrieved the blackened bundle from the flames, stamping on it and beating it with the stick to put it out, but instead it disintegrated into a thousand tiny pieces which went on burning as they scattered, and seeing the money now irretrievably lost he felt strangely elated!

Then he went outside again. He inspected his hand and forearm in the sunlight once more, sat down on the doorstep for a moment and then got up again. He felt restless. Realizing he must find something to do, he went back into the house. The flames had now gone out and the room and bed were covered with particles of charred clothing, but all evidence of the crime had vanished. He felt satisfied. He decided to do some work in his garden and took down his hoe. Setting about it briskly, he hacked away at the fallow land to tire himself out, hoping through hard labour to forget what he had done that night, and every so often the hand that had wielded the knife would catch his eye and he would check that it had washed clean.

He had toiled away like that all afternoon and gradually calmed down. He now knew without a shadow of a doubt. He was a killer! He himself had committed murder. He had murdered for the sake of Margarita, whom he now must marry! What good would worrying, remorse and self-laceration do him? The past could not be undone. He wished he had not done the cruel deed, but since he had he should make the most of it. Now he even felt vexed that the money had burned, what would it have mattered if he'd kept it, as it was after all his. Yes, he would marry her, he would make her his wife, he would have her when, how and as often as he pleased, he would control her absolutely! That's what he had committed murder for! His hand had changed the course of Fate. He was superior to other people, because he dared!* Who had witnessed the murder? Who suspected him? Who could possibly suspect him? Life had now opened up before him, a life of happiness, the months of fretting and frustration were now over, Margarita would belong to him!

He recalled the rapture of the previous day which had ended in that savage night, his passionate intoxication which had ended in the murder. And in his heart he felt a cruel pride at having been bold enough to do it! But a moment later he felt ashamed and, glancing at the hand he'd seen all bloody, realized that his soul would not find true peace until he either stopped trying to justify the crime or managed to forget it, and again he began hacking vigorously at the soil to tire his body out and drown his oppressive imaginings in labour.

Meanwhile evening had set in; he was about to call it a day when suddenly he noticed Tourkoyannis there before him. He was carrying his little bundle on a stick over his shoulder and was deathly pale and trembling. He watched him stop and stand there silently for several moments, looking at him searchingly with tears in his eyes, and he felt afraid . . . Tourkoyannis had sensed his trepidation and now said to him in a subdued voice, 'They brought him back in the cart!'

'Who?' he asked, terrified despite himself.

And Tourkoyannis, his suspicion now confirmed, continued with a sigh: 'Oh, Judas, why did you kill him?' and then he began to weep.

He had not replied, but had realized with dread that if Tourkoyannis were to speak out he was doomed, and rushing from his garden he soon found himself among the crowd in the centre of the village, where everyone was talking about the murder. He knew he must say something, express his sorrow, deflect people's suspicions onto someone else, and was himself the first to mention Tourkoyannis' name, telling people about his expulsion from Arathymos' home, though without appearing to condemn him. He also knew he must be among the first to be seen beside the corpse and hastened to the church.

But when he saw the murdered man he nearly fainted and had to muster all his self-control not to give himself away; he could see people had noticed his inner turmoil, but fortunately they put it down to his grief over the iniquitous death of his friend; this made him realize that even if Tourkoyannis talked he would not be believed and that he was safe.

Then he saw Margarita come screaming into the church, followed by her children, also in tears, and start wailing and lamenting in front of all the villagers, blaming herself for causing the tragedy by having insisted on the sale of the oxen. He had been the first to comfort her with consoling words, and had persuaded her to leave the church when the priests were about to begin their chanting over the corpse.

By now he was completely rational again.

But when the funeral service commenced, he again felt somewhat uneasy, noticing that many eyes were watching him. He was wearing his jacket slung over his right shoulder and suddenly felt his hand tingling beneath it when he imagined it all bloody, and this perturbed him. The sight of the murdered man, with the gaping wounds he had inflicted, now became utterly intolerable. He also kept thinking obsessively about Tourkoyannis.

Eventually he had caught sight of him inside the church, his little bundle in one hand and his crooked stick in the other; then he had watched the policemen throw him to the ground and tie him up, at which his heart rejoiced and from that moment on he considered himself totally secure.

Now he could no longer remember how the ensuing days had passed. He had been in a sort of stupor. He had avoided company, worked hard then slept a lot, and begun to drink alone. All he could remember was that he had concentrated all his efforts on forgetting the savagery of the murder and on justifying himself to his own conscience by claiming he had done the deed in the conviction that it was necessary. At times he even admired his own daring. He had laboured arduously that spring, but even he couldn't remember much about it. So arduously indeed that the following summer he had had a bumper crop. During all that time he scarcely saw Margarita, only occasionally passing by her house, fearful lest confronted by her grief he might betray himself, and aware that she was surrounded by male and female relatives keeping her company to help console her.

Then the inquest had begun. He realized that he would again need all his self-control when facing the authorities to avoid giving himself away, and he imagined himself locked in hand-to-hand combat with Tourkoyannis, who doubtless would speak out in his own defence, tell all he knew about his affair with Margarita, reveal his suspicions, and so everything would come out and be made public . . . He recalled that it was during this same period that he had met Margarita alone in the deserted hut for the first time since the murder. He had waited many hours for her and felt he might perhaps have been in too much of a hurry. And on that occasion they had not enjoyed love's passionate intoxication as always hitherto, indeed from the very first moment they had both felt an intolerable tension. They didn't know what to say to one another.

She frequently looked down at her black mourning dress, he kept glancing furtively and fearfully at his right hand. Even now Petros could recall what they had said that evening. Both feared Tourkoyannis might be talking, making his suspicions known. And she kept asking him what to do to avoid being slandered, as she felt deeply ashamed and fearful that even marriage could not extinguish such dishonour. He did not know how to answer, as he had his own oppressive secret, which must be kept even from her and which Tourkoyannis might reveal too as he had guessed it!

Thus their conversation faltered and they didn't dare embrace, as if they feared some spirit from beyond the grave might suddenly appear, and they nervously cast their eyes about, convinced they would see some apparition in the hut that evening.

They talked about Tourkoyannis. Margarita did not believe he could be guilty. He tried to convince her that Tourkoyannis was indeed the murderer and urged her to testify against him, without telling any lies, but Margarita would not agree.

Then there had been an awkward pause.

Eventually both of them had felt the need for love's consoling moments, after so much time apart. But from the very first kisses they realized at once that sadly those moments would never be the same, as the soul of him who had suffered so unjust a death now came between them . . .

It was on a later occasion, after the trial of Tourkoyannis, that Margarita first broached the topic of the intolerable unease that came over her when they were together. Now it was no longer fear that caused it, because poor Tourkoyannis had said nothing, sacrificing himself to his bitter love, and she was both a widow and a free woman whom nobody controlled; and gently she asked him whether they shouldn't perhaps sever their ties once and for all and each seek solace elsewhere. At this he at once became enraged, his eyes blazing so fiercely that Margarita was thoroughly alarmed and started trembling. And Petros recalled how that day for the first time in his life he cursed her, clenching his teeth as he had done that night in the act of killing, and how in his rage he anathematized the man he had unjustly murdered. And suddenly Margarita panicked at the spectacle of such ferocity, the suspicion flashing through her mind that Petros was indeed the murderer, and scared out of her wits she told him so, bowing her head as if expecting him to strike her. But instead his ire had suddenly abated and he had begun to weep, realizing how his fit of fury was destroying everything. Margarita had wanted to believe in his innocence, and in the moments of rapture that ensued they managed to recapture something of their former love and agreed on a formal festive marriage! . . .

They had now been married since Carnival time,* shortly after the year of mourning had concluded, and that day were working together on her property. The ploughman with his two huge beasts had meanwhile left the field and from a distance had wished him a good night, but Petros had not heard him. The children had also departed with the sheep and it was now beginning to get dark. Margarita shouted to him anxiously 'What are you doing down there alone so long, aren't we going?' and she sighed, reflecting that she was no longer happy . . .

'I'm coming, I'm coming!' he replied as he approached, and his face looked tired and drawn after his lengthy ruminations. His eyes were dull and staring and took nothing in. He came up to her without a word.

'What's the matter?' she asked.

Petros couldn't find anything to say. He knew he ought to discuss the day's work with her, the seed they still required, the tasks yet to be performed, but he felt completely tongue-tied because that evening his soul was in revolt, compelling him to take some drastic action and liberate himself from the intolerable secret that tormented him.

She looked at him anxiously. 'Things were better when he was alive!' she said.

'Much better,' he answered with a sigh.

'Even in your wildest dreams you never thought I'd be your wife! Are you dissatisfied?'

'Even in my wildest dreams,' he replied sourly, 'how could I be dissatisfied?'

'I don't know!' she went on, 'but even in your sleep you don't seem to find peace!'

'The soul,' he replied seriously, lowering his voice, 'is a precious thing, as Tourkoyannis used to say, and our sins weigh us down. This is why, ever wakeful, it disturbs us in our sleep, seeking its deliverance . . .' And as he said this he looked about fearfully, thinking for a moment he had given himself away. He shuddered.

Meanwhile Margarita, smiling uneasily, replied, 'But for goodness sake, your sins are not that great! . . .'

He stood there motionless for a few moments, then looked her in the eyes with a glazed expression, and suddenly he felt an irrepressible urge to speak out and at last unburden himself of the oppressive secret suffocating him. His face assumed an unusual ruthlessness and he clenched his teeth as he had done in the act of killing. She became even more afraid of him and didn't know what she should do. She sensed that he was about to say something appalling which she ought not, did not, want to hear, and anxious for the scene to end, she bent down, rearranged the things in her basket and putting it on her head said gloomily, 'Let's go now, it is getting late.'

'Wait,' he replied huskily, 'I have something I must tell you.'

'Oh, don't say anything!' she pleaded in alarm.

'Wait,' he repeated resolutely.

The two of them fell silent and looked into one another's eyes. All about them quiet reigned in the gathering gloom of dusk, as if life on earth had been extinguished, and the mystery of that hour made their inner turmoil all the more unbearable. Margarita, her basket balanced on her head, stood trembling in anticipation, then Petros came up close to her and in a dead voice whispered in her ear, 'I killed him!' Immediately he stepped back, thrusting out his hands in a gesture of denial, and stared at her wild-eyed and breathing rapidly, not quite grasping what he had just done. Margarita swayed as if about to faint, then slowly lowering her basket sank panic-stricken to the ground, feeling the urge to weep but quite unable to. She couldn't believe her ears. Yet his words resonated grimly within her soul and she knew her husband had just told her the truth. This explained all the mysteries. This was why Petros had wanted to send Tourkoyannis to the gallows. At last tears came to her eyes and with heaving breast she sobbed aloud. 'You, you!' she cried. 'Oh, what have you done, what have you done! . . .'

'It was me,' he affirmed sadly and despairingly, for even this confession had brought him no peace. 'I murdered him! It was at night, in a deserted spot near the church of the Holy Virgin by the Wayside, and I slaughtered him there like a sheep. I'd lain in wait for him! . . .'

'You, you?' she cried. 'How can I go on being your wife?' And she looked at him in horror out of the corner of her eye, and cringing as if to avoid his blow added with hatred, 'Oh, I can't bear to look at you, you murderer! You orphaned my children and then you married me!'

Seeing the whole structure of his life collapsing after he had worked so hard to build it, he suddenly became enraged, and while not regretting his confession yet wanting this woman to love him for the man he really was, he cried out, 'Because I loved you!'

'I can't bear to look at you,' she repeated, 'you are the murderer!'

For a moment he did not answer, then finally he said to her brutally, 'I control you! You're my wife! My wife you will remain!'

She made no reply. Getting to her feet with a sigh, she replaced her basket on her head and started out for the village. He followed her in silence, now rediscovering within himself the resolute man who had murdered Yoryis Arathymos in the dead of night.

XI

'Because in this world,' Tourkoyannis was saying in the prison yard, 'only those who always do good, or who having done evil repent, are happy.'

'Is that why you robbed and murdered, so you could then repent?' laughed a convict sitting near him, a swarthy middle aged man with a fierce expression.

'Not me!' said Tourkoyanis. 'It is written, thou shalt not kill, and I did not kill. It is written, thou shalt not steal, and I did not steal!'

The other convict looked at him sceptically and said with a sarcastic chuckle, 'This is not a courtroom and you've no need to hide things. Sins are treated sympathetically in here because all of us are sinners and the greater the crime the greater a man's prestige, so some are proud of what they've done!'

Two or three others who had been listening thoughtfully, smiled. A small but sturdy man standing in front of Tourkoyannis stroking his chin remarked, half-closing his eyes, 'Tourkoyannis is a just man, and he is unjustly held in here.'

This man had grown old in jail, he already had white hair and a little white moustache, and premature ageing had given his face a serene expression.

Tourkoyannis looked at him gratefully, knowing him a friend. This man had been the first to speak to him in prison, the day he emerged from his cell dazed and faint with hunger. He had cautiously put his head out, after the guard unlocked his cell door, and seen the prison yard full of strangers talking quietly among themselves or strolling in the sun. No one then had given him a second glance, and slowly he had ventured forth, sitting on the doorstep of his cell and hiding his face as best he could. He had remained there for some time alone, hungry and awaiting food, and the convict who was now his friend had approached and spoken to him quietly: 'We're not wild animals in here,' he told him. 'We are human too. If you're suffering we'll console you, and if people hate you for what you've done, here you will find sympathy!'

They had sat together for several hours. Tourkoyannis had had his first taste of prison food with him, and by the end of the day had heard many horrific stories about the prisoners strolling past. When Tourkoyannis had asked his name, the man had replied, lowering his eyes, 'In here they call me Cain! But in the world outside I had another name! . . .' It was evident that the man was suffering at the recollection of his crime. Tourkoyannis had then remembered a girl he had known somewhere abroad, with a rosebud face and a pure and charitable soul . . . This girl had sinfully fallen in love with a married man and become so deeply depressed that her life was in peril. Feeling sorry for her, he, Tourkoyannis had wanted to rescue her, and disregarding the derision of the world had offered to marry her, take her far away and support her by his labour. But the man who had wronged her intervened, determined she should marry his brother who was expected home from overseas, and from then on God's curse had descended like a whirlwind on that family. Things got very tangled and one brother wound up six feet under, the other locked away in jail.

But on that first day Tourkoyannis had not pressed him further, nor revealed that he himself was implicated in his story, merely gazing at him with tender sympathy, yet from then on he had felt a bond of affection for the man.

In response to Cain's remark about his being held unjustly, he replied, 'Who can know the will of God? Why do the innocent suffer in this world?'

The other convict laughed derisively and shaking his head got up and started strolling about the prison yard alone.

Some people,' Cain observed with a sigh, 'are proud of what they did. Not me though!'

'Has God set you on His path then?' Tourkoyannis asked him

delightedly, for a moment forgetting his own pain.

'My soul is damned!' replied the other gloomily.

'But haven't you repented? Then why should you despair?'

Cain's eyes blazed harshly. 'I have not repented,' he replied. 'If the man who landed me in here were still alive, I would murder him again!'

Tourkoyannis gazed at him sadly and said nothing. He recognized a kindly light in his fierce eyes and realized that this man who had killed his own brother was trying to harden his heart, nurturing the bitter hatred his brother's wrongs had sown there, and did not want to repent, however much he might have preferred not to have been obliged to kill him.

And suddenly Tourkoyannis' heart was illuminated by a ray of hope: perhaps he himself might be destined to guide this man along the road to his redemption, possibly other fellow prisoners and future inmates of the jail as well, and as he imagined himself benevolently cast among them by the Will of Providence to save sinful souls, his face at once resumed its usual cheerful and serene expression and his troubled soul grew calm. Within his heart the mystery of it all was being dispelled. His life in prison had a purpose, a higher purpose than in the world outside. And since that was the case, what did it matter if he had suffered, been maligned, condemned unjustly and had yet to suffer more? What did it matter if Arathymos had been killed? By these means a Higher Will would redeem many people, or this one soul at least. This would be the final fruit of all his adventures.

Gently he said to his companion, 'My brother, I can see your deed oppresses you.'

Scowling, the man replied, 'I wish I'd never been born!'

'Or never had him as a brother!' added Tourkoyannis, looking him in the eye.

Cain flushed and the veins in his neck stood out. 'Ah, yes,' he said, 'then I'd not have ended up in here!'

At that moment Tourkoyannis sensed that Cain was beginning to accept him as a friend as well and this brought him new joy. 'However badly your brother treated you,' he then said to him, 'you treated him far worse You took away his life! . . . You could not have exacted more. You should now be content to atone for the injustice here!'

'Ah,' sighed the other man, 'how could he be so wicked!'

Then he went on to relate how he too was a lifer, condemned initially to death, how he had grown prematurely old in jail and seen a lot of people pass through the place — some had arrived before him and completed their sentence, others after him and were already free, still others would soon be released — and all that time he had been rotting away in there, having given up all hope of receiving a pardon. He knew each and every convict, their histories and character, and Tourkoyannis ought to get to know them too, since he would be spending the rest of his life in jail, no matter how long he lived. Then he went on to explain how his brother, the man he had murdered, was the real villain and had only received his just deserts, far less in fact, but despite this the law had decided that he deserved to suffer! He told him how he too was a villager, peace-loving industrious and respected until the day he committed his crime — not through any fault of his but because of his brother's outrageous conduct. He had sent him abroad for years, reduced him to penury, not given him any of their father's land, married him off the day after his return, and then seduced his wife, whom he had believed honest and had loved more than all the world, more than himself. People said his brother had deliberately chosen her so that he could enjoy her too, since he also loved her and had refused to let her marry a stranger. And so he had killed him. But the court had not believed his testimony. It had wanted to make an example of this fratricide, especially in view of the brutal manner of its execution, for Cain had disfigured the corpse, driven to exact every last ounce of vengeance . . . Then he recounted his long years in prison, his monotonous and sterile life, though still so young, mixing with hardened criminals who had gone from bad to worse and were impressed not by all he had unjustly suffered or his harsh and unreasonable sentence, but by the gravity of the offence and the savagery of the murder. He himself had never bragged about his deed, but he did mention that today he ranked first among the prisoners. His orders were carried out, grudgingly or by coercion, because the other felons feared him and deferred to him. Then he told Tourkoyannis how, many years back, he had twice tried unsuccessfully to escape from prison and a third time had succeeded, managing to reach his native village. There he had seen his unfortunate wife, who by then was living quietly with a stranger, and found his children begging in the street. He had not revealed himself to her, not wishing to shatter the tranquillity of the longsuffering woman. No one in his village had recognized him except her, and she had taken fright, thinking he would kill her, gone into hiding and turned him in at once.

As he related these events, his eyes blazed and he clenched his teeth. His own story enraged him, his voice grew harsh, his face flushed red and the veins in his neck expanded. Even after all these years, Cain's fury had still not abated, and love had turned to hatred in his passionate heart. Finally he said, 'Well that's true, isn't it? If my brother had not been so wicked, would I be stuck in this place? Of course I wouldn't! I'd be at home with my wife and children . . . I would not be a lost soul!'

'It is written,' Tourkoyannis replied earnestly, 'that the angels in heaven rejoice at the repentance of a sinner. And the sinner who repents is worth more than him who has never sinned . . . My brother, I feel sorry for you!'

The convict looked at him deeply perturbed, his whole body shook, his face went pale and two large tears trickled down his cheeks onto the ground, thereby sanctifying the prison soil. Tourkoyannis got up to return to his cell, looked him in the eye for several seconds and then also heaved a sigh. Suddenly he found himself remembering Arathymos' home, his oxen, his children, and hearing the enchanting voice of Margarita, who perhaps at that very moment was remembering him fondly too.

But Cain was now on the road to his redemption.

XII

Some time had elapsed. The nights were still long and it was late one evening. In Arathymos' house they had not yet gone to bed. Petros was absent, the two boys were seated on the floor in a corner of the large room reading a battered schoolbook. Leni, now a grown lass, was sitting weaving at her loom and Margarita was standing beside her daughter, stooping a little as she watched the shuttle whizzing to and fro between the warp. The blackened oil-lamp attached to the frame cast a dim reddish light across the dark room, while the wooden comb clacked rhythmically, and every now and then Leni would hum a traditional song.

'He's still not back!' Margarita anxiously remarked after a while, glancing at the stairs.

The wooden comb clacked away.

'I'm tired,' said Thanasoulis. 'Look mother, he's fallen asleep on me already.'

And true enough, the smaller boy was fast asleep with his head on his brother's shoulder, his whole body lurching forward now and then.

'Leni can keep you company waiting up,' Thanasoulis told his mother.

Then he shook his brother awake, took him by the hand and together they went downstairs, where ever since Margarita's marriage to Petros the three children had been sleeping.

The wooden comb clacked on. 'Good night,' their mother called out yawning as they disappeared.

'Thanasoulis,' Leni remarked smiling, 'looks after his brother like a second mother!'

Margarita sat down on the chest beside the loom and for a while said nothing. Then gazing into the darkness of the room she said a little plaintively, 'When your father was alive, this was a blessed place! A true Paradise! . . . What should one remember him for first? His honesty? His kind-heartedness? His common decency? . . . May he now bless us from on high . . . He'll be resting in God's bosom, after such a gruesome death! . . . She sighed then lapsed into silence for a while, following the shuttle with her eyes as it traversed the warp and hearing the comb clack twice. Then she continued, 'Now you've been orphaned, I must take charge of you myself! . . . You've grown up and need a dowry . . . Who else is going to see to that?' She again fell silent for a few moments.

'He can't seem to settle down at home!' she added.

'Why not?' asked Leni, pausing in her work and looking directly at her mother.

Margarita gave a shrug: 'Who knows! Something comes over him in here! A kind of madness . . . And he spends all day drinking in the wine stores with his friends . . . And what money he has, he squanders . . .

'But he loves us!' said Leni clacking the wooden comb again. 'He's a good man. And the children love him — in fact they fear him, because he knows how to command.'

'True enough!' said Margarita bitterly, 'he knows how to command! No one can deceive him! Your poor father was different. He and Tourkoyannis never looked up from their tasks all day . . .'

'Tourkoyannis!' said Leni smiling, 'he certainly didn't know how to command . . .' She yawned and turned to her work again. For a while neither of them spoke. Then Margarita said, 'He's quite late!'

'Let's go to bed . . .'

'Ah, no!' sighed Margarita apprehensively, 'then he startles me in bed, returning in the dead of night the way he does!'

'Who knows if he'll come at all!' said Leni. 'Didn't you say the police were after him? Perhaps they've caught him?'

'D'you think they might have caught him?' asked Margarita smiling faintly, pleased at the thought. Then she added doubtfully, 'Ah, he knows how to look after himself! He'll be back shortly!'

And she glanced at the stairs. 'Your warp has snapped,' she observed after a while. 'Tie a knot in it!'

'Oh, mother, I'm so sleepy!'

'Not already, surely! There's a long night ahead still, plenty of time to say a prayer in bed before dawn! I don't want to wait up alone!' A moment later she added, 'Your father was always home by dusk. He didn't get involved in other people's business.'

'Who's going to blame him for doing what he did? The village now considers him a hero!'

'Well, let him go to jail for it!'

'The law goes after people who do good. Even Tourkoyannis is locked up — the man who didn't commit murder!'

'What business had he, interfering in the village!' said Margarita stubbornly.

'But if he happened to be there, what was he supposed to do? And all those people gathered in the square, were they to stand by and let the bailiff haul the poor man off, just for being in debt? . . . Besides, they say, if the nobles start playing that game again, then woe betide us all! Today it's Spyros, tomorrow it'll be Kostas, the day after Yeoryis, they say. We'll be bond-slaves as of old, they say! He did the right thing!'

'He resisted the authorities! And he'll go to jail for it!' she smiled.

'He'll go when he decides!' said Leni proudly and began clacking the wooden comb again.

Margarita got up to trim the lamp and went on brooding anxiously. Yesterday had been alright! He had come home early when all the children were still up and, blind drunk, gone straight to bed and fallen asleep at once. He hadn't even spoken to them! But tonight? And Leni was exhausted — she kept on yawning, and no wonder. Children need a good night's rest, and she was being an absolute slave-driver. They were being made to pay for her mistakes! . . . Tonight he'd be back much later! And he'd find her alone . . . Oh, she didn't want him near her as a husband. What torment whenever he embraced her! . . . Her heart stopped beating every time . . . her blood froze in her veins . . . and she didn't have the strength to evade him . . . She even feared he might kill her with those powerful hands of his . . . He could easily squeeze her throat like some little fledgling . . . She looked across at the loom and told her daughter, 'You've botched the edge. The fringe won't lie straight. Unravel it! . . .'

'Not now!' she replied, 'I'm going to bed!' and started to get up.

'Just a little longer,' said her mother and continued her own train of thought. Last night she had had a lucky escape. They hadn't been alone together even for a moment. She hadn't gone to bed until she heard him snoring, she had tiptoed in so as not to wake him and risen before dawn, she had woken her children early . . . and then left to see to her affairs down in the valley . . . And he had spent all day in the village! Just as well he was fond of the wine store! If he were like Arathymos, spending all day at home, it would be worse than hell! . . . At least now he would be going to prison for a while . . . she would be left in peace for a few months! Perhaps he'd come home blind drunk again this evening, and leave her alone . . . Oh, how terrified of him she was! . . . Her children on the other hand adored him . . . Little did they know, poor things, that he had murdered their father . . . But had she herself not loved him, the very same man? Had she not sinned with him, deceiving her own husband, regardless of the consequences, in that confounded hut! . . . And had she not considered being in his arms like being in the bosom of God? . . . But in those days Petros had not yet killed, he did not have that steely look which made her shudder . . . He was like other people . . . and his love was sweet . . . Sweet in those days maybe, when she didn't understand him, when she never imagined him capable of such injustice! . . . Of murdering her husband and becoming father to her children . . . Of sending an innocent man to the gallows, a saintly man . . . poor Tourkoyannis! . . . Ah, how well she remembered him, with his bashful love and dreamy eyes, gazing at her as if she were the sacred icon of the Virgin in the pretty village church . . . and the way he would stand before her, thin and slender, his head bowed . . . the way he would speak to her in a tremulous voice, the man who submitted to his bitter fate and did not know how to command! . . .

Leni had by now quietly risen from her loom and after saying goodnight was going downstairs. Margarita thought to herself with a shudder, 'Ah, poor thing, she must be exhausted! And tonight, how am I to escape from him tonight! . . . He'll be here any moment now!'

And fearfully she imagined him coming upstairs, emerging at the top of the stairs and standing there before her! . . . Ah, he was not like Tourkoyannis! nor Arathymos! . . . He was tall, broad-shouldered and extremely handsome, with a dark curling moustache and flashing eyes! . . . How high he held his head! . . . Who would dare to cheat him, to play games with him? . . . His sonorous voice alone inspired fear! . . . And he knew what it was to desire and to command . . . he knew what he wanted and how to subjugate Fate! . . .

And ah, how insatiable his love was! Whenever he heard her voice it struck such a sweet chord within him that he would respond at once, enchanted by her looks, her glance, her rosy cheeks, her little mouth! . . . That's what he would tell her! . . . If his heart were at peace he would never leave her even for a moment . . . but wherever he went he would hear the blood crying out, and since she had learned his hideous secret, the tremor in her voice would remind him of his crime and he would turn for solace to wine and gambling with friends! . . . But ah, he loved her so! Oh, how insatiably he kissed her as she swooned away, on the cheeks, the eyes, the mouth! How he cradled her small head in his broad palm! His hand was powerful, the hand that had committed murder! . . .

A deep sigh escaped her lips. Would that she were dead! Let her orphaned children wander the earth alone! She didn't want this grotesque and terrifying love of his, for her a torment, no she didn't want it! But she was afraid of him and didn't know how to go about resisting. If only she were old, if only she were losing her beauty and sensual appeal! Then, surely, his eyes would rove elsewhere! Perhaps he would take that Paraskevi girl to the hut where Areti had lived, or that other fallen woman like her, who did the rounds of the big houses as a servant, producing a child a year with each new master! That was the only way she would be left in peace! Oh why didn't her eyes lose their lustre, why didn't her face become eyebrowless and ugly like that leper woman, why didn't her mouth swell up disgustingly and make others pity her?... She was so miserable she felt she had need of such compassion now!... And in her despair she beat her breast, drew blood from her cheeks with her own nails and wailed aloud...

The distinct sound of Petros' footsteps on the paving just below the house alarmed her. A fine sweat chilled her brow. She heard him coming upstairs and a moment later he was there before her. He was wearing his jacket slung over one shoulder, held his head up proudly and looked very dashing standing there twisting his dark moustache.

'Ah, so my good little wife has been waiting up for me,' he said tenderly.

Shuddering she bowed her head. 'You'll be sent to jail!' she ventured timidly.

'What did you expect me to do,' he replied, enchanted by her voice. Let them drag the man away in front of us? And then have the bailiffs in our village every day, harassing the poor, impounding goods and detaining people, back to the old days with the villagers in bondage to the nobles and the rich!...'

And seeing that she did not reply he continued, 'I happened to be in the wine store, we were having a drink and playing cards... Suddenly a man came rushing in, pale and out of breath. Two policemen and the bailiff were on his heels and arrived a moment later. Outside a crowd had gathered. I became enraged! I flung down my cards and went over to the door. From there I shouted, "The whole village will be dishonoured if we let them haul this man off under our noses!" And suddenly there was a commotion in the crowd, and a moment later the man had escaped the bailiff's clutches — amazing that they didn't lynch the bailiff!... Who'll say I did wrong? The village now considers me a hero. But the police are on the lookout, to take me off to jail...'

'Why wouldn't he pay up?' asked Margarita again timidly.

'Because he didn't have a bean!'

'How is the nobleman to live? If everyone won't pay, he'll become as poor as us. That is not God's will! . . .'

He looked at her strangely; but gazing at her pretty face he could feel his heart begin to pound. 'I'm not worried about prison,' he said, 'except that we'd be parted. Because, you see, your love's a wine that one savours more the more one drinks!'

'Oh!' sighed Margarita, shuddering again.

He embraced her and tried to kiss her on the lips, but he wasn't quick enough and merely brushed against her clammy brow. 'What's the matter?' he asked.

She did not reply and turned her head away. She closed her eyes, felt her heart freeze and miss a beat, and her whole body broke out in a cold sweat. Her mind refused to function and she couldn't move her hands. He was now holding her firmly by the waist and frenziedly kissing her pale cheeks; he had raised her from where she was sitting and was pushing her towards the bed. Suddenly opening her eyes wide, she stared aghast into the darkness and in a faint quaking voice said, 'We're being watched!'

'All the children are asleep!' he answered with an ugly laugh.

'It's not them!' she said. 'No, it's Yoryis . . .'

For a moment he relaxed his grip and instinctively glanced down at his hand. Ever since the murder, he would always do this when he got upset. 'Yoryis,' he replied with a forced smile, 'he's long gone, he's six feet under!' And as he couldn't reach her lips he kissed her forehead ardently and noticed how cold it was. Drawing back he looked at her. She was white as a sheet, her eyes were closed, she looked half dead and was trembling from head to foot. 'What's the matter?' he asked again.

'Oh, not now, not now' she pleaded. 'I daren't open my eyes because I can see him. He's in here, close beside us, watching us — oh, leave me alone, I beg you! . . .'

He thought she was about to faint in his arms and became incensed. He shook her violently, going red in the face and glaring at her fiercely, and when she opened her eyes a little she was terrified. It struck her that his expression must have been just like that when he seized hold of Arathymos and stabbed him.

In a voice thick with emotion he said brutally, 'I got rid of him to have you when and where I wanted! . . . You're my wife!'

He was holding her tightly. She squirmed a little trying to evade him, half opening her eyes again.

'What sort of a man would I be,' he added, 'if I had you only when you want! . . .'

And he thrust her violently towards the bed and stretched her out on it. She went even colder and began to shiver, there was a buzzing in her ears, her lips went dry and, as her husband frantically tore at her garments trying to undress her, she could feel a chill sweat pouring down her body.

Petros was by now on top of her. She turned her head away and kept her eyes tight shut to avoid seeing his glittering eyes and smelling his breath. His lovemaking was a torment! Then she lost consciousness! . . .

Petros felt as if he had an icy corpse in his embrace, but he did not relinquish her for all that . . . Finally he rolled over beside her and without another word fell into a deep sleep.

XIII

It was summer and early in the morning, but already the sun had made the earth and air stiflingly hot. There was no wind and the occasional breeze wafting in from the pale calm sea was hot as well; the cicadas were singing incessantly on every tree; everywhere the grass was dry and the whole valley looked parched and thirsty.

At this early hour the convicts were already out on the hill behind the penitentiary, making tiles and bricks. All were dressed alike in plain shirts, thick canvas trousers and crude straw hats. Four of them were wielding heavy picks, hacking away at the quarry face and every so often detaching large lumps of clay, which others took charge of as they came loose and laid them out in the sun to give them time to crack open. Two others were carting clay across to the clay puddle in the middle of a wide pit, where four convicts were vigorously treading it, thrusting their feet in knee deep, while still others delivered the well-mixed clay over to the cutters, who were working at their rickety mud-spattered trestles in the sun, using moulds and dies to cut out bricks and tiles; these finally were handed on to the layers, who would lay them out on the wide drying-floor in the sun to bake. A number of uniformed policemen were keeping an eye on the convicts, and all around soldiers with fixed bayonets were on guard.

Tourkoyannis was working with a heavy pick. He hacked away vigorously and rhythmically at the hard clay, never pausing to take a breath or mop the sweat from his brow; and it was he who extracted the largest lumps from deep within the quarry face. He looked pale and ill. That morning he had just emerged from eight days' solitary confinement in his gloomy cell, following a prison riot that had erupted, no one knew quite why. The prisoners had come to blows amongst themselves, and the guards and all available soldiers had laid into them left and right with their rifle butts, beating some so severely that they became ill. The guards had reported Tourkoyannis as the likely culprit, having often heard him talking to the other prisoners about redemption and sweet liberty, and Tourkoyannis had been unjustly punished, but he had cheerfully accepted the punishment, not wishing to shift the blame onto anybody else.

The root cause of the disturbance was that one group of prisoners hated Tourkoyannis and ridiculed his preaching which they found disquieting, and they had found a thousand ways of harassing and insulting him in prison, all of which he accepted with a smile of forbearance. But on that particular day Cain had become incensed and struck the first blow against one of Tourkoyannis' foes, after which the violence rapidly spread throughout the prison. Despite this, no one had laid a hand on Tourkoyannis.

Now Tourkoyannis was working in the open air again and felt contented. And as he dug into the hillside with the heavy pick, he pondered whether Divine Providence was making him pay for the misdeeds of others so that sinful souls might be redeemed, or whether he was perhaps suffering in vain because this world was governed by a blind irrational will. Cain had known him for so long now and yet still remained remorseless: he hated his brother as bitterly as he resented his imprisonment.

To his left, two other convicts working at the same task were talking in an undertone. 'Another sixteen years!' one of them, a youngish man with lively cunning eyes, was saying. 'A whole life! Ah, if only I could find some way to escape! I could live in hiding, as the cash I stole is well concealed!'

And in response his companion, also young and serving a long sentence, a former icon painter who had forged a few banknotes when art no longer provided him with enough to sustain his wretched existence, observed, 'I'd follow you! But how can anyone escape from a jail like this? Besides, we're on an island and they'd soon catch up with us . . . Cain succeeded once though. He could show us how it's done! . . .'

Cain was also working nearby, on the other side of Tourkoyannis. He was slowly hacking away at the soil with his pick and seemed preoccupied. On hearing his name mentioned he gave them a sharp look.

'Would he trust us,' the thief said slyly, 'after we got Saint Yannis Tourkoyannis here confined in solitary?'

'It's not that,' sighed Cain, 'but I've grown old! How would I survive in the outside world? By robbing others, since nobody would take me on as a day labourer . . . And what sense would there be in burdening my doomed soul with further crimes? Might as well sit tight! . . .'

Tourkoyannis glanced at him and smiled.

'But if your soul's already doomed,' said the thief, 'what more can happen to it?'

'The soul!' scoffed the icon painter. 'Man dies the same as any old donkey! Everyone in here agrees, except for the priest who's paid and Tourkoyannis who is stupid. I painted the saints, but I don't believe in them!' He laughed, bringing his pick down with force.

'No!' said Tourkoyannis, pausing in his task and sighing gently, 'no one should despair. Look at me, I'm a convict and I'm innocent!'

'But you had a rare old time with your Margarita!' said the thief to needle him. 'Now you no longer have her, you act the saint with us — a wooden one! . . .'

'I am innocent,' Tourkoyannis continued, as if he hadn't heard this, 'and so I should have more right to despair of God's justice, if I didn't see His hand at work in all my suffering! I was twenty years old and wanted Margarita to be my wife, I, Yannis the son of a Turk! She was right to turn me down! . . . I went abroad to make my way in the world. I began to prosper and thought the daughter of the house where I was working might become my second Margarita, but they threw me out, and then I gave away my savings to the poor, put my little bundle on a stick over my shoulder and left to become a monk, despairing of this world. Fate brought me to the home of a wise teacher, whose benevolent heart enabled him to understand the mysteries of God, and had he not been called to His bosom I would still be with him. Then I returned to my village and ended up here among you. And now I know why all this happened — so I could provide consolation to tormented souls. That was my destiny!'

Noticing the guard approach, he resumed his task, adding thoughtfully, 'What Cain says is right. Why should he escape? Soon he will receive his pardon and taste sweet liberty. Instead of talking shamelessly, confess where you've hidden your loot and get rid of it. Don't drag others into a life of hell where they'd have to rob people or live off your ill-gotten gains, for it is written, thou shalt not steal, and you should not have stolen . . .'

No one said anything for quite some time and they all went on with their task.

Then the icon painter remarked, 'I was right to get you locked up in solitary! You deserved all of those eight days! . . .'

'And why?' Tourkoyannis asked him gently.

'You lousy mongrel!' said Cain glaring at the thief with hatred. 'You and your mate are both spying for the guards!'

'Yes, so you watch out,' replied the icon painter brazenly. 'This way I have an easier life, while they mistreat the rest of you! . . .' and he laughed.

'But to betray Saint Yannis Tourkoyannis!' protested Cain, appalled.

'If I'd betrayed anybody else,' replied the icon painter, 'who knows if I'd have saved my own hide! . . . And I don't want to part with it just yet! . . .'

'A stinking hide like yours! . . .' muttered Cain contemptuously.

'That is part of God's creation too!' said Tourkoyannis with a sigh.

And a moment later he added, 'Sentencing brings punishment to all but not enlightenment!'

The thief laughed. The icon painter looked at Tourkoyannis thoughtfully a moment, considering his calm intense expression, then he too laughed and said, 'What a stupid fellow you are, Saint Yannis Tourkoyannis!'

Then the four of them fell silent, as the guard was now watching them.

XIV

Soon a loud whistle summoned the convicts to their breakfast. They all downed tools at once and assembled next to the guards in the shade of a few scrawny trees. They helped themselves to their bread and cheese and most of them settled on the ground to eat.

But Cain was not among them, as Tourkoyannis noticed. He had withdrawn on his own to the shade of a small tree and was eating slowly and thoughtfully, as if his mind were in another world. It was not the first time Cain had sought solitude. The other convicts had observed the change in his behaviour for a while now, and his workmate the icon painter, suspecting him of plotting another escape, concluded that he was keeping things to himself, either because he didn't trust him or because he considered him a hindrance to his scheme. And it was true enough, he reflected, Cain and the thief would escape more easily without him and survive longer on the hidden booty in the world outside. When he noticed the thief approaching Cain and secretly addressing him, his suspicions hardened into certainty. Suddenly he was so overwhelmed with hatred for his two workmates that he went up to the guard with a smile and pointing to Cain under the tree and the thief about to join him, whispered confidentially, 'They're planning an escape!'

Tourkoyannis, who had registered all this, was suddenly at the icon painter's side and in a voice quivering with sorrowful indignation said, 'Oh, Judas, you're betraying the man in his most holy hour!'

He was about to dash over to the guard and intervene, but another guard restrained him and prevented him from speaking! 'Where d'you think you're going?' he shouted grabbing him by the sleeve and shaking him roughly.

'Ah!' cried Tourkoyannis sadly, looking at Cain with tears in his eyes.

Meanwhile in two swift bounds the other guard, the young one with the placid expression, had reached the tree ahead of the thief, seized Cain by the arm and was now shaking him angrily. 'What are you up to here by yourself?' he asked aggressively. 'Why did you come over here? Why are you waiting for that fellow?'

Cain turned pale and couldn't find anything to say.

'What are you doing here alone? Why aren't you with the others?' he yelled without letting go of him.

Cain remained silent.

'Why did you come over here?' the guard bawled again in mounting fury.

'I just came, what of it!' Cain now replied offhandedly.

At this the guard dragged him to his feet and slapped his face hard four times, palm then backhand, giving him a bloody nose and mouth. Cain's eyes suddenly blazed with fury; he clenched his fists, felt his blood seething and rising to his head, and recalled how a similar dizziness had come over him when he struck down his brother. He looked round as if seeking assistance from the other convicts, and saw Tourkoyannis standing not far off, pale in the face and gazing at him with his serene expression. He again remembered the terrible ordeal of murdering his brother and with a sigh submitted without further protest.

Trembling, Tourkoyannis murmured, 'In his most holy hour! . . . His most holy hour!' and raised his eyes to heaven.

Meanwhile, cursing and swearing, the guard was driving Cain up the hill, led him to a post sunk into the ground and tied him to it in the sun, snatching his straw hat off his head.

When the whistle called the men back to work, Tourkoyannis passed the post where Cain was tethered and by now in tears, and said to him respectfully, 'Rejoice, brother! He has treated you unjustly in your most holy hour. You have been redeemed!'

Overhearing him, the icon painter and the thief burst out laughing.

'After those slaps,' said the former, 'he's redeemed himself alright!'

Work continued until midday. And then the whistle again summoned the convicts to their meal and a two-hour rest. The guard with the placid expression went over to the post and untied the convict.

Cain was drenched with sweat and blackened by the searing sun; the rope had left welts all over his body; the flies had tormented him; but inwardly he felt an indescribable serenity tinged with the sorrow of repentance, and looking at the guard without hostility, he heaved a sigh and said sincerely, 'You've done me a good turn. I shall remember it!'

'You see?' the guard replied smiling without malice. 'You'd have been a goner too, as the soldiers would have shot you, and you'd have put paid to me, a family man! You see? I shan't report you.'

Then they both joined the other convicts underneath a tree.

By now all were eating. Tourkoyannis, pale and trembling after witnessing the mystery of redemption, was talking to some of them and saying, 'When I saw them leading Arathymos' oxen to the slaughter (may he bless us, as he paid for his sins with his unjust death), his fine Perdiki and his fine Paraskevas (we called him that because he was born on a Friday), I reflected that good animals suffering such a death must also in some way be redeemed, in another better world! Otherwise God, all glory to His name, would be unjust! He'd also be unjust if He condemned human beings, His own creatures, to eternal hell, since He created the world the way He wanted it to be, but repentance sanctifies, repentance redeems — it has redeemed Cain! A sinful soul can be redeemed in the fearful hour of death, it can even find repentance in the next world. Why should the contrition of a living soul be fruitless there? That's what the wise teacher would explain to me, when I was wandering all those years abroad. I would never have left his side, had God not called him to His bosom, His hand wishing to guide me here to console tormented souls. Indeed he would say that an evil soul, whether of beast or man, might at most terminate in death, having fulfilled its earthly destiny as a means of testing goodness and allowing it to triumph, and that eternal hell does not of course exist, which is why it is written, he who dies in sin, has died for ever. Once and for all. The good teacher had read many wise old books explaining how God, all glory to His name, had created the world because He wished to love. He wished to love good creatures who resembled Him. But goodness is manly and manliness can only be recognized through danger, and that is why in this world goodness is tested by temptations. And there is another holiness, that of cheerful serenity which repentance bestows. This is why God permits His creatures to sin. Cain, the murderer of his own brother, has now repented, suffered and been redeemed!'

The convicts glanced at one another and then looked respectfully at Cain, who had been listening to the sermon thoughtfully and now heaved a sigh and smiled.

XV

Autumn had arrived and it was afternoon. The sun was flooding into the prison yard from the deep blue sky, across which white clouds were gently sailing. The prisoners were chatting among themselves in little groups, some standing, others seated, others strolling up and down. Cain was no longer among them, having received his pardon, nor the icon painter, who had contracted consumption, infected others and died alone in his cell one night, nor the thief who had managed to escape and gone to live off his hidden stash. And of the rest some had been transferred to different jails, others were now at liberty; and new faces had recently replaced them, now that the criminal court was back in session, some sentenced for many years, others for a few and one even for life. Just then Tourkoyannis was in his cell and had stretched out pensively on his hard bed. He was as much involved in his mission as ever, but prison had aged him. His shorn hair and untidy moustache had turned white, his shoulders were more hunched, his brow had become furrowed, but his expression was as cheerful and his innocent eyes as serene as ever.

The iron gate opened and Petros Pepponas entered, attended by a guard. He had been sentenced that same morning.

He eyed the convicts one by one, as if to see whether there was anyone he recognized, and smiled at them, as the guard with his heavy keys unlocked a cell.

'You'll be sleeping in here,' he told him casually; the other convicts surmised that he would only be spending a short time in their jail.

The lifer approached him and said, 'Welcome. Come and join us and tell us what's happening in the outside world!'

Three or four others then silently came over and gathered round him in a circle. 'Is it true,' asked one of them, 'that there's been a change of government and they intend to grant more pardons?'

'I don't know,' replied Petros, 'I've been in custody for six months.' Then noticing their gloomy disappointed looks he added sympathetically, 'But I did hear rumours — they say it's fairly certain!'

'Maybe the food will improve too,' remarked another. 'What they serve now has made us all sick. Our governor, they say, has his hand in the till. He was a bigwig in the previous government, you see.'

'Ah well!' said another, 'we know our fate! . . . Things go from bad to worse! . . .'

'And how long are you with us?' the lifer asked Petros.

'Another six months,' he replied looking at him benevolently. 'The charge was serious, but I had solid witnesses — the whole village was on my side, but the affair has cost me dearly . . .'

'That's no time at all!' sneered the lifer.

'In my case,' remarked another, 'the court did not believe the witnesses I'd paid. One of them nearly landed behind bars himself. They sentenced me to twenty years. A lifetime!'

'I should be thankful,' said Petros, 'for by the time the maize has been sown and ripened I'll be home again, reunited with my wife! . . . And in the village I'll be popular of course, because no bailiff with a requisition will dare set foot near the place again . . .' Proudly he gave a brief account of what he had done, then looked at the convicts one by one and after a pause added, 'I got off lightly! . . . Once I'm safely out of jail, brothers, if I run into any of you, I'll cook him a meal! And all the wine he wants! . . .'

'I'd like to bet,' sneered the lifer again, 'you're some tame village landlord, quiet and law-abiding! You won't displace me in the pecking order here. My name is well known in good society, nor will it be readily forgotten. What's your name?'

'Petros Pepponas!

'And where are you from?'

He mentioned the name of his village and glanced toward the cell occupied by Tourkoyannis, who was sitting on his doorstep talking to a juvenile offender squatting before him, and saying, '. . . because no one can be happy here on earth, save those who do good or those who, having sinned, are truly contrite and repent. For even the soul of the evil man retains a divine ray to light his path. This too is part of God's creation. And that ray is called compassion. When the mind is not exerting its control over the soul, especially when a man is about to fall asleep, then compassion dominates and his conscience reproaches him for his evil deeds. It will be similar in the fearful hour of death, when to the murderer Death assumes the semblance of his victim. Likewise, when people have some deep sorrow hidden in their heart. While they are awake and their mind is in control, that sorrow is forgotten and seems dead, but the moment sleep closes their eyes it revives and will not let them rest!'

The young man listened attentively, gazing at him fondly with tears in his eyes.

On hearing the familiar voice so close by, Petros turned pale, involuntarily checked his hand, and stared hard at him, never having seen him shorn and shaven. Then, hoping it might not be the same man, he asked, 'Who is that?'

'It's Saint Yannis Tourkoyannis,' one of the convicts told him.

'He goes on and on like that all day,' said the lifer jeeringly. 'He's stark raving mad, and no one knows why they've left him here so long. He says it doesn't matter, and he browbeats us all day long — theology, theology and yet more theology! It's no longer possible to tell what sort of place this is — church or prison!' He squinted grotesquely in Tourkoyannis' direction and laughed.

'He's from your village!' said another prisoner.

'You tell us,' asked someone else, 'did Tourkoyannis kill anyone or not?'

Petros did not reply to this. By now he had recovered from the shock and, as if in response to Tourkoyannis' words, said seriously, 'There's another form of happiness on earth which is the true one — that of the man who knows how to command. He controls his fate, his will dictates and overcomes all obstacles!' He looked round at his audience with a smile and then continued, 'What would I be, were I not such a man? The plaything of Fate! Whereas now I have property, a wife and one day will have children, and people envy me, they even revere me now, I tell you!'

'And are you happy?' asked someone else.

'Tell us,' persisted the same prisoner who had asked before, 'Did Tourkoyannis kill anyone or not?'

Petros glanced at his hand again uneasily.

'And will you take your possessions with you to the next world?' asked another convict.

'The next world!' sneered the lifer, glaring at the speaker.

'Tell us!' the prisoner asked Petros yet again.

'Petros is right,' said the lifer, 'but a man needs to stay on top of things. In my case, Fate had it in for me and I very nearly forfeited my head!' Then he shouted, 'Yannis, Tourkoyannis, come over here. There's someone from your village!'

Turning his head towards them as if emerging from a dream, Tourkoyannis first looked at the lifer then riveted his eyes on Petros, who looked down immediately, whereupon Tourkoyannis' face changed colour more than once and with a sigh he went back into his cell.

Petros went deathly pale and remained silent for some time, twirling his dark moustache.

'Tell us,' the same prisoner pressed him once again, 'did Tourkoyannis kill anyone or not? Why won't you answer?'

Weighing his words, afraid he might betray himself, Petros replied, 'I don't know! He was always an obstacle in my path. He would lie in wait for Margarita, the murdered man's wife. He was omnipresent and I was in love with Margarita, obsessed with her, my heart was totally in thrall. Today she is my wife. With her husband, fair enough. But not with him as well! Margarita wouldn't come to meet me and I was sweating blood . . . Then her husband was murdered. He pleaded innocent but I testified in court and cooked his goose! . . . I nearly sent him to the gallows. But Margarita says he's innocent and pesters me to find a way to get him out of jail! . . .'

'He is innocent!' said the prisoner.

'Come and have a word with him!' said the lifer and seizing Petros by the hand led him towards Tourkoyannis' cell.

The little door was open and he was sitting on his bed, his head in his hands and deep in thought.

'Saint Yannis, Tourkoyannis,' the lifer greeted him.

He raised his eyes and looked at Petros sorrowfully for some time. 'Did God permit you,' he sighed, 'to commit another crime so you could repent and His name be glorified?'

'Did Tourkoyannis kill anyone or not?' asked the lifer.

'I don't know!' said Petros, instinctively glancing at his hand again.

'Ah, Judas!' cried Tourkoyannis, 'you know full well I did not kill, which holy writ forbids! And you persecuted me, me an orphaned human being, and tried to send me to the gallows! What harm would I have done to you?' And his lips went on trembling, as if he were muttering something more.

'Who killed then!' the lifer demanded impatiently.

'Let him tell you!' said Tourkoyannis, greatly agitated. 'I did not!' He was now looking at Petros, his lips continuing to tremble; he wanted to say more but seemed afraid to do so. Finally, lowering his eyes and sweat starting from his brow, he asked him softly, 'And Margarita?'.

'She's my wife!' Petros replied at once with trepidation.

'Oh, you married her!' he cried out in horror. 'You married her? How could you!'

Suddenly the lifer looked at Petros and, slapping him on the shoulder, declared with an ugly laugh, 'I'll bet the head I nearly lost, Petros Pepponas, you killed him yourself to get your hands on his wife and then framed this man!'

By now Tourkoyannis had risen from the bed, his whole body was shaking, his face was pale and there were tears in his eyes. Petros felt his throat constricting and looked from face to face utterly dumbfounded. His soul was in turmoil. His mind was no longer in control. Suddenly all the details of his crime flashed before his eye: the night of the murder, his lurking in the dark, the butchered Arathymos, the suffering of the man condemned by his false testimony, his own marriage. And in that same instant he again felt the urge to unburden his hard heart and confess everything. He wrestled with himself for several moments and the struggle was reflected in his face, which turned red, then blanched and began to sweat, in his distracted frightened look, his bulging neck-veins, taut lips and fumbling fingers. His secret was suffocating him! The powerful urge to speak out was irresistible. Closing his glazed and staring eyes, he said to Tourkoyannis, 'Oh, forgive me!'

Bewildered, he began to shake from head to foot, tears started to his eyes, and he sobbed aloud. Deathly pale and drenched in a cold sweat, he longed to vanish from the spot and escape the other convicts' stare, suddenly conscious that his horrific murder had outraged them all, and hiding his face in his hands he flung himself sprawling to the ground. Now he could no longer resist the power driving him inexorably to his own destruction. With his head hunched between his shoulders, he cried out in a dry rasping voice, 'It was I who killed him! In the dead of night. I lay in wait for him!' He felt as if a flame had escaped from him, searing his vitals.

The other prisoners stood round him, as if awed by the terrifying scene, and looked at one another pale and shaken.

Only the lifer went on laughing his ugly sneering laugh and said, 'You didn't keep up your high and mighty manner to the end!'

Tourkoyannis had by now emerged from his cell, a smile on his frightened face, tears in his eyes and trembling from head to foot, ready to give Petros his blessing. Suddenly the image of Margarita flashed through his mind and he remembered Arathymos' orphans. Then after a few moments' reflection he announced in his usual calm manner, 'He didn't kill anyone. I've been deceiving you!'

Petros was on his feet at once and approaching him fell on his knees before him, weeping copiously without uttering a word. But Tourkoyannis continued calmly, 'He's lying, it was I who killed him, and I have been punished. All this time I've been deceiving you!'

'Ever since I killed him,' Petros now confessed, 'his ghost has not given me a moment's peace. He would appear in my dreams, begging to be killed a second time, because I'd married Margarita, and he still refuses to leave me alone!'

'He's lying!' repeated Tourkoyannis, 'I killed him and was punished.'

'Oh, forgive me!' Petros begged him again. 'They'll grant you a pardon now!'

'And where would I go?' sighed Tourkoyannis, 'I, an orphaned human being? Margarita must never know and must live contentedly with you, I no longer have anything to live for in the world outside! This prison is my world. I don't want a pardon, and this is where I'll die, for souls in torment need consolation while they are repenting!'

Just then the guard with the placid expression shouted, 'Petros Pepponas, your wife is asking for you at the gate, she's come to say hello!'

Tourkoyannis turned and looked toward the iron gate, caught a glimpse of Margarita through the bars, and heaving a sigh went tearfully back into his cell.

NOTES

*The notes correspond to asterisks in the text and each begins
with the number of the page on which its asterisk appears.*

HONOUR AND CASH

5. Siora Epistimi Trinkoulos. The local form of the Italian title
'Signora' followed by the Greek name deftly suggests the bilingual
culture of Corfu Town, dramatized more fully in the market scene
(Chapter XII, pages 64–70). The family name Trinkoulos is clearly
related to Trinculo, a character in Shakespeare's *The tempest*, which
was well known in Corfu from the translation by the Corfiot Iakovos
Polylas.

5. twenty-four francs. The French franc was the most extensively
used of the major currencies in Europe during the nineteenth
century. The drachma, originating in Antiquity, was reinstated in
1832 under King Otto, and after Greece joined the Latin Monetary
Union in 1868 it became equal in value to the franc. 100 francs were
worth about 4 pounds sterling, a currency then tied to the gold
standard.

10. What happened to the sugar? In 1911, Sophie Atkinson
published the following amusing account of sugar smuggling on the
island: 'The Kaiser's holiday [visit] not only caused fluctuations in our
egg market, but indirectly put a stop to "jamming" operations.
Cherries and strawberries were ripe, but there was no sugar! [...] The
accustomed supply of duty-free sugar was per force temporarily cut
off, and of course no one would think of buying expensive duty-paid
sugar for preserving [...] I was told about one sack in a hundred
might pay the almost prohibitive duty [...] Indeed in a country as
poor as Corfu, with ruinous duties, accommodating shores, and the
free-trade coast of Turkey [Ottoman Albania] so very handy, smuggling is inevitable, and is almost openly practiced' (Atkinson 2015,
82–3).

10. Fifty-five okas, that's a hundred and fifty-five pounds; sixty-two francs all told. The Turkish oka weighed 1,282 grams, thus 55 okas = 70.5 kilos = 155 pounds, which at 40 cents per pound amounts to 62 francs.

11. He has already left Mandouki. Theotokis satirizes such corrupt use of political connections more extensively in *Slaves in their chains*. Mandouki on the north-eastern shore of Corfu Town facing Albania would have been the logical place for a customs inspectorate's headquarters.

14. a couple of pints. The Greek *kartoutso* denotes an eighth of a gallon, possibly a leftover from the time of the British Protectorate.

15. you should all vote for the minister. Later referred to as 'the Corfiot minister' (p. 33), this is Yoryos Theotokis, from a different branch of the Theotokis clan, who was elected mayor of Corfu in 1879 and launched a programme of road building and other public works. From 1886 he served as naval minister under Charilaos Trikoupis, and from 1899 was for ten years prime minister of Greece. In times of rapid change and revolutionary ferment, his instincts were reactionary, favouring his own class and facilitating jobbing and corruption. In 1910 he was succeeded, after two short interim governments, by the liberal reformist Eleftherios Venizelos, whom the novelist admired as much as he despised his own namesake.

15. Kostandas. Apparently a local politician.

23. so people will take him for the Kaiser. 'The Kaiser's brown motor-cars, matching the brown and gold of his liveries, and with pretty silver bugle calls, were soon well known on all the passable roads of the island. Taking into consideration the unsophisticated ways of the peasants, who take no notice of a bicycle call, and of their animals, which know no rule of the road, the entire absence of accidents was remarkable, especially when the mile-long hills and passes are considered, with their broken surfaces and alarming corners' (Atkinson 2015, 111).

23. napoleons. Gold coins issued by Napoleon I and worth about twenty francs.

25. It's her proud secret. This is part of the ironic Greek idiom *o kosmos to echei boukino, ki emeis kryfo kamari,* meaning roughly 'it's the talk of the town, and we think it our proud secret'.

31. Sayada. A town on the Greek–Albanian border, opposite Corfu.

44. Carnival time. This seventeen-day period of revelry preceding Lent, also known in English as Shrovetide, was less important in Orthodox than in Catholic countries, but in Corfu had become a major celebration as part of the legacy of Venetian rule.

51. D'you think I'd be frightened of old Trinkoulos? Had the Trinkoulos family had a strong father or brothers capable of avenging Andreas' dishonourable conduct towards Rini, he might well have been wise to emigrate.

64. Spilia. Then the main marketplace of Corfu town, close to what was later known as the Old Harbour.

64. it was the time of day when the affluent went shopping. That is to say, in the cool of early morning.

65. the last of the old nobility, would cordially greet each other in Italian. Italian was only gradually replaced by Greek as the administrative language during the British Protectorate, and many old aristocratic families, including that of Theotokis, continued to use Italian domestically.

65. holding his baton erect like an officer's sword from inside his pocket. This naughty satirical sketch is a reminder that Theotokis was a near contemporary of Aubrey Beardsley and influenced by aestheticism. There is an early photograph of the young Theotokis looking every bit the Parisian dandy.

THE CONVICT

78. one was named Perdiki, being russet brown, the other Paraskevas, as he had been born on a Friday. The names are from the Greek for 'partridge' and 'Friday'.

78. thick taper-like strands. The key Greek word here is *phytilia* which can refer either to the wicks in candles or to very long thin candles, sometimes called 'tapers' or 'taper candles' in English, which are often carried in religious processions or stuck in trays of sand in Greek churches. Similar references to Tourkoyannis' hair occur on pages 86, 121 and 137.

78. elaborately patched old trousers. Extensively patched garments were common among the rural poor of Corfu at the time, and occur again as emblems of abject poverty in *Hangman Thomas*. Theotokis often uses naturalistic details symbolically, in this scene Margarita's scarlet band for instance, or Tourkoyannis' taper-like hair suggestive of his inner light (see previous note).

98. "Sacrifice and eat!" He said Himself. A reference to the Feast of the Passover, linked in Christian tradition with the Last Supper and with the symbolism of Jesus as the Paschal Lamb.

99. She was Albanian [...] but like us a Christian. There was a sizable number of Albanian migrants, Muslim and Christian, working in agriculture on Corfu, often on a seasonal basis, the men recognizable by their sheepskin capes and pleated kilts, the women by their smaller size and less erect bearing than the Greek women, from carrying panniers and pitchers on their shoulders rather than their heads.

101. I enjoy working in families with children. The tradition goes back to Christ and in literature includes Blake's *Songs of innocence and of experience* and the figure of Alyosha surrounded by children in *The brothers Karamazov*, Dostoyevsky believing that 'the soul is heeled by being with children'.

104. and woman is a weak vessel. See I Peter, 3.7 — said of the wife as compared with the husband. This standard Christian doctrine is central to Milton's dramatization of the Fall in *Paradise lost*.

110. Areti, number one whore! Areti in Greek means virtue or chastity, so the joke and the irony are diminished in translation.

115. his crook, which he sometimes took with him at night to ward off wild dogs. 'When summer heats come and fruits ripen, the peasants build themselves huts, arbors, and tree platforms, where they sleep among the olives beside their crops, to ward off marauders, and especially dogs. One of these thieves will ruin a vineyard in a single night, so they are consequently shot at sight' (Atkinson 2015, 74).

121. *tsarouchia*. Rustic Turkish shoes.

121. blue ribbons in her hair and sash. Brightly coloured ribbons and streamers by contrast were a feature of traditional Corfiot wedding dresses.

128. Death the Comforter. *Charos,* the common word for death, derived from Charon, the classical Greek god who ferries the dead across the Styx, is associated by Tourkoyannis with *chara* meaning joy — a pun that is lost in translation.

131. Lombardo. Not traced.

133. to Lombrozo, to Krafft-Ebing, to Carrara. Cesare Lombroso (1835-1909), an Italian criminologist and physician who believed that criminality was inherited and could be identified by physical defects; Richard von Krafft-Ebing (1840-1902), an Austro-German psychiatrist, author of *Psychopathia sexualis* (1886) and an authority on sexual deviance, who coined the terms 'sadism' and 'masochism'; Mario Carrara (1866-1937), an Italian professor of forensic medicine at Turin university.

133. guillotine. The guillotine was introduced into Greece in 1834 and last used in 1913.

134. triangular yard. This is a feature of the British-built hilltop prison on a wooded hill on the edge of Corfu Town. It consists of a large circular enclosure with circular administration block in the centre, from which radiate narrow cell blocks, creating triangular exercise yards between them — the panopticon principle, for more efficient surveillance of prisoners.

153. he was superior to other people, because he dared. Nietzschean sentiments which also recall the credo of Raskolnikov, the protagonist of Dostoyevsky's *Crime and punishment.*

157. Carnival time. See the note to page 44 above.

BIBLIOGRAPHY

1. WORKS BY THEOTOKIS AND HIS CONTEMPORARIES IN ENGLISH TRANSLATION

Karkavitsas, Andreas, 1982. *The Beggar,* translated by W. F. Wyatt Jr with an appendix by P. D. Mastrodemetres (New Rochelle, NY: Caratzas).

————, forthcoming, 2021. *The archaeologist,* translated by Johanna Hanink (London: Penguin).

Papadiamantis, Alexandros, 1987. *Tales from a Greek island,* translated with an introduction and notes by Elizabeth Constantinides (Baltimore: Johns Hopkins University Press).

————, 2011. *The murderess,* translated by Liadain Sherrard (Limni, Evia: Denise Harvey).

————, 2011 & 2019. *The boundless garden,* 2 vols, various translators (Limni, Evia: Denise Harvey)

Theotokis, Konstantinos, 2014. *Slaves in their chains,* translated with an introduction by J. M. Q. Davies (London: Angel Classics).

————, 2016.*The life and death of Hangman Thomas,* translated with an introduction by J. M. Q. Davies (London: Colenso Books).

————, 2017. *Corfiot tales,* translated with an introduction by J. M. Q. Davies (London: Colenso Books).

Verga, Giovanni, 2003. *Life in the country,* translated by J. G. Nichols, with a foreword by Paul Bailey (London: Hesperus).

Vizyenos, Georgios, 1988. *My mother's sin and other stories,* translated by William F. Wyatt Jr (Hanover, NH: Brown University Press).

————, 2014. *Thracian tales,* translated by Peter Mackridge (Athens: Aiora).

————, 2015. *Moskov Selim,* translated by Peter Mackridge (Athens: Aiora).

2. CRITICAL AND BIOGRAPHICAL STUDIES

Chourmouzios, Emilios / Αιμίλιος Χουρμούζιος, 1979. *Konstantinos Theotokis: the founder of the social novel in Greece / Κωνσταντίνος Θεοτόκης: ο εισηγητής του κοινωνιστικού μυθιστορήματος στην Ελλάδα* (Athens: Ekdosis ton Philon).

Dallas, Yannis / Γιάννης Δάλλας, 2001. *Konstantinos Theotokis: a critical study of his career as a prose writer / Κωνσταντίνος Θεοτόκης: κριτική σπουδή μιας πεζογραφικής πορείας* (Athens: Ekdosis Sokoli).

Davies, J. M. Q., 2014. 'Konstantinos Theotokis and Giuseppe di Lampedusa: literary responses to troubled times', in Hirst and Sammon 2014 (below), 385–94.

———, 2020. 'Reflections on translating Konstantinos Theotokis' *Corfiot tales* and *The life and death of Hangman Thomas,*' in Nikolaou 2020 (below), 218–31.

Philippou, Philippos / Φίλιππος Φιλίππου, 2006. *Konstantinos Theotokis: slave to passion / Κωνσταντίνος Θεοτόκης: σκλάβος του πάθους* (Athens: Elektra).

Theotokis, Spyridon M. / Σπυρίδων Μ. Θεοτόκης, 1983. *The early years of Konstantinos Theotokis: a biography / Τα νεανικά χρόνια του Κωνσταντίνου Θεοτόκη: βιογραφία,* ed. Tassos Korphis (Athens: Prosperos).

3. HISTORICAL AND CULTURAL BACKGROUND

Atkinson, Sophie, 2015. *Artist in Corfu* (London: Forgotten Books); first published 1911.

Beaton, Roderick, 1999. *An introduction to modern Greek literature,* revised edition (Oxford: Oxford University Press).

Campbell, J. K. 1964. *Honour, family and patronage: a study of institutions and moral values in a Greek mountain community* (Oxford: Clarendon).

Crawley, Roger, 2011. *City of fortune: how Venice won and lost a naval empire* (London: Faber).

Dakin, Douglas, 1972. *The Unification of Greece 1770–1923* (London: Ernest Benn).

Durrell, Gerald, 2006. *The Corfu Trilogy* (London: Penguin). Includes *My family and other animals* (1956), *Birds, beasts and relatives* (1969), *The garden of the gods* (1979).

Durrell, Lawrence, 1945. *Prospero's Cell: a guide to the landscape and manners of the island of Corcyra* (London: Faber).

Flamburiari, Spiro L., 1999. *Corfu: the garden isle* (London: Murray).

Fleming, K. E., 1999. *The Muslim Bonaparte: diplomacy and orientalism in Ali Pasha's Greece* (Princeton: Princeton UP).

Gallant, Thomas W., 2001. *Modern Greece* (London: Arnold).

Gilmore, David D., 1987. *Honor and shame and the unity of the Mediterranean* (Arlington, VA: American Anthropological Association).

Herrin, Judith, 2007. *Byzantium: the surprising life of a medieval empire* (London: Penguin).

Hirst, Anthony and Patrick Sammon, editors, 2014. *The Ionian Islands: aspects of their history and culture* (Newcastle upon Tyne: Cambridge Scholars Publishing).

Holland, Robert, 2013. *Blue-Water Empire: the British in the Mediterranean since 1800* (London: Penguin).

Jenkins, Romilly, 1981. *Dionysius Solomos* (Athens: Denise Harvey); first published 1940.

Jervis, Henry Jervis-White, 1970. *History of the island of Corfu and the Republic of the Ionian Islands*, reprint (Amsterdam: Grüner); first published 1852.

Lancaster, Osbert, 1947. *Classical landscape with figures*, illustrated by the author (London: Murray).

Lear, Edward, 1988. *The Corfu Years*, ed. Philip Sherrard (Athens: Denise Harvey).

Mackridge, Peter, 2009. *Language and national identity in Greece 1766–1976* (Oxford: Oxford University Press).

Nikolaou, Paschalis, editor, 2020. *Encounters in Greek and Irish literature: creativity, translations and critical perspectives* (Newcastle upon Tyne: Cambridge Scholars Publishing).

Peristiani, J. G., editor, 1966. *Honour and shame: the values of Mediterranean society* (Chicago: Chicago University Press).

Potts, Jim, 2010. *The Ionian Islands and Epirus: a cultural history* (Oxford: Signal Books).

Pratt, Michael, 1978. *Britain's Greek empire* (London: Collings).

St Clair, William, 1972. *That Greece might still be free: the Philhellenes in the War of Independence* (London: Oxford University Press).

Ware, Timothy, 2015. *The Orthodox Church: an introduction to Eastern Christianity* (London: Penguin); first published 1963.

Young, Martin, 1977. *Corfu and the other Ionian Islands* (London: Jonathan Cape).

Lightning Source UK Ltd.
Milton Keynes UK
UKHW010033020121
375981UK00001B/2

9 781912 788